Scream at the Sea

Scream at the Sea

Christopher Murphy

ST. MARTIN'S PRESS
NEW YORK

Library of Congress Cataloging in Publication Data

Murphy, Christopher.
  Scream at the sea.

  I. Title.
PR6063.U729S3   1982   823'.914   81-23179
ISBN 0-312-70587-5   AACR2

First published in Great Britain by Martin Secker & Warburg Ltd.

To G.L.M. and in memory of J.V.M.

with much gratitude for their help and enthusiasm to
Peter Jago
Maurice Hynett
David Thurston
Paul Murphy
Gay Wallwork
Felicia Liddell
Andrew Osmond
John Tilley
Kenny-John McKenzie
Kenneth McKenzie
Dr Dorothea Gall
Keith Beck
Carol Manderson
Peter Grose

One

That morning in the Western Highlands was bright with distance. The sun sparkled the water as Loch Kishorn thrilled to the stiff northerly breeze. Its sound was a background to the clinking of the chisel, and it made the treetops duck and weave as it swept in descent to the loch, accelerating in furious downdraughts. The gusts played on the water in urgent, darting thrusts and away from the shore the only Teal Amphibian in Europe reared and jostled against its mooring line. I was pleased with my work and the croft cottage was beginning to look quite pretty, at least compared with its former grey, rather forlorn aspect. It looked as though spring had really started in earnest, irresistibly dispelling my gloomy feelings. Fergus, the lurcher dog, seemed even more active than usual, re-appearing frequently as if to show I wasn't the only creature busily engaged. He had the bright, hard gaze of a humourless professional, heedless of friendship, detached and rather sceptical.

Fergus' real master was a poacher, who was currently doing four months at the taxpayers' expense which should have carried him through the lean winter months had he not misjudged the trial date and suffered doubly. The dog's normal function was to be an early-warning system. I was tending to avoid visitors at the time, which seemed to suit him, and if anyone approached the isolated cottage he would appear quite silently, turn his head in the direction of the intrusion and slink away into the trees. Occasional visitors, prompted by kindliness or curiosity or for a closer look at the little aeroplane, would simply not find me at home.

The warning he gave this time was different. He appeared quite suddenly and gave a quick, low snort to pull me out of my absorption with the window frame I was trimming. For once, he positively acknowledged my presence and stopped quite close, unblinking. His tail, which normally swung with rude enthusiasm, was stiff and still. From my muttered conversations with the poacher, I understood the sign to mean business, to bury the rod and traps and assume innocence, while the dog would melt away with the shadows.

I put the hammer and chisel on the windowsill and moved quickly to the nearest part of the wood. The dog moved silently with me, his legs taut in a tip-toe gait. As soon as we were in cover, he turned and faced past the front of the cottage, crouching motionless. In some way, I sensed he was behaving more tensely than usual about approaching visitors. Stealth for him meant hostility, and besides that, the approach was not from the road as it had always been before. The other way, there was nowhere to come from except a rocky, deserted shoreline which climbed abruptly into awkward, tumbling scrub and heather.

Across the clearing, the foliage moved to the wind and just as I felt the dog's hackles raised to full elevation, my eye was caught by the stoppage of movement in a single low branch. Through it, the head and shoulders of a man were just visible, stealthily examining the whole area. For half a minute he stared fixedly at the plane where it tugged and sheared about a hundred yards offshore, then his gaze returned to the cottage. Without any restraint from me, Fergus stayed put, confrontation not being part of his duties.

I'd begun to foster hopes of light-heartedness, but now I shed them with slow reluctance as suspicion deepened. Confirmation was quick and unambiguous. The stranger stepped into the clearing with a decisive movement, a big man with his right hand strongly curled and largely smothering heavy black metal. He could have knocked on the door and shoved his gun up the nostril of anyone gracious enough to answer, but he must have been trained in a tank regiment for, without breaking stride, he planted the heel of his shoe against the lock with great force. Curiously, the lock held but the hinges collapsed on the other side and the door went down with an abject crash. He moved inside without hesitation, crouching and quick for his size. I felt sure I'd seen him before, but I couldn't place him.

It didn't seem the moment to play the deeply affronted

householder so I stayed where I was, seething nonetheless. More than a mile away across the loch, I saw small white sails being hoisted. There must have been twenty-five knots of wind from the North, but I'd seen her out in worse weather and sometimes wondered about her.

There weren't enough belongings in the cottage either to impede a search or make it worth while, nor enough rooms to make it extensive. My intruder soon reappeared, walked to the water's edge and looked carefully each way, I assume for some kind of boat. Seeing nothing, he took off his jacket and shoulder harness, holstered the gun, then removed shirt, shoes and trousers. He dumped the clothes in a pile under a bush, replaced the harness and strode down to the water's edge in his shorts. He wasn't the hesitating kind, and forged straight into the water without flinching. He was heavy and solid, about 220 pounds, though not a practised swimmer.

Once deep enough, he surged into a rather inexpert crawl straight towards the aircraft, which was attached to the shore on a tripping line. He must have been mystified as to how anyone approached without a boat, but the high tide covered the inner end of the line at the edge of the water. I used this arrangement so that the Teal could be kept floating even at low tide. She could be taxied out on her wheels but the scattered rocks made it rather tricky; with the tripping line, all I had to do was to slip a hitch at the inner end and pull on a continuous rope running through a fixed pulley moored to a buoy at the outer end. The amphibian's painter was attached to this line and moved with it.

It was early May, and the swimmer must have been very cold moving away from the shore, his head held awkwardly high out of the water. I wondered whether he meant to set the aircraft adrift, damage it or steal it, and I quickly dismissed the last because of his clothing left behind; but he still had a gun and didn't seem to mind it getting wet. They still work if you shake the water out of the barrel first. From where I stood the wind direction seemed on a line with the extensive bank of sedge on the far side of the loch, so I ran to the waterside pulling the aircraft's keys from my pocket. The keyring had a penknife on it, and I lifted the submerged tripping line from the water, slipped the hitch and began cutting ineffectively at the rope. *Harold Klumb, Scrapmetal*, quoted the label on the knife, and rather late I remembered that the steel was so poor that it wouldn't hold an edge even after sharpening a pencil. I didn't have time to go and fetch something better because the swimmer was making steady progress.

Urgently, I put the knife edge on a stone and struck it with another, taking a chunk out of the blade. Forty yards to go, maybe less. The damaged blade was more effective, dragging at the Terylene strands, and, after some vigorous tearing, the rope parted. There was a fair strain on it and the two ends disappeared quickly when I let them go. I turned at once and retreated into cover again, since I expected him to come back in a surly frame of mind.

The Teal is a two-seat amphibian, twenty-three feet long with a thirty-one foot wingspan, but with flapless wings, tip-floats and a pylon-mounted engine on top it has a considerable drag factor. The rate of drift in a breeze is quite startling, since the draft is only eighteen inches and the tail keeps it weathercocked into wind – which is probably why my visitor took so long to realise that his quarry wasn't much nearer, plus the fact that he had no reason to be proud of his swimming ability.

Once I saw him look back at the shore, but, with extraordinary single-mindedness, he started to put real muscle into his task, churning the water white in a frantic effort to catch the plane.

For a few worried moments I thought he might make it, though his efforts were bound to exhaust him and the gusts played him cruelly, teasing the plane on ahead. I wondered when he would see sense and turn back – the water, relatively smooth near the shore, was much rougher out there in the full force of the wind – but he kept going even when the aircraft was obviously increasing the distance between them. His stupid persistence was almost like a shock to me as I realised what was happening. Steadily he began to bob more and plough water less, the effort diminishing until I simply lost sight of him.

I felt astonishment and a tremor of guilt. Effectively I'd removed the only thing that would keep him afloat, and I felt certain it would be useless to go in after him. Even if I could find him I would never be able to bring him back. But whatever his purpose, it's a tremulous thing to watch a man die. I came out into the open and started to wave my arms about.

To the south-west, the dinghy was now moving fast, hard on the wind with the mainsail only half full, its luff full of tremors, a necessary prudence in that strength of breeze. Abruptly, it came round onto the port tack, heading straight towards where I was

10

standing. I wondered how much she had seen, whether her attention had only been drawn by the sight of the drifting Teal. I had never met her; we had just exchanged waves a few times as she sailed past, not near enough for me to have formed an idea of her features. I had bleakly assumed she would be either attractive or unattractive and relished neither, one being a nuisance, the other a shame. I waved and pointed in the direction of the plane, now quite a way downwind, but she didn't acknowledge beyond maintaining her course towards me.

As she came nearer to the land and the lee of the hills the gusts became more fitful, requiring much more care and anticipation to avoid a capsize than further out where the windspeed was more constant. As the clouds jostled for position in the urgent wind, magic cards of sunlight scattered across the water and the light blue dinghy charged in towards me in a sparkling patch of green and white. Soon she had the mainsail in tight, and the boat chuckled along still at speed but now in flatter water. Judging it perfectly, she came up into the wind about twenty yards away, reaching forward to raise the centre-board. With its sails flapping their irritation, the dinghy had just about stopped when the nose grounded on the edge of the grass just a few feet in front of me. There had been no exchange of glance or word as she was concentrating, and she tossed me a light line so that I could pull the dinghy to a firmer seat. She had short, dark brown hair and a fresh, open-looking face, nicely coloured by the wind and sun.

She was frowning, and called over the noise of agitated sails, "Didn't I see someone swimming out there? What happened? What about the plane?"

I really wanted to simulate, being so averse to the sinister aspect of the business, but one look at her eyes was enough. I told her what had happened quite tersely, making it clear what I'd done.

She didn't comment, but said, "I don't suppose there's any chance now, but we could go and look for him in the dinghy. You never know."

I nodded, whipped off my socks and shoes and waded out, pushing the boat until she floated clear. I scrambled aboard while she let the wind push us away. The dinghy swung, heeled and immediately began to plane downwind at about twelve to fourteen knots, the rudder humming with the speed. Further out she rounded up and we tacked back and forth making a thorough search of the area where we'd last seen him, but there was no sign.

She made a wry face and called over the wind, "You've no idea who it was?"

"None at all," I answered, "though I think I've seen him somewhere. I don't think there's any chance now, it's very cold and he was all in."

She swung the helm and freed the mainsheet, and in a moment we were surging off again to the south. It was quieter and less chilling, though the bigger waves further out were beginning to lick their tops over the gunwale. There was a fair bit of water in the bottom and she reached down and opened the automatic baler. The water gurgled out quickly under suction and I glanced at her, thinking she must have got pretty wet while she was on the wind coming over to me. In fact, she was uniformly soaked through her navy blue sweater and jeans, which is why I hadn't noticed, but she didn't seem to be concerned.

The Teal was about a mile away, still pointing at us but set fair towards the sedge beyond which should stop her harmlessly. We were silent for a while and she just said, "No, I'm fine," when I asked if she was cold.

"There've been a few mutterings about your aeroplane, but I can't imagine anyone round here would want to damage it. You're not exactly obtrusive, are you?"

"I suppose not."

"You shouldn't feel guilty, you know. I was thinking, suppose a thief reaches for your wallet, you snatch it away and he falls flat on his face. You could hardly be blamed for his broken nose. Still, I suppose you'll have to tell the police. Any of those busybodies could have had the glasses on you. There'll be all sorts of questions, I should think."

"Yes." I looked gloomily ahead to where the Teal was now stranded.

"I'll tell you what I saw," she said slowly. "There was this man in difficulties, and you set the plane adrift to give him something to grab hold of, but he didn't make it."

I looked at her in surprise, and she was sitting contentedly with the tiller crooked in her arm. She smiled and looked away archly.

"It would certainly be less complicated, but I think we ought to

12

give it to them straight. Thanks anyway. What's your name? Mine's Seamus."

"Cloudy," she answered, "Cloudy McNeil."

That was a new one to me, and I learned later that it was spelt "Cleodie".

She went on, "I didn't know your first name, but the gossip's told me the other. Squire, isn't it?"

I nodded and she gave me a little smile. "Why Seamus? Are you Irish?"

"No, but my mother was half. She stuck me with it while my father was away during the war. He never found out; probably just as well."

"Was he killed?"

"Yes. Anzio."

We were nearly over the other side of the loch by then and during this last exchange she had veered off to port so we didn't hit the plane or the sedge bank at a dead run.

She said, "Could you put the centre-board down when we gybe, then be ready to ease it up a little if we touch bottom?"

I nodded briefly and squatted down in the middle of the boat. She was so polished, I really enjoyed watching her hand the mainsheet, call the gybe and put us neatly on the other tack, parallel to the shore, the wind now on our starboard beam. With that amount of wind and unskilled hands we'd have been for a swim ourselves. The Teal had grounded on a clump of spiky grass, but still bobbed to the waves, which made loud slapping noises under the nose. Occasional louder slaps could be heard as the wind picked up a wing and slammed the opposite tip-float on the water. The waves were short and steep, sloshing continually over the boat's gunwale and even onto the Teal's nose.

"Can you climb on there, or is it too slippery?" she asked.

"No, that'll do fine. Say when."

About ten yards off, she put the helm down and carefully held the dinghy's head to wind as we drifted backwards. Clutching shoes in my teeth by the laces, I clambered aft and she made room for me to step across or make a fool of myself. I got two hands and one knee onto the Teal's short nose, slipped and just managed to hold on by thrusting hard against the dinghy. It looked as though that's what I meant to do.

She turned to organise her bits of rope, then shouted, "I wouldn't mind a go in *your* boat sometime."

"Well, maybe tomorrow, if it's fine. Can you phone the police for me? I don't have one and it's too rough to take off. Tell them I'll be over as soon as the wind goes down. If they think it's urgent they'll have to come to me."

"OK, will do." With a wave she was gone, perched high on the gunwale as the dinghy heeled and sped away.

I got the cockpit open and everything seemed to be in order, so I started up and taxied back to the north side. The waves being so steep, I had to go very slowly, but even so the water sloshed over the nose and frequently obscured the windscreen. When I finally reached calmer water, the tide had ebbed just enough to reveal the top of the buoy on the mooring, so I rethreaded the tripping line and taxied into the beach. I had to step out into two feet of water, then pay the line through my hands until the Teal was back on station. I wondered what would have happened if the intruder had seen and recognised the system, but it was pointless speculation.

With annoyance, I realised I'd left my shoes in the aircraft, but I had some gumboots somewhere inside the cottage. I decided not to try on the shoes of the dead man, out of distaste, or superstition. I used to declare I was free of them after surviving so many single magpies and painters' ladders, but we're all bolder in our youth.

The thought made me glance towards the pile of clothes, and then I went cold and tense. They weren't there any more. I felt exposed, standing in my little clearing, baffled and alarmed. I weaved quickly to the trees and waited stock-still for the slightest sign of movement, and after a few minutes of gathering cramp I was startled by Fergus as he came out of the undergrowth swinging his tail, giving the all-clear. I was very relieved to see him.

He gave me a cursory glance, spent a few moments snuffling where the clothes had been, reclaimed the contaminated area with a brief cock of his leg and went off again. I went inside, boiled the kettle and sat down with a cup of tea, feeling rather drained. I was so sick of trouble.

Often enough I had tried to convince myself that, compared to innumerable millions, I was extremely fortunate. I had a pension from the RAF, which was boosted by the fact that I was carried rather than ordered out, and I was gratifyingly firm in my decision to leave the world of undercover work and espionage when two of my friends were more or less jettisoned on the Chief's orders

14

and I escaped by a whisker with a bullet in my right lung. I recovered and was sent off to Norfolk for a field refresher and to learn a few more ways of killing and maiming people. I was drafted in the first place by the Department of Intelligence, I thought because I had read Modern Languages at Cambridge, little knowing that they had apparently decided that I had other questionable qualities which got me processed to be a field operative. The training was vigorous and very interesting and restored my health, but the sordid reality was a different matter. DI6 were upset to have miscalculated over my killer instincts and tried to keep me in a domestic post, but I wanted to be right out of it.

Cherishing a new independence, I started a Flying Club and, with a little help, built the clubhouse myself in a corner of Shoreham Airport in Sussex. We progressed over a period from a tiny, cramped Cessna 150 to two 172s, we gained another instructor and, through stringent economy, I had a livelihood which I loved and an engagement to a spirited, pretty lady.

There are people in Brighton who've made it the hard way to a shady respectability after making fortunes in the metropolis from ruthless, effective crime. Such people are not usually given to empty words; Old Man Shriver wasn't, anyway. When his son was killed in mid-Channel, I think he resolved to ruin me by stages until my life was tattered and sterile and ultimately he or I would end it.

As sometimes happens when a man believes he is starting a dynasty, Shriver loved his only son inordinately, with a fierce pride and indulgence. Rather than speak ill of the dead, I would say that I never understood his affection, and I knew the son well. I taught Eddie to fly and he treated me with grudging respect once he understood that rudeness and belligerence wouldn't get him a licence from me in the air and would earn him a broken back in the clubhouse.

One day on the cover of an American flying magazine I saw the most seductive little amphibian just coming into touchdown on a blue patch of New England water. It appealed irresistibly to the sailor and the pilot both, and after negotiations I obtained the European franchise for it and the first model was shipped over from David Thurston's factory in Maine to Le Havre, France. At the time there was a lunatic forty per cent levy on imports which you could get round if you brought them in yourself as personal property.

One fine spring morning, with no one else knowing our real purpose, we set off to France in one of the Cessnas to assemble the Teal and fly it home. I didn't even tell Ruth because it was to be a surprise for our honeymoon, touring all the best watery parts of Europe.

Eddie Shriver flew the Cessna and, after some badgering, I agreed to let Bob Large, the engineer, sit in the co-pilot's seat while I sat in the rear. Eddie was competent, if aggressive and spoilt, and as long as I was firm with him he did as he was told. Even he didn't know the purpose of our trip and Bob kept the assembly handbook to himself.

The modern aero engine doesn't fail. So they say. Only if the pilot maltreats it or the engineers on the ground neglect it. Statistically, it may be true. I wasn't able to discover for myself why our healthy Continental gave up the ghost, without warning, in mid-Channel, forty miles from the nearest land. Long after, I learnt that it was a mixture of kerosene and turbine oil in the crankcase. We were at 3000 feet, Eddie was alert but relaxed, Bob was humming quietly to himself, the sun blazed down, the sea sparkled to a strong south-westerly and I was contentedly jotting some notes, when in the space of about three seconds the propeller went from 2300 RPM to a dead stop as though a giant hand had crushed the engine block into a congealed lump.

Eddie knew all the emergency procedures backwards since I'd been particularly thorough with him; one cocky maverick can ruin the whole show. But I couldn't change his character. He looked in horror at the stopped propeller, then down at the waiting sea and began a string of violent obscenities whilst doing all the wrong things to the control column.

I whacked him sharply on the ear and said quietly, "Go through your checks. Trim to glide, seventy knots, turn head to wind, pass me the microphone."

He quieted down slightly, but the look of horror remained fixed in his eyes. I reached over to grab the handset and spoke urgently into it, straining my eyes to read the bearing on the radio-compass.

"Mayday, Mayday, Mayday, London, Golf Alpha Tango X-ray Alpha, mid-Channel, bearing 235 from Seaford, approximately forty-five miles, ditching in one and a half minutes, over."

London FIR came back immediately. "Golf Alpha Tango X-ray Alpha, Roger your Mayday, alerting search and rescue, confirm passengers and safety equipment."

I suppose some people lie on their flight plans, say they can't afford a liferaft, and would change their stories under those circumstances.

"London, X-ray Alpha has three persons, three life-jackets, one liferaft."

"Roger, X-ray Alpha, S and R scrambled, good luck."

Eddie meanwhile had trimmed nose-down and too fast and was futilely twisting the starter key. Getting not the slightest response, he began shouting again. Briefly I wondered if there was time to get Bob Large to crawl into the rear seat so that I could change places with him, but I couldn't trust Eddie to stay calm and Bob at least deserved his chance in a tightened seat-belt. There wasn't much time and I'd wrestled the liferaft onto the other seat anyway.

I tried to slap Eddie again to make him get a grip, but it only transferred his venom into threats on my obscene person. Speaking very quietly into his ear, I told him to turn onto 260 degrees, apply full flap, trim to sixty knots, tighten his belt, unlatch his door and prepare for the mushiest, stall-on touchdown he'd ever tried in his earliest days. I reached over and tied the laces on his life-jacket and made sure Bob did the same, all the time keeping up a soothing patter to Eddie.

As the last of our height diminished, the waves grew alarmingly in aspect, green phalanges with white frilly tops, force 4/5, a perfect yachtsman's day.

"Now, Eddie, when you judge it right, ease back very slowly on the column, all the way back, just like a practice stall – NOT YET!" – urgently, because we still had two or three hundred feet left. He eased off the pressure slightly, but not enough, and I sat leaning forward to keep talking to him. My harness was still loose, which probably saved my life. My guess is that Eddie was in hypertension, over-straining both his feet on the rudder pedals when one of them slipped off. He had reduced the airspeed too much to survive the sudden veer to starboard and with a sickening roll the wing dropped and we were pointed nose first at the ocean with no chance of recovery.

I dropped down behind the front seats in the second that remained, but Eddie and Bob would have taken the full force of the water crashing through the screen at nearly a hundred miles an hour. I've never felt such acute pain as the sudden pressure in my ears; we had nothing but solid water growing darker by the second and I knew she wasn't coming up again. The overhead one-piece wing had been torn off.

My heart began to scream for air as I clawed my way over the front seats. Fumbling, desperate, I got the lap-straps off Bob and Eddie and forced them both out of the huge opening in the roof, where the wing had been, groping for their jacket inflation lanyards as I got them clear. Reaching back for the liferaft, I got my own clothes caught on a projection. It was almost the end: my face felt purple, my chest under an hydraulic ram and a little voice saying, "Calm or die, calm or die," over and over.

Deliberately, I abandoned the raft, picked myself clear and floated out through the hole, the increasing pressure telling me we were still going down. The effort not to inhale was absolutely shattering, the hardest I have ever made; somehow I held it as I wrenched at my lanyard, felt the life-saving CO_2 inflate the jacket and haul me accelerating to the surface. I looked up to see the pale green barrier of life so far above that I despaired of reaching it. I clamped both hands over my nose and mouth, closed my eyes and begged for strength to endure. Then I passed out.

I came round on the surface, my head back and nestled on the collar of the jacket, coughing sea-water in spasms of nausea. It cleared eventually and I looked round to see Bob and Eddie floating similarly about twenty yards away; beyond them the wing floated soggily, making sucking noises through the cable holes. The skin was largely intact even though it was distorted, but it didn't look like keeping its buoyancy. It amazed me that it was still afloat with the weight of a stout metal spar in it.

I paddled over to the other two but they were both quite lifeless, their faces horribly damaged. The horizon was empty, the sea cold as winter, and the liferaft was presumably still going down with the fuselage. The chances of being spotted were very poor and an extended search would be fatal. I knew that survival would be half an hour in that temperature, an hour at the most, while the helicopters were some forty minutes' flying time away. The wing, painted pure white, would stand out well but must surely sink as the waves jostled out the last pockets of air. It became obvious what to do.

Laboriously, I dragged the two bodies one at a time and with

18

numb fingers tied them to each end of the wing, threading the laces on their jackets round the aileron hinges. Then I tied myself to the centre section and rested my arms on top of it, just out of the water. The waves slopped over my head one after another and the cold continued its creeping, soporific advance to the very core of my bones.

I was unconscious when the Whirlwind arrived from Thorney Island, and I came round on the return journey with a huge crewman pumping heavily on my chest. Another had my trousers off and was rubbing vigorously at my legs. I looked round and saw the bodies of Eddie and Bob slumped unattended. The big crewman saw me looking and ceased his grunting efforts.

"Both dead, mate. Sorry. Did you go in fast?"

I nodded. "Vertical." My voice sounded very old.

"You were lucky with the wing. Good idea. Sank as soon as we cut you off. Nearly took you with it. We did the ends first. Rum do. Feeling better?"

I nodded again, although the pain of returning circulation was intense. The pain of life returning and another venture finished on a stretcher.

"I started with the RAF," I said.

He continued with his ministrations. "Oh yes. When was that?"

"About five years ago. Only lasted six months, though."

"How come, what did you do?" He showed a sort of gleeful interest.

"I had a flame-out just after take-off. Jet Provost."

"Oh. Blimey. Did you eject?"

"Yeah, but she'd rolled on her side. Chute never opened fully. I ploughed a hundred yards of field and finished in a ditch. Broke everything."

The big man rolled his eyes up, put some blankets over me and stood up. He looked scared to be around me. When we landed, however, he helped pass the stretcher down to the waiting ambulance and called out to the other crewman on the ground.

"Careful with this cat, John. He's on his third life."

The inquest cleared me completely, although there were questions as to why the man with the most qualifications was sitting in the back seat. It was quite legitimate since Eddie Shriver had a full Private Licence plus a limited Instrument rating and about 150 hours in his log. After the hearing, however, his father came up and stood in front of me, his face full of venom, florid, with flattened greying hair and bulging eyes. When he spoke, his voice carried strong tones of London's East End.

"This'll be the finish of you, boy."

I started to ask him what he meant but he turned away and left immediately. I had in fact tried to see him very soon after the accident but was met with a blunt refusal. I found out what he meant about a week later when one of my students lost his elevator control shortly after getting airborne and hit the hill below Lancing College. He survived somehow, but the second Cessna was a write-off, and two days later the clubhouse was burnt away to nothing. My house was rocked by a "gas" explosion and declared unsafe to live in. My car was hit from several different directions by anonymous trucks. I was attacked by a single heavy and unfortunately gave a good account of myself, so they sent two the next time and gave me a real going over. The insurance underwriters' man came to see me in hospital armed with some heavy cheques and politely refused any further cover once I'd explained the circumstances. Ruth came to see me once, and the following day a registered letter arrived, causing some interest in the ward. There was a diamond ring in it, but no note.

Once recovered, I slipped off to France unseen, assembled the Teal with some local help, cleared Customs at Gatwick and headed north for some empty spaces. Later on I learnt that Shriver had been jailed for life but I wasn't tempted to start again with the sticky memories.

Based on Glasgow I was hoping to instruct on the Teal, but it soon became obvious that there weren't enough takers during the week to make it worthwhile so I went looking for another job. With my training I was tailor-made for a security company, but when my credentials were checked back to London the old firm picked it up and I was called in by the Navy as a Security consultant. My predecessor had not, apparently, been thorough enough and the particular project required an absolutely watertight system. It was centred round the building on Clydeside of the latest and most secret nuclear deterrent, a massively fast and powerful submarine which could stay at sea for three years, operating in an entirely random and unpredictable pattern. The Navy had its own vast security system, of course, but my role was to check on it, to operate on my own and without routine, even playing the part of enemy agent. This had a lot of stimulus since I was constantly trying to outsmart the regulars but largely without the risk of being shot.

After eighteen months, the new ship completed her trials and we watched her departure from the Holy Loch with a sort of blank relief. The job had paid well enough that I didn't need to instruct on the Teal and I had bought a remote cottage on Loch Kishorn for my time off. The Government were still debating on whether to build another ship of the same class, trying to make an equation out of defence requirements for the voter against the vote-losing cost of about £240 million. Meanwhile, I faced redundancy and another decision, and renovating the desolate croft was a useful distraction from pointless brooding.

Now the placid rhythm was broken. I had no idea of the origin of the swimmer, nor why I or the aircraft were under threat or scrutiny, but I'd had enough ill-treatment at the hands of Shriver to be viciously averse to any more.

About an hour after I got back I heard the sound of rotor blades and an Air-Sea Rescue helicopter put down on the far side of the loch, lifting off a few minutes later. Starting on a line between my house and the sedge bank, it quartered the area very precisely, working steadily seawards with the ebbing tide and after about two hours it went away. I'd have told the police about the clothes disappearing but they didn't come at all, and I didn't see the point of running two miles in Wellington boots to set them after someone who was long gone.

That evening I rigged up some crude alarms and a trip-wire near the mooring stake. I was morose but not nervous because Fergus trotted by several times looking relaxed and eager. I slept all right after spending the evening renewing my doorpost, although I had a slightly nasty feeling about the drowned man. I didn't like the idea of being the innocent instrument of someone's death whatever his purpose, but I was coldly furious about the intrusion. I couldn't see that I had any importance now that the job was done, but I guessed I'd better report it to Security anyway. Perhaps it would all have been a lot more depressing if I hadn't kept thinking of the girl with the clear gaze and wind-fresh face.

The sunset had plenty of crimson in it as it faded behind the Cuillins, the Red Hills on the Isle of Skye which crouched on the Western horizon, so I hoped for a fine morning.

Two

The wind went down during the night and the new day was hazy but promising. I suspect an early morning swim is not so much masochistic as showing off to oneself but I did it anyway and was soon at work cleaning paint and plaster off the joists in what was to be a little study. The baby Honda generator was humming outside to provide power for the drill and Fergus came by several times, busy with his rounds. As far as I could tell, if he wasn't chasing his dinner his day was spent tirelessly quartering the area, single-minded in his search for possible gamekeepers. His ears were always at half-cock and his eyes bright with suspicion.

About mid-morning, I still hadn't had a visit from the police and my arms were red hot from working overhead, so I stopped, got a shopping bag and went to pull in the aircraft. Fergus watched me go and then lay down contentedly to sun himself in the clearing. It was nearly eleven o'clock and the day was warm and calm so I had to paddle out and turn the plane round before starting the engine.

Chugging slowly away as I let her warm up, I felt a small relief at being on the move but still rather confused about my situation. The first chore was to call on the police at Lochcarron, so once the engine temps were in the green I did my cockpit checks and took off. I was still quite low when I passed over the cottages on the southern side and I looked down to see a figure jumping about and waving. Pulled up on the grass was a little sailing dinghy, so I rolled the Teal into a steep turn and landed back on the loch, sweeping towards the shore in a high-speed curve. As it turned out, Cleodie thought I was just attracting her attention; she came down to the water's edge smiling, but when I switched off and had drifted in near enough, the first thing she said was, "Show-off."

When I answered, "Don't be so predictable," she looked at me curiously and waded out to my side of the aircraft and I had to say, "Other side, please."

"Oh," she said with a smile, "not like motor cars." She moved round to the right-hand side, tossed her pumps in the back and climbed in. She sat down in the puddle her feet had made on the seat, took the end of the belt I offered her and fastened it, all without comment.

She didn't need reassurance, offered no silly remark and just looked relaxed and eager as I turned the nose round with the paddle. She was wearing some flowery jeans and a check shirt knotted above the waist, showing a light brown midriff and a pale bronze bikini top. Her eyes were very dark, the kind that make you look into them for secrets, and her profile, high cheek bones and a slight tilt to her nose, very special. The eyebrows, her own, were quite arched and gave her either a surprised or quizzical expression and she began to worry me. With a jolt I realised that her looks were actually making me hostile so I busied myself with controls and instruments and said nothing. Neither did she, but just sat there watching my hands and taking it all in.

I started up and she looked round at the propeller spinning behind our heads as I taxied into deeper water.

"The police sergeant is away over at Applecross this morning and says can you meet him there?"

"I suppose so," I answered. "I wonder why he didn't drop in on his way."

"He was in a hurry, he phoned me just before he left. He couldn't come last night because his fan-belt broke or something and anyway he said, 'Tus no a mahter o' life an' death uf he's daid a'ready.' Maybe he's scared of you."

"That great bull? You're joking."

"Yes."

With a smile I ran quickly through the checklist again and made sure both side-windows were tight, otherwise you get a few pints of sea-water in your lap during the surge before she begins planing.

"Will there be an inquest if they don't find the body?" she asked.

"Only if someone gets reported missing and looks like the man I saw."

"Either way it's a damn nuisance."

"Well, just leave it to me, say you were too far away to see anything. You don't want to be embroiled with coroners and so forth; really there's no point."

She didn't argue, so I opened the throttle and in a few seconds the screen cleared as we came up on the step of the hull and the airspeed indicator began to read at around forty mph. At sixty-five she came off cleanly, and, feeling a little churlish about my previous reaction, I glanced across at Cleodie and her eyes were shining, and this was a feeling I knew very well, as it happened for me every time. She looked across and we smiled to each other. It's more than twice as good to share it. Keeping low, about ten feet above the water, I let the speed build up to about a hundred mph, then eased back on the throttle to a cruise setting of twenty-three inches (Manifold Pressure) and coarsened the propeller pitch to give 2300 rpm. A slight breeze ruffled the water and the sun was behind us, so judging the surface was no problem. When it's glassy calm, it is quite impossible to judge low heights off the surface, the denial or ignorance of which fact has claimed many lives in unexpected touchdowns at high speed. There is a marvellous exhilaration in flashing across the water like that, so mesmerising that you have to keep looking around to keep a sense of proportion – rather like when driving through a winter snowstorm you get that great temptation to gaze up a seemingly endless tunnel of slanting snow, and you wish you were the passenger so you could relax and enjoy it.

We stayed down and headed west at first, since a direct route would have required a climb to over two thousand feet over Cattle Pass, where one of the most tortuous roads in the country crossed the Applecross peninsula, sparsely populated, mountainous, almost Icelandic in its air of remoteness. We turned north round the point between the mainland and the little Crowlin Islands, passing within about thirty yards of a solitary figure crouched in a rowing-boat, holding a rod; something I would not have done normally but he appeared suddenly as we rounded the point. Instead of shaking his fist, he calmly and politely raised his deerstalker, and Cleodie and I both waved to him through her side-window as we passed. She smiled at me and made an expression of surprise.

24

After a few minutes, Applecross bay opened out to starboard; the sea was still very calm, so I just brought the throttle right back, adding a little pressure towards me on the stick to maintain the height whilst bringing the speed down. At about fifty-five, the Teal quietly stopped flying, there was a slight check to our forward movement, and then we were skidding along in near silence but for the chuckling of the water under the hull. With the speed still quite high, the propeller is windmilling softly, and for a few brief moments you're in a blissful water-glider, which responds like a speed-boat with touches of rudder. To keep planing requires the addition of power, unfortunately, but the response is then better since the rudder is directly in the engine's slipstream.

About fifty yards from the beach, I brought throttle and stick right back, and with this increased drag angle of both wings and hull she stopped very quickly. Lowering the wheels in the water is a bit of a palaver, because of the different mechanisms required to force the wheels down against the buoyancy of the tyres, a force not required in the air and positively dangerous if so used inadvertently. When they were down and locked, a tickle of power eased us towards the beach, the water-rudder, which is combined with the tail-wheel, giving directional control at slow speed. Once the wheels touched the sand, we stopped, and the engine roared uncomfortably as it heaved us out; I took her up well clear of the incoming tide, in case I was put through a session of form filling.

Cleodie just watched with great interest, and I guess she had thought of our earlier exchange and decided on a change of tactic, because she said, "That was marvellous. You seem to be terribly expert."

As the engine died and I unstrapped to climb out, I considered my reply quickly and settled for being unpredictable again, there being just a hint of ingenuousness in her look; it turned to outrage and a helping shove out of the hatch as I said with a heavy, mock-Texan drawl, "Ah wouldn't do it if ah wasn' good."

She glared and then suddenly gave a big smile which was for me like climbing out into the sunshine from a layer of stratus cloud.

I said, "Could you stay with the plane and try to stop the children from tearing the ailerons off? Here comes the first lot now, they can never resist it. I'll be back as soon as I can, OK?"

"I've a good mind to tear one off myself – what are they? No,

25

go on, I'll be fine." She smiled and gave a little wave so I stumped up to the road where the police Land Rover was parked.

Sergeant McFadzean was the only person ignoring me, sitting inside writing in his notebook, since everyone else was out looking at the funny little monster sitting on their beach. I tapped on his window and he opened the passenger door, motioning me inside. For a few moments he eyed me sternly, disapprovingly head-masterish, and I quickly concluded that deference and not winning ways was the approach. He was very large with thick black eyebrows.

"Good morning, Sergeant, I'm afraid I've got a nasty little problem."

"Aye, ye have that." His glance wandered out to the Teal. He was all sweetness and light, that one.

"I'm in the little white cottage on the beach, on the north side of Loch Kishorn, just this way from the Russell Burn. I suppose Miss McNeil told you what happened?"

"Aye, but I'll be hearing it from you."

"Well, I saw a man drown. I don't know who he was. He left some clothes there, but when I got back after fetching the plane they'd gone, which is a complete mystery. There must have been someone else about. I've a feeling I've seen him somewhere but I can't be sure. Also he was carrying a gun."

"Go on," he said, without expression.

"Well, that's all except that he searched my house first and broke the door down."

"And ye saw him going for the plane and set it adrift?"

I nodded and he wrote the whole statement laboriously for me while I waited to sign it. Down on the beach, Cleodie was sitting on the Teal's wing surrounded by a crowd of children.

"Occupation?" McFadzean rasped suddenly.

"Security consultant."

"Up here?" he queried suspiciously.

"Glasgow, with the Navy. I'm on long leave at the moment."

He wrote that into the statement and said, "Aye, ye've the look about ye. I'll ask ye to stay in the area till this is cleared up, meanwhile, guid day to ye."

When I got back to the Teal, Cleodie was still sitting on the starboard wing with her legs swinging, telling a group of small children a far-fetched story about some Bigglesey character dropping midget guided torpedoes on hostile submarines. They were enraptured and failed completely to associate me with the hero – I told Cleodie later that a lesser man might have been piqued at being so rudely ignored and moaned at for being a possible interruption. Actually, her voice was so animated, at the same time high, clear and confidential that I became enthralled myself. Even the older children were failing in their efforts to look bored, and were all listening intently even if pretending to give the aircraft a professional once-over.

Cleodie brought the story to an end when some of the parents came and called their children away. Then they all moaned and booed and cried, "Where are you going, where are you going?" in chorus and Cleodie answered, "For a picnic in Plockton," whereupon they all cheered and I added for good measure, "And a pint of Plonk!"

We could hear them repeating all this as we strapped in and we laughed delightedly together. With the engine high out of the way, you can start up without fear of anyone getting hit by the propeller, and the noise usually has the effect of scattering them to a safe distance.

The engine was still hot and needed no warm-up time, so as soon as we were back in the water, I was able to raise the wheels into an immediate take-off to give them a bit of a show. I wondered if McFadzean was watching with his thoroughly disapproving scowl.

We climbed away to 1500 feet and turned south-east for Plockton, just ten miles away, and off to starboard we could just see the three-masted schooner, the *Captain Scott*, returning from her latest sail-training cruise. In the virtual calm, she was under engine with all sails furled, but was still a fine sight on the placid, clear blue surface, which was now quite glassy in patches. I love those calm days during the big spring tides, when the flood seems to have a special quiet mystery, gently tickling the weed on the rocks, exploring the creeks and refilling the pools, gradually lifting the smaller boats left high and dry on the ebb. It's the mucker-about-in-boat's dream of heaven, and when I get there, I'm going to get special permission to do it all the time. I said as much to Cleodie, who nodded her agreement to all but the last notion, and asked, "Isn't there something missing in your life?"

"To philosophise as heavily as I intend to on this fine day," I answered, "the essence of the idea is of heaven as a state of mind, needing nothing. If you include the waterside pub with a little jetty,

27

George in the pub launch to bring you a pint when you give one blast on the foghorn, and ten naked naiads to swim out and minister to your needs on two blasts, I guess it implies the tiresome factors of want and satiety. Our earthly affliction is to want satiety, and when sated to realise that the wanting was perhaps more fun."

I realised this might sound a bit pompous, and added, "You do understand that I am merely discussing wants, and not putting a pint on a par with ... er ... "

"Yes I do, but you shouldn't have mentioned it first, it's too rugger."

"OK. I'm not going to show off this time, we'll land well outside so's not to annoy anyone."

She gave me a sideways smile, and we began to descend; the water below was very glassy, so I explained that we might touch before I meant to, and she should place her arms, flexed, on the top of the instrument panel. When the water's like a mirror, you make a faster approach, but with a low rate of descent, not more than 150 feet per minute at the end to minimise bounce. The fact that there are no waves obviates the effect they would have combined with the higher speed, when the thump is like a sledgehammer on concrete, and wings fall off, spines get impacted and so on. My experience with the Teal had shown it to be very forgiving, as indeed it needed to be, since there had been no one in Britain to teach me how to handle it. If incorrectly balanced, stabilised or trimmed, an amphibian has a tendency to "porpoise", which is an accelerative pitching condition and has to be controlled early, otherwise the last bounce is usually *your* last bounce. The Teal handles very well at speed and it is a great delight in calm conditions to skim along the surface, even holding her down at well over flying-speed just for fun. The tight turning ability is also very useful, since if there is no wind to assist take-off, or the piece of water is limited, you can approach the starting-point and swing into it so as to begin the take-off run at about forty mph.

I ran through the landing checks: water, wheels up, instruments all correct readings, fuel, windows and seat belts. Prop to fine pitch, throttle back to fourteen inches Manifold Pressure, then trim to eighty mph.

If you do that all in good order and keep the wings level, she virtually lands herself, and it's essentially an instrument landing, less the need for precise location on a runway. On glassy water it's compulsory because the mirror effect of the water makes it impossible to judge height accurately above it, so you keep your eyes on the horizon and just let her sink down quietly on her own. Sometimes you get an inkling that you're about to touch and can ease back on the stick and throttle for a slight "flare", but it's tricky. If it works and you get the final rate of descent down to about fifty feet per minute, you can touch so gently that for a few moments you don't realise it's happened, as the Vee of the stepped hull absorbs the downward movement. It's magic, and it worked perfectly this time because there was plenty of sea-room and I had eased back at just the right moment.

While I was concentrating Cleodie sat expectant and still, then as the swishing became audible under the hull she relaxed and beamed at the sheer joy of it all. You don't need a lot of power to keep planing once you're there, and we swept round the corner at speed until the village opened out, when I cut the throttle and let her ease off by herself with no drama. The tide was half-way in, leaving plenty of room on the sand to taxi out on the wheels up to the wall in front of Plockton's one main road, where shops and little houses huddle on the far side. The harbour side of the road is lined with palm trees, a completely unexpected feature which seems to transpose the place to some dreamy tropical setting, although there aren't that many days warm enough to support the image. I wondered if social status had anything to do with propinquity to the pub, in housing that is. What little movement there was seemed to be heading in that direction, except for an ancient riderless horse plodding quietly the other way. Plockton is such a very pretty place that I wished the engine could be more subdued as we rolled out of the water, but after all the events with the film not long before, nobody seemed to think anything unusual. In summer, the road is quite chock-a-block with tourist cars, but this is tolerated for the revenue they bring. Well, they do have the rest of the year to glory in the setting. On a day like this, you have a misty view of peace all the way up Loch Carron to the east, and across the harbour the sun rises over the purple hill, in whose shadow lies the castle at Duncraig, huge and mysterious-looking. Curious to build there on the north side, and see little of the sun.

As we climbed out, a head popped over the wall and said, "Good morning," in an English sort of way.

"Oh, hello, Mr Plumley," I answered, "how's everything?"

29

He nodded politely to Cleodie and said, "Fine, thanks. I'm glad you've come over, you remember I told you my son Jack is a Navy pilot? Well, he came down from Lossiemouth yesterday morning, I'd like you to meet him if you're staying for an hour or two, um?"

I didn't really want to but he'd been very kind to me, giving free access to his roomfuls of books.

"Yes, OK. This is Cleodie McNeil . . . Mr Plumley."

They smiled at each other, then he said, "I hear there was someone drowned over your way yesterday."

"Yes. Nobody knows who it was, though."

"I've worked out that the body will come ashore in the next forty-eight hours, between Scalpay and Kyleakin."

"That reminds me, I've got your chart here, many thanks for the loan of it."

"Keep it, keep it as long as you like. It's years out of date anyway. Going shopping are you?" he added.

I nodded and grinned at him. Up on the road, Cleodie said, "Shall we have that picnic lunch, then?"

"Yes, great, what shall we have?"

"Leave that to me. I expect you're going to get a week's supply of sausages and frozen chips for your 'shopping', am I right? You could ask the pub to put some wine in the cooler for us."

"Drinking and flying?" asked Plumley, good-humouredly.

Cleodie dismissed that airily. "Well, we could taxi home on the water. Could you ski behind it, by the way?" She turned to me.

"I don't see why not, but no one's tried it yet. Would you like to have a go?" I couldn't help warming to her, it seemed so rewarding.

"Yes, sure. Look, shall I meet you in the pub in twenty minutes or so? OK, see you later perhaps, Mr Plumley."

We watched her swing off gaily, Plumley watching her, fascinated. He said, "Golly, cool one, eh? Won't it be dangerous?"

"Well," I considered, "there'll be a lot of slipstream from the prop, and she'll be a slow starter because of the extra drag. If we use a long line and plenty of slack, it should be all right. I'd have thought the only benefit over a speedboat is that if we can get the plane off the water she'll have perfect calm to play in, but for that we'd need about sixty-five miles an hour, which is bloody dangerous if you fall badly. Better see how good she is first."

"Jack's bound to want to have a go," he said. "Stops at nothing. He's thirteen stone, probably rip your tail off."

He thought for a moment and said, "I'm sure you'll like him, but try not to encourage him, will you? I'm a retired Sassenach from Sussex as you know, and it's a bit embarrassing when he's gone back to Lossiemouth, leaving the pub in a shambles and I don't know how many filthy stories circulating round the village. Marjorie has to go round with her nose in the air, trying to dissociate herself."

"Well, I'll do my best, but don't forget it was you who wanted to introduce us."

"I thought he would like to talk aeroplanes with you," he answered, looking a trifle inadequate. He was white-haired, clean-shaven and healthy-looking, with a kindly expression. I guessed retirement had lifted some burden from him, since none of the expressions I had seen him use looked likely to have caused the deep furrows of frowning, and only the laugh lines round his eyes and mouth seemed to have a function now.

He was about the only person I'd become acquainted with in Plockton, as a result of asking in the pub about a library. The landlord directed me to Plumley, who was very amenable and lent his books gladly. Still, he had never pressed me about myself and we hardly knew each other.

We separated and agreed to meet in the pub later. I glanced over the wall and estimated about two hours before the tide would reach the aircraft, but no doubt I would keep checking. You always worry about boats in possibly vulnerable positions – "At sea, if it *can* happen, be sure it *will*."

Cleodie appeared down the street then vanished again, so I decided to get my shopping done with. I did get plenty of sausages, of course, plus toothpaste and a few other things, including a box of 4.10 cartridges for the only weapon I normally possessed. It's an ancient double-barrelled pistol, rather heavy and complete with curly hammers which catch on everything, but specially adapted to take the shot cartridges. The range and spread are terrible; really, if you're close enough to kill with it, the rabbit or whatever would have had a heart attack first. I just thought it might be a comfort to have under the pillow. They'd trained me with all the modern automatics, of course, but I didn't keep one since a gun like that has only one possible function, the killing of men. It was a subject I'd developed strong feelings about.

31

From the call-box I tried to phone the Security head, Admiral Sir Adrian Feather, who was known as Poofy because he looked like one even though he had five daughters. He too was on leave so I left a message with his stand-in and said I would call back if there was anything more to report. He didn't sound particularly interested, which annoyed me.

Still, I was surprised to find how little effort it was to be light-hearted and to suppress the earlier feelings of foreboding. Usually, when things become habitual, even gloom, you let them go reluctantly.

Three

"Yes, I did some competition stuff a few years ago," said Cleodie in answer to my query, so I probed a bit further.

"What sort of speeds do you get up to, do you know?"

"Well, I was told we could be touching sixty when you cross the wake really hard. I think it depends how much strain you can take on your arms."

"Ever fall at speed?"

"I don't think so, but I once saw a chap fooling about and buzzing this sailing dinghy; going flat out and he misjudged it – he let go the rope and tried to jump over the stern, but instead he went straight through the mainsail, all arms and legs *and* the dinghy capsized. A show-off that really went wrong – it was right in front of the yacht club." She laughed delightedly at the thought. "That expression you used at Applecross – it sounded like a quote. Was it?"

"Yes. Sammy Davis Junior was on stage doing fast draws and shooting out lightbulbs, and you know he's supposed to be the fastest gun in Hollywood? Well, the audience went absolutely wild watching him, as he finished by tossing the gun in the air and turning round, and it fell straight into the holster. He just held up his hand till they quietened, and said, all mean and cowboy-like, 'Ah wouldn't do it if ah wasn't goord.' I think it's a glorious remark because it expressly implies exhibitionism, to use with the kind of skill you'd privately practised to perfection before loosing on the public."

We were sitting on tall stools in the bar, and the door opened to admit Plumley followed by a burly man in his late twenties. They stopped to exchange good mornings with some people by the door, and Cleodie said, "Oh – oh, that must be Plumley junior." He had close-cropped brown hair, a slightly droopy moustache, and his attention wasn't really on the pleasantries, since he turned and made a gesture to the landlord, who nodded and began to pull pints.

"Young Jack looks dangerous," I said.

"Why do you say that, particularly?"

"Eyes. The kind that look beyond you, beyond the horizon, you know, cold. The kind you associate with assassins and fighter pilots."

"But yours do just the same. Actually, they're worse, being a sort of Baltic blue, instead of nearly black like his."

"Oh." I thought it was time to change the subject, but at that moment Plumley senior finished speaking and came over to us. Before he could say anything, Jack came to the bar, seized the two pints and gave him one, so his father said, "In a bit of a hurry aren't you, lad?"

"Well, it's Saturday, you never know, they might close early or something."

His father turned his eyes to heaven, for our benefit, I think, because he said to us, plaintively, "It's only quarter past twelve. This, you will have gathered, is my son Jack." He made the introductions and Jack insisted on getting our glasses refilled, while his father told him that the aircraft outside belonged to me. Jack was much more interested by this, and started asking a few technical questions, so his father gratefully cottoned on to Cleodie.

Jack's initial glance had already told me that he had singled her out as a possible "kill", but for the moment he left her filed in "pending". For some reason, this annoyed me. I even had one ear cocked to her conversation, since we hadn't spoken very much, and I enjoyed hearing her voice.

Jack's accent was quite different from his father's, in that it had that special Fleet Air Arm exaggeration, sort of Oxford and then some. There is the hearty stress on certain syllables, like "su*perb*" and "*certainly*", and "no" is pronouced "nao". The laugh is a pronounced "whaw, whaw, whaw", but devastatingly infectious.

"What are you flying?" I asked him.

"Phantoms. Will be for some time, I should think. They've just switched me to teaching others all the naughty things I've learnt. Not that I mind, you know, you really get hooked on those things."

"Why?"

"Don't know, really. I think it's just the incredible amount of power at your disposal. Doing some combat training the other day, burnt up the entire fuel load in eleven minutes. Supposed to last an hour and a half."

"Even that's not very long."

"Ao, yes but of course we do get to go a fair way in the time. You must realise that a strike aircraft is designed round the pilot, who has to be a drinking man or he wouldn't do it, and he, poor lad, has simply got to pee – quite often, actually. Whaw, whaw."

In case this was a hint, I ordered a refill. Jack moved into overdrive, and started telling airy anecdotes. At one point I went out to check the aircraft, and when I came back in the tableau was completely altered, with Plumley talking to the landlord and another character about fishing; Jack had cornered Cleodie, who was listening with mock intent to some of his doings. He drew me into their conversation, and we heard about when he was flying a Messerschmitt 109 for the Battle of Britain film, and was alongside the camera aircraft just above some low cloud, when the engine started to cut out, " . . . so I said to myself, 'Now look here, Jack, you've only got two thousand feet, you don't know what's underneath, time to get out' sort of patter, she was going like a porpoise, in and out of the cloud tops, 'cos the donk kept missing and then picking up again, so I unstrapped and got the canopy open, got one leg out of the cockpit, and gave a thumbs-down to the cameras. They were all waving to me frantically, and I couldn't make it out, and then I realised the director was up there, looking really spare. Well, they'd pranged so many planes during the filming, I expect they were running short of ME 109s, not that that meant a thing to me, I wasn't even being paid as we were supposed to be enjoying it, but just then the donk picked up again and seemed to be quite smooth, so I got back in and carried on. I'd left her all trimmed, and can you imagine if I'd got out and she'd carried on without me till she ran out of juice? Thing was, when they developed the film, they invited all the other pilots to come and see the rushes of young Jack doing his hands-off bit, but I shook 'em when they asked me to make a speech after the

35

showing. I told 'em how after I got back, I checked my parachute and found some props man had stuffed the bag with an old blanket, 'cos he didn't think we used those things any more!"

His father and the landlord and several others had heard this last bit, and had joined in the chorus of horrified delight, so naturally another round was called for, but Cleodie looked across and said what about our picnic, so we said we might see them later. After collecting the wine, I turned back and said, "Jack, have you got any water skis and a rope?" I wasn't going to tell him what for, but of course he guessed, and said he would commandeer a friend's speedboat with all the kit and meet us out in the bay later on. He looked fascinated like at the beginning of a new adventure, and just as we got through the wall I heard another burst of laughter from the pub, with Jack's "whaw" prominent.

We taxied out round the corner and passed the *Captain Scott*, which was now made fast to her mooring. The cadets were all on the yards making shipshape, and stopped to watch us go past. When we were about a mile offshore to the east of Plockton, I switched off and let us drift on the oily calm. There was just the vestige of a swell.

"Right, what have you got for us, then?" I asked, as I opened the hatch, transferred the seat cushions onto the cabin top and turned the propeller by hand until it was horizontal. Gingerly, we arranged ourselves underneath it, leaning against the engine pylon. I had no corkscrew, so had to push the cork in with my finger, but Cleodie had thoughtfully managed to get hold of two clear plastic glasses. She produced pâté and smoked salmon and some fresh rye bread. It was very hot by then, so she unsettled herself again to remove shirt and trousers and sat there looking very contented with her munching.

"The wine is just right," she said, "well done. Aren't you hot? Why don't you take your shirt off? Are you shy?"

I slipped it off, but kept it between me and the cushion to avoid getting sticky. I closed my eyes in blissful content; there was just the faintest movement from the water, and no sound at all. I murmured, stretching my glass out, "Refill, please, I think you are nearer."

The only reply was a sleepy "Um", so I sat up to reach for the bottle. She must have opened one eye because she said, "Crikey, where did you get that scar? And another one here. What happened to you?"

"Well, it's a long story, and Jack'll be here any minute. Go back to sleep."

She was silent for a while and then asked, "I was going to ask you what you do, but instead I'm going to guess. You're a cat-burglar, aren't you, but not a very good one, hence all the punctures. Am I right?"

"First time. You must come and see my collection of cats sometime, it's terrific."

She closed her eyes again, smiling. I forced myself not to look at her for two reasons, one because it disturbed me, and the other because I thought I might lose a few Brownie points if she caught me at it. Behind closed eyes, however, was firmly ensconced a photo-image of her lying there looking very relaxed, and it took a grievous effort not to be wistful, but simply to enjoy. Eventually I managed to doze off while the photo-image was still dressed in the bikini, and was woken some time later by the sound of a high-revving outboard breaking the stillness. As Jack came up to us and slowed down, it was the noise of Jack rather than the outboard which woke Cleodie, and she opened her eyes to see him taking a photograph of us. He said, "Got the skis for you. Mono or two?"

"Mono and one to kick off, I think. I imagine she'll be slow off the mark. If you've got two ropes, it might be an idea to knot them together, to reduce the slipstream on her, and give me height for turning."

"Would you like me to try first?" offered Jack.

Cleodie was awake properly now, and she said firmly, "Certainly not. It was *my* idea, and I've been mentally preparing myself, as you can see, while you've been boozing it up. Let me come across and get organised. Wow, the water's freezing."

Jack reached out a paddle, and we manoeuvred the boat gently alongside our bows. Cleodie chucked her shirt and jeans across to him, and helped me put the picnic things away in the rear of the cockpit.

"Now," I said, "I've got a mirror here, and I'll be watching for all your hand signals, but I'll need about sixty-five to get off and give you clear water. I'll make the turns gentle, but if airborne I'll need to go up a few feet to turn, so's not to dip a wing. If I start getting too high, signal me down, and remember I might have trouble judging the surface, although the angle of the rope should help."

Jack said, "What shall I tie the rope to?"

"There's a tie-down under the very end of the hull. Don't tie it to the tail-wheel because that moves with the rudder. Now, are you sure, Cleodie?"

She nodded confidently, and looked quite sure, so I clipped on the side mirror, waited till they were organised and had fixed the rope to my stern, then started up and moved slowly away to warm the engine. Once the oil temperature was well into the green I went back and they signalled they were ready; making a wide circle round the boat, I trailed the long rope into them. I watched as Cleodie took seven or eight large coils in her hand, inched her bottom to the side of the boat, and gave me a vigorous nod.

I opened the throttle wide, and everything was quite normal for the first few seconds, and the Teal was practically planing before I felt the strain and the distinct check to the acceleration. The mirror was still obscured by the spray, but I could feel that the speed was still picking up, and in a moment it cleared and I could see Cleodie back there still on two skis but looking all set. Once the nose had levelled at about twenty-five, she kicked off the spare and did a few little zigs to show all was well. She then had the sense to keep straight to help me get the speed up, and the Air Speed Indicator began to register forty, forty-five, fifty. She took one hand off the handles, gave me a thumbs-up and go-faster motion, and at sixty the plane began to hop to a very slight long swell. Cleodie looked fine, the ASI showed sixty-five, and I eased back slightly on the stick. Cleodie skied right through the the final pencil-line drawn by the Vee of the hull, and then was flashing along in her own patch of glassy water, dipping occasionally to the long undulations. The speedboat was left far behind, and we were still at full throttle just touching seventy. I decided to try a long slow turn to the left so that I could keep an eye on the angle of the rope. Using this as a guide, I gained about fifteen feet and gently banked to port. All went well until we were out of the turn and heading south, back towards Plockton, when I saw Cleodie leave the water a couple of times, muff a landing and let go of the rope. She stayed upright for a few seconds, and then came a terrific purler, like Barnes Wallis' bouncing bomb. Very worried, I came round as fast as I dared and as I passed I could see her head bobbing as she trod water. She gave a little wave which was a great relief, but knowing it was very cold, I got down as soon as I could, just missing the ski as I touched. Turning, I could see the speedboat approaching, but still about half a mile away, so I went back and picked up the ski and then stopped alongside Cleodie. She was cheerful, but her teeth were chattering, so I said, "Let me help you out, he'll be here in a minute with your clothes."

"No," she shouted, "just give me the ski and take off straight away. Out of the sun – NOW."

She had the ski on in no time, but it took me a few moments to start up and bring the rope round to her, and in that time Jack roared up and did a great circle round on us, churning up the water. He stopped somewhere behind my tail, and I could see Cleodie in the mirror waving "go" to me, and "go away" to Jack, who was leaning over the side of the boat. He straightened up suddenly, and zoomed round in front of me, whirling something over his head like a dervish, and suddenly I understood her urgency – it was Cleodie's bikini top. Jack looked as though he'd won a prize or something. When he was clear, I opened up, and in a moment felt the huge drag as the aircraft tried to pull Cleodie up from a submerged start with a single ski. We began to accelerate very slowly, and I couldn't see how well she was making out, only feel by our sluggishness that she was still there. So was Jack, moving abreast of us, holding the bra over his head with both hands, and grinning from ear to ear. Knowing he'd be eyeing Cleodie from a range of about a foot for at least half a minute until we drew away from him, and feeling so helpless, made me hopping mad. Using the rudder gently, I turned towards him and for a long moment it looked as though the wing-tip was going to hit him in the chest. Just in time he got serious, sat down and moved away at top speed. We were just about planing over the water by then but without enough speed for the ski which was still ploughing and wobbling at the tip. Finally she came over the hump and we started accelerating much better, turning gently towards Kishorn.

I checked again in the mirror and did an instant double-take for she was quite naked, and thinking on it I wasn't surprised because a fall at that speed can tear skin off let alone clothing and could have hurt her very badly. We should definitely have let Jack go first. I could see him following but at a good distance, probably sulking because he was unable to catch us. I saw Cleodie turn and look for him, and then she was smiling. She waved me faster, so when the Teal was ready I lifted off again. Seventy-five mph seemed to be about the limit and it became quite calm again as we rounded Kishorn Island. Cleodie took a hand off and pointed straight ahead, then made the cut-off signal, so I gathered she wanted to borrow a pair of *my* trousers rather than rush home.

She was zigging and gaily tossing her hair as she threw up sheets of spray from the ski. I wished I had a 360° picture of the whole scene, the mountains with their streams, pines and heather, the sea and sky a hazy bottomless blue, the dotting of islets and the legendary Skye to the west – and the most graceful centrepiece, a gleaming naked naiad skimming the mirror surface with such easy flourish.

As we neared the northern shore, I turned gently to starboard to move along it so that Cleodie could choose her moment to let go, but as we passed the cottage, two of our lads in law-and-order blue were standing on the grass, watching us. Cleodie must have seen them as well, because she stayed with me, and suddenly I was in real trouble because the bay ended just ahead and the land climbed quickly to over 400 feet. There was not enough room for a crash stop, so the only choice was a tight turn round to starboard. Cleodie was unlikely to realise that her drag coupled with the tight turn could stall me in and so she probably wouldn't let go until too late. I couldn't shake her off by just heading straight at the south shore, since she mightn't be able to stop in time at that speed, neither would I be able to touch down and slow up enough to make a turn on the water. There was just no choice, so I pulled up as high as I dared without losing too much speed and hauled her over into a steep turn, still at full throttle, and the stall warning horn came on with the red light almost at once. Still in the turn, I grabbed the undercarriage lever and put the wheels down, thanking heaven that I had obeyed the rules and changed from the water mode after leaving the shore, otherwise they would have slammed down and broken something, being over-powered by the anti-buoyancy mechanism.

The horn blared on, the slip indicator showed we were falling into the turn, and I had to decrease the angle of bank hurriedly. She struggled round gamely, but when I levelled off, the speed was down to under sixty, and the stick was held alarmingly far back in my left hand as I tried to keep her flying. The speedboat was stopped about half a mile ahead, and I knew Jack would have been watching with interest, being familiar with such problems. I decided we had no choice but to land and get Cleodie's clothes from him, and anyway I was sweating by then.

I started to ease her down, and remembered the wheels only just

40

in time, which made the perspiration break out afresh. Just as we touched, I saw Cleodie cut across to my left, which kept the aircraft between herself and Jack in the speedboat, so I dug the nose in by pushing the stick forward until the speed was below anything at which the plane might be tempted to fly again, then brought it hard back, and she stopped very quickly. As Jack eased the boat over, Cleodie left the ski and hauled herself in on the rope. By now, she would have been very cold and short of options, so she swam to the boat, and Jack hauled her aboard making a real effort to keep his glances discreet. She accepted the towel from him without a word, so he leaned across to me and said, "You had a spot of bother there, lad. Why on earth did you put the wheels down?"

"Well you may ask," I said. "This must be the only aircraft in the world which actually flies faster with the wheels down than up. You see the angle at which they are now, swept back, they create more drag than when they're down, and the legs are vertical and presenting their edges to the airflow. See what I mean? You cruise with the gear down, the difference is about four or five knots, and I needed all the help I could get in that turn."

"Extraordinary," was his only comment and then he said sideways, "Are you decent yet, Cleodie?"

"Yes, all right now," she shivered, "that's better, thank you. You didn't find the other half of my thing, did you?"

Jack shook his head, so she made an "Oh, well" face and said, "I wouldn't have missed that for anything. Skimming along in flat water at that speed is simply electrifying, fantastic. But when you turned back into the sun and we met those long swells, I couldn't see the surface and got quite disorientated. Did you see? I just let go and curled up into a ball and bounced and bounced. The water is rather hard at that speed." Jack and I raised eyebrows at one another in admiration of her lack of melodrama. She finished tying her middle and then said, "Why don't you come over, both of you, Carruthers has made some scones and we can have some tea. Not too early, is it?"

"Great idea," I said, a bit surprised at myself. "Will you go over with Jack? I think I'd better go square it with the boys-in-blue and follow you later. Could you take the rope off me?"

Jack started to ask what I meant, but Cleodie said she would tell him in a minute. They sorted themselves out and went off, and I taxied towards the cottage. It must have been almost the very top of the tide and they were standing there waiting, two of them, the burly figure of McFadzean looking particularly menacing. As I got out, he said, "Muster Squire, what d'ye think ye're aboot? If ye're thinking o' turning this neck o' the woods into a nuddist colony, I'd best be warning ye ... " With a sudden shrug, he seemed to dismiss the matter and gestured towards the cottage. "Well, we've looked around, but we may require ye further if anything turns up, and we'll be asking ye to remain here for the present or let us know if ye're awa' at all, clear?"

I nodded and they went off to the Land Rover which was parked at the edge of the clearing. In McFadzean's presence, I had hardly noticed the slight and gangly constable, who had been almost hiding behind him. I didn't envy the constable.

Fergus was nowhere to be seen, but then he'd been trained never to be in the same square mile as the law.

I dumped my shopping and taxied over to the south shore, which has fewer rocks than mine; I put the wheels down and parked the plane right at the edge of their lawn, leaving room to complete the turn out again. Walking along the wing, I was able to step off onto the grass dry-shod, something you can't do when she's floating as your weight pushes the tip float under water.

As I walked up the grass, I realised I still had reservations about being sociable, though not quite so strongly. I didn't dwell on it since I'd long been in the habit of dismissing confused thoughts.

Four

Carruthers turned out to be her mother. Cleodie explained the nickname was invented by her two brothers, who wanted to keep their end up at Harrow in the pretence that they had servants at home just like the other sons of the privileged. She was in her early fifties with dark hair swept back and beginning to grey, fine features which Cleodie mirrored, and a serene expression from large brown eyes. We had tea and scones on a little terrace and they chatted while I tried hard not to stare morosely across the mile of water where McFadzean's Land Rover was still in evidence. The day was still very warm, but the sun had begun to turn its attentions to the west in earnest, and shimmered vividly in the slow movement of the water. Still no breeze stirred the new leaves, and the total quiet gave a most unreal atmosphere.

Carruthers reached into a pocket and passed me a small coin, black with age and tarnish, and I examined it in answer to her raised eyebrows; it meant nothing to me, so I passed it on to Jack, who also shook his head. He broke the silence, saying, "Did you find it in the garden?"

"Yes, in the flower-bed there," answered Carruthers. "Do you know what it is?"

"No, sorry. My uncle Wilf could have told you, he was a fiend for that sort of thing, but I killed him last year."

He looked a little crestfallen at the thought. Cleodie and her mother immediately said, "You did what?" in unison, so Jack had to explain.

"He had one of those metal detectors, and was always off on the downs hunting, but it wasn't much use, in fact I could hardly get it to register a man-hole cover at two inches, so for his birthday I got a pal in the Guards to purloin one of those hypersensitive jobs. Damn thing would pick up a milk-bottle top at the depth of two feet and the first morning he went totally bananas and dug about sixteen deep holes in the front lawn and had a heart attack just before lunch. It was his seventy-fifth birthday and I know he died in a spasm of total bliss." He paused for a moment, then added, "Wilf and I got on famously, he was always laughing and saying, 'You'll be the death of me.'"

Jack paused to check his audience reaction, and predictably Cleodie and her mother were looking concerned and trying not to smile, unsuccessfully. I had choked on a mouthful of tea and my subsequent coughing bout must have made me look singularly callous perhaps; but it set them all off as Cleodie slapped my back, having carefully taken the tea-cup from me first, and they ended up shuddering with laughter. Carruthers was shaking soundlessly with tears showing on her face, and Jack's infectious "whaw whaw" compounded the reaction.

I don't know how it would have stopped, but suddenly the phone rang inside, and Cleodie went inside to answer it still neighing with indrawn breath. She was gone a minute or two so we had a chance to simmer down by the time she came back to say, "Jack, it's for you. Your father. Just on the right of the door as you go in, on the window-sill."

Cleodie sat down as he went in, and said, "Well, Seamus, tell us what you do with yourself when you're not bashing the blitz out of that cottage. Sometimes we can hear you clear across the loch. We imagined you'd had an unhappy life and were taking out your frustration on the stonework."

I fielded that one with a big grin and said, "Well, it's really good therapy and I've lost half a stone. Only thing is, by evening I'm usually so exhausted I'm past enjoying the total bliss of being without television, and I must say that mental stimulus is a little lacking round here, except for reading. I'm thinking of writing a book."

"What about?" asked Carruthers. "And I noticed you hedge the question."

"About perfection, I think. I'd certainly give your scones a mention."

Before they could dig any further, Jack came outside and I asked, "Everything all right?"

44

"There's a flap on. I've got to be back in the morning." He finished his tea and said, "Can I have a gander at the plane, Seamus?"

We walked down the lawn together and I asked, "What's the flap, Jack?"

He groaned at the pun but answered, "Not sure I can tell you – Classified Information and all that."

"It's OK, I'm sworn in."

"Oh?"

"Yes, I work for Poofy Feather in Glasgow, on leave just now. Have you heard of him?"

"*Cer*tainly, who hasn't? You know, I don't care how many daughters he has, and I've even, er, *been out* with one of them, that man has got to be a fairy. Anyway, he'll be doing his nut. Somehow his protégée has blown a gasket and heads are going to roll, by Cecil."

Jack was neatly testing me but I didn't need to spar with him. He could see my concern.

"I take it you mean UNS1 is in trouble."

After a pause, he nodded. "Yes, she's surfaced and stopped but they can't get near her. She's got more defence systems than the rest of the Navy put together and they daren't set them off. Meanwhile, we all go on Full Alert because the Reds are delighted and sending relays of Antonovs over to have a look. We don't know if they know that their proximity can make her self-destruct but we have to intercept and keep them away. I'm supposed to be instructing these days, but I'm back on Ops from tomorrow, while this thing lasts."

"Where's she surfaced?"

"Out in the Atlantic. Once they get a carrier there it won't be so bad, but until then our chaps are having very long sorties, refuelling in the air."

"I phoned in this morning and nobody mentioned it."

"It only happened this morning."

"I'd better call back then, see if I'm wanted. Poofy wasn't there, and they weren't very interested in my intruder."

"What intruder?"

"The man who drowned. He'd actually come on some bad business, armed, forced entry and so on."

He looked at me closely. "Did you fix him up, then?"

"Not really. He was a rotten swimmer." I explained briefly what

45

had happened. "Also, there was someone else with him, whom I didn't see."

"Golly. Are you thinking there's a connection?"

"No idea. I've got nothing to go on, and I haven't had any bother before. We cracked two Red infiltrators in the shipyard and another at the electronics testing lab, but I'm reasonably certain she was quite secure for at least the last three months. Tightest operation ever – anyway that's what Poofy said. Don't know how they got any work done, the screening was so intense. I myself wasn't allowed on board, which I said was a mistake, but only because I was curious. There's only one thing about this intruder: I think I've seen him before."

"I was going to ask you to take me for a spin but I think you ought to make that call."

"Yes. I'd want a return match anyway."

"What do you mean?"

"Phantom."

"No chance."

"Get stuffed then," I said good-humouredly, and we walked up the lawn after Jack had peered in to the cockpit and given it a quick once-over.

Back on the veranda, Carruthers asked Jack, "Is it your lot that scares all the drivers on the road to Kyle? Cleodie and I were going down there the last time she was here, you know where the road goes alongside the loch but high above it? Cleodie was trying to do the ton as usual and I was trying to stop her, when there was this terrible rending noise and I thought all the wheels had come off. We both sort of looked round in a panic and there was this jet fighter at the same height about fifty feet away, but going a bit faster. We nearly had a fit."

"What sort of car have you got?" said Jack innocently. "I'll find out who he is and have him court-martialled."

"We were in Cleodie's red Lotus," she said, clearly impressed, not realising that I and several others to my knowledge had had the same experience. It was after all one of the areas where they practise their low flying, but it does give you such a fright that I'm surprised a suburban committee hadn't been formed to have it stopped. It seems they're less like that in Scotland than in the grey old South, just as there was no legal reason for me not to land on the lochs, which are public property except for a few on private estates, and there's no law of trespass in Scotland. Conversely, in

46

England you are not allowed to land on any inland water without express permission, which is almost never forthcoming for the public places – committees again. They haven't yet found a way to stop mountaineers, potholers and yachtsmen, but eventually they will.

"Did he have dark hair, black eyes and a Zapata moustache, Cleodie, by any chance?" I asked.

She affirmed it vigorously but Jack interrupted.

"You didn't see what colour socks he had as well, I suppose? You're forgetting about the helmet and oxygen mask."

"I'll get to the bottom of it for you," I said, ignoring Jack. "He's going to take me up. Says he's got lots of pull, back at the base."

Jack tried to say he'd never said anything of the sort but Cleodie just carried on talking to me.

"Are you going to land on a carrier?"

"Yes, of course," I answered airily.

"How exciting. Or terrifying."

"Well, he's the best pilot in the Navy, so it's no problem."

"Who told you that?"

"Who do you think?" I pointed a thumb at him. He was flapping his arms helplessly by this stage, torn between modesty and not wanting to deny his skill in front of her. With an anguished grin, he said he had to be going.

"I'll have seen nothing of Mother, though she'll never approve of me until I'm a teetotal Rear-Admiral."

He turned to go and then said, "Oh, oh."

"Yes," I said. "Boat-pushing detail will now volunteer, by the left."

The speedboat was high and dry, so we all trooped down to give him a shove. Jack larked around giving orders about where to push, and we all pretended to strain and groan like mad, getting nowhere until he was forced to give a hand. We then piped him aboard making sure he got his feet wet. After a lot of noise and palaver, he finally got sorted out and made off, waving.

Unexpectedly, it was Carruthers who turned to me and said, "Couldn't we creep up on him in the plane and give him some of his own back? It probably was him, you know. Come on, let's give him a fright."

I looked at her in momentary surprise and then nodded. Cleodie followed us down to the Teal wailing, "What about me? I suppose

47

you've no room and I can make filthy gestures with the best of them."

"Go on, squeeze in the back," I said. "It's all right, we're not trying to climb mountains. Quick now."

We piled in and were soon on our way, doing up straps and windows as we accelerated, with Cleodie leaning between the two seats from behind. Her head was close and I was very conscious of her. Because of the extra weight it took quite a distance to get off, but eventually we were airborne in hot pursuit of the speedboat, which was plainly visible leading an arrow of white water to the south-west. I climbed a few hundred feet so that we could approach with the power reduced and not give ourselves away prematurely by the noise.

We came up on his left as he sat there idly with one hand on the wheel, and we were all eagerly watching as we came abreast of him unnoticed; then I gave her full power and swept over the boat with the starboard wing about four feet over his head. It was beyond our wildest expectations to see his reaction, which was that of a lone fighter on his way home with empty guns being jumped by a pack of bandits out of the sun. He looked up in sheer horror, slammed his throttle closed, and when we circled to pass over him again, we saw him sitting there stopped in the water, just hugging himself. It was too good to believe and the girls were waving gleefully and making peculiar noises.

"Rat-a-tat-tat, you're dead," I muttered to myself, in the manner used in mock combat, but aloud I said, "Let's go home, I think he's had enough for one day."

Cleodie, however, said, "It serves him right, he's a cad and a bounder."

Carruthers thought she was being a bit hard on him, but Cleodie didn't bother to explain. I assumed it was because of the episode with the bra, unless he'd made a pass at her while bringing her ashore.

When we got back I asked to use the phone, which they let me do privately. This time I was put through to the chief himself.

"Got your message, Squire. You'll have to sort it out yourself, there's a panic on."

"Wait," I said before he could hang up, "what about UNS1, what happened?"

There was a long silence before he said, "How did you know?" in a quiet, ominous tone.

48

"I bumped into a Navy flier who's just been recalled because of it."

"Then you'll both face a court martial for discussing Official Secrets."

"Yes, all right," I said in a bored voice. Sometimes Poofy could be a real pain. "Actually, I called in to see if there was anything I can do."

"Hmph, think about it. Give me your number, I'll call you back."

There was no problem about waiting for the call because the McNeils made me stay, saying I had to do the washing up, then it was time for a drink and finally they insisted I stay for dinner, which was a real treat, and I didn't demur. They were both in high spirits.

The sunset had curious greeny-grey tinges in it, which I should have taken as a warning. With the mellowing effect of the good company and a delightful meal, plus the fact that a call hadn't come through, I left it too late.

Poofy finally rang back at 8.00 p.m. He'd done some fast homework since I hadn't given him Jack's name.

"I want you to go to Lossiemouth with Commander Plumley in the morning. Is your aeroplane functional?"

"Yes."

"Well perhaps you'd like to fly him back, he hasn't got transport at the moment. See Briggs, the Security Officer – he'll brief you. Did you get a make on your visitor, by the way?"

"No, just a familiar feeling. Do you think it's important?"

"I've no idea, but you shouldn't forget faces in this business. Can be costly. Well, that's all then. Good night."

He had a clipped tenor voice, which could be quite irritating, but it was easy to come back to the present as we talked and listened to the sunlit music of Vivaldi and Handel on the record-player. Then a sharp wind came up from the south-west, sending a steep nasty little chop against the ebbing tide; drops of rain rattled on the windows to underline my alarm when I realised I wouldn't be able to get back home, at least not with the Teal. Cleodie sensed my concern and promptly suggested that I stay the night.

"That's all right, isn't it, Mother? The spare room's made up."

"Yes, of course. Go on with what you were saying, Seamus."

I'd forgotten what I was saying because of my consternation. If I was still someone's target, and there was no reason why not,

49

my presence might endanger anyone near me, but even if I asked Cleodie to give me a lift home by road, the aircraft remained a pointer to my presence, real or not. At least there was no dilemma; I'd have to stay with it and stay awake.

Meanwhile they had an urgent need to categorise me – not, admittedly, the prerogative only of women. I gave them a brief CV but contrived to make it sound boring so their curiosity wasn't aggravated by mysteriousness. I was able to say that I had no surviving family, but without saying that my mother had died when I was ten in a quiet despair because my father hadn't actually been killed at Anzio, just shell-shocked into a helpless moron, dying in an institution a few years before. I turned the subject to do some quizzing of my own.

Cleodie had a degree in English, which she taught at a school near Edinburgh, along with various games and general Physical Education, which accounted for her fitness. The school had just been through an epidemic of flu, and those who had escaped had been sent home, with Cleodie among the lucky ones. Another week's grace would lead into ten days for half term, so she was feeling very pleased about it. So was I, and all the danger signals were howling at me. I suppose I had begun to miss amenable company quite badly without being fully aware of it, and now it was there with a vengeance.

When they felt it was time for bed, I made an effort to conceal my anxiety. "Look, if you're sure it's all right for me to stay, I'd better bring the plane up a bit. It was after high water when we stopped and this wind will pile up the next tide, I should think."

Cleodie came out of her chair in a single fluid movement, now pleasingly familiar. "I'll come and show you where, you mustn't carve up Carruthers' lawn."

I went outside and waited a moment while she fetched a jacket. The wind was still fierce, but seemed to have dropped slightly. I had an urgent need for positive action and felt frustrated and helpless. I thought again of Shriver and further violence and felt very bitter until Cleodie came out and we walked down the lawn. On my own, I had strong feelings of foreboding which I couldn't explain, but Cleodie was almost a complete distraction.

"Have you found anything out yet? I didn't ask you in there because I told Carruthers about the drowning but nothing about the sinister part. I don't think she's very well really." Her voice

50

dropped to a conspiratorial whisper. "What's it all about? I've a feeling you haven't told me something."

"Not really, but I've got nothing to go on, at least until I can remember where I saw the man before."

Curiously, she left it at that, and we walked to the water's edge in silence. Her coolheadedness and control were to be a constant surprise to me, especially in one so vital and eager.

"It's quite rough," she said. "Could you get back if you really had to?"

"Perhaps, but it's not worth it. There's no one to show off to in the dark."

She laughed gaily. "You're really scoring today, aren't you? I'll have to brush up my repartee. Inside, you made a remark about you having secrets *too* – obviously meant to draw me. But I'm not going to ask."

"Then you'd be missing a compliment." I was thinking of those deep, dark eyes, but she made no response beyond a quick snort.

"Now, she wants to be facing into wind. Can I go on that patch of rough there?"

"Yes, that'll do fine. Perhaps we'd better pull the dinghy up as well, just in case, but I don't think this is a big blow coming, do you?"

"I'll see what the altimeter's done. It works like a barometer." I got into the Teal and she leaned in after me.

"This one here. It was zeroed at sea-level and it now says nearly ninety feet, which is a drop of about three millibars – not too significant in, what, four or five hours? Should be all right."

"Do you have to zero it every time you fly, then?"

"Sort of, yes, but at higher levels everyone adopts a common setting so that the relative heights of aircraft to one another remain the same. The pressure can change from place to place, like during a flight, so it's very necessary. It can make a difference of many hundreds of feet. Now would you mind taking your head away, today has been far too intimate and it's getting me rattled."

"I'd never have noticed, you haven't moved a muscle."

"Neither does an empty tiger, then suddenly he springs!"

I made a deep bass "Miaow" in her ear and she withdrew quickly in pretended fright. I started the engine, let it warm for a minute then taxied up onto higher ground. When I'd finished, we pulled

51

up her sailing dinghy and ran back to the house chased by a shower of rain.

Carruthers was clearing up, and we all went to bed soon after on the buoyant note of a day thoroughly enjoyed. Cleodie showed me to my room, fussed around with towels and found me a toothbrush and then said goodnight at my door. The air between us was full of many unspoken things.

"Thank you for a super day," she said.

I held up my hand palm towards her as if to protest and she looked at it curiously, her head on one side, and since it went with the gesture, I said deeply, Indian fashion, "How."

"Easily," she answered, then touched her finger-tips to mine and turned quickly away.

Without Fergus and the trip-wires I had to be my own sentinel, and the dog had had the added bonus that, having seen me put them in, he didn't set off any alarms himself but stepped over them with gingerly suspicion. I didn't want to alarm the McNeils either, so I had to be very quiet myself.

The house was completely quiet by 10.30, a good rural hour for bedtime. I slept for two hours, leaving the rest of the night for watching like a single-handed yachtsman in the shipping lanes – up every twenty minutes for a good scan. Once you get the idea of it, you don't mind too much.

My room overlooked the back of the house, but the bathroom was opposite so that I could watch all approaches as well as the Teal. The rain had stopped and the clouds broke frequently; the faint starlight and later the appearance of the waning moon would make an unobserved stalk very difficult. I felt a curious sense of vitality mingled with worry and responsibility. It's next to impossible to anticipate moves against you if you don't know what the opposition wants. All I knew for sure was that the swimmer was not alone because someone had removed his clothes, an extraordinary act in itself unless they contained identification.

At 3.13 a car passed on the road about a quarter of a mile above the cottage. At 3.35 another passed in the opposite direction. Too much traffic – the same car? It went on, and the sound faded too quickly and did not recur, although the road was winding with plenty of hilly bits. I dressed quickly and, knowing that the stairs creaked, let myself out of the window and dropped from arms' length. As I came out of the landing crouch my adrenalin was all

52

over the place as my right thigh brushed against an upright bamboo stake firmly planted in the flowerbed. A bit close, worth a shudder.

I made my way up to the road, and then along it, keeping carefully to the edge and the shadows, in the direction the car had taken, east towards Achintraid. After going gingerly for nearly half an hour, I had seen and heard nothing, and was just about to give it up as a wild goose chase when one of the frequent cloud-breaks let the thin crescent of moon show the silhouette of a black car parked well off the road to the right. There was no one to be seen, and once I'd got close enough to establish that nobody was in or near it, all the alarm bells went off in my head. They must have taken the direct route either across the fields or down to the shore and along it, and they would have had enough time to be at the cottage by now. They might be just lining up a bazooka or something, and there was no chance of getting back in time to stop them. I tried the car door, and it was locked, so I smashed the quarter light with a stone, and jammed a piece of stout twig between the door and the horn, which was on a stalk. I left it blaring, and raced back the way I had come, and it could still be heard quite clearly from the track leading down to the cottage. I approached slowly in a crouch to keep behind the hedge, and tried to control my breathing. A light came on upstairs, but I didn't know whose room it was, and I ventured a cautious look over the hedge. About three fields away, I could see two figures running in the direction of the car, but could make out no detail of size or shape, or what they were carrying, although the first tinges of dawn had appeared. The wind was dying too, and in a few minutes the horn had stopped, followed immediately by the sound of the car accelerating away.

Relieved and at the same time vaguely disappointed, I walked towards the house and scrunched across gravel.

"Who's that? What are you doing?" came Cleodie's hushed voice from an upstairs window. The light had gone off, and I could just make out her face framed in shadow.

"Me, Seamus. Did you hear that horn? Thought there might have been an accident, so I went to have a look, then it drove away. Did you hear it?"

"Yes. I didn't hear you go out."

"Jumped. Is the door locked?"

"Yes, hang on, I'll let you in."

53

When she came down and had the door open for me, she whispered, "Proper little hero, aren't you?"

"If only you knew." I told her about the bamboo in the flowerbed, and she said, "Ugh," and huddled herself more closely. She was doing this already because of the flimsiness of some ridiculous wispy thing she was wearing. I gave a resigned sigh and looked pointedly away, and she said, "Whatever you say, I feel I have no secrets any more after yesterday. If you must know, I don't own a dressing-gown, and I only put this stupid thing on to come down in. What are you looking like that for? I bet you think I fell off the ski on purpose. Mother saw us go past, you know. She said, 'I didn't know you had a white bikini, Cleodie,' without being at all pointed, so I don't know if she realised or not."

"Well, she'll think twice if she comes down now. Can't you put a mac on or something, before she throws me out?"

"Oh, don't worry. She found a chap pawing me once, and do you know what she said?" I shook my head, waiting. "She just said, 'optimist', and walked out of the room!"

"Did that spur him on to greater efforts, or did he retire in confusion?"

"Full of clichés at this hour, aren't you? No, he just sort of lost interest."

"Must have been purely physical, and the mental obstruction was too great. Was this recent?"

"Course not, I'm a big girl now, nobody paws me any more."

"So there."

"So there," she smiled back. "Would you like a coffee or anything?"

"Anything sounds great, but I'm going back to bed."

"Oh come on, I'm wide awake now. We could stoke up the fire and get warm. I'll put a mac on if you like."

"I'll still know what's underneath." I gazed at her long and hard, and she returned my look with a charming, guileless smile, which was just too much. I went up to her and held her tightly by the arms. I said, quietly and closely, "I will *not* treat you as a creature comfort I have been without for some time. There's a pleasure in saying close and cosy things for their own sake, but we've both got to know that I mean them. I anticipate mightily, and I want to be allowed to enjoy it, even if it's just optimism. I hope you're not too big a girl to need respect. See you in the morning."

She actually helped to turn me round, and I went resolutely

54

upstairs without looking at her expression. That was her problem, I had enough of my own.

It took me a long time to get to sleep even after getting my pulse down to normal. I distracted myself by wondering whether the boys would be back, since they would think I would think it most unlikely, which would make it a perfect opportunity, but then they might think I would think of that. I should have stayed up, I suppose, but by the time that argument had gone several full circles it was too light anyway. It doesn't feel right going to sleep when the birds have started singing, and the memory of ancient boozy nights tells you to feel ghastly as soon as you wake.

In fact I felt marvellous, for Cleodie was standing there fully dressed for a change, drawing my curtains and cheerfully announcing breakfast. I pretended to look scared and hugged the bedclothes tight around me, but she laughed gaily and went out. I wondered if she'd been teasing or testing, which was sceptical, I suppose, but she was too good to be true.

After breakfast I flew away south to Plockton, still wondering about the intruders. It felt a lot better now that there was a possibility of having the Navy to call on, especially with my clear memories of how helpless the police had been in the face of Shriver's rampages against the flying club. Even when I was under full surveillance, his rented heavies had got through, untraceable to him, of course, and the surveillance had effectively prevented any counteraction on my part. Naval Security has a more right-wing approach for, as I was certainly aware, if they found someone to have acquired knowledge which it was dangerous for him to have, that person simply ceased to exist. And there were no complaints, either.

In this case, if someone could afford to lose a man and still keep coming with reinforcements, a couple of sceptical policemen serving several hundred square miles would simply not be able to afford much in the way of protection.

Life for the lone wolf must be as tough as anything one can imagine, especially if he has memories of better times.

Five

Plockton was delightfully picturesque in the early sunlight, with the tide at half-ebb. By the time I had taxied in between the stones and the smaller boats lying aground, Jack was standing by the gap in the wall with a duffel bag on his shoulder, his mother and father next to him. She smiled as she said good-bye, so I assumed he hadn't disgraced himself the night before. Or perhaps she hadn't heard about it yet. When his grinning face appeared at the window, and he had pushed his bag into the rear compartment, I asked him if he'd stayed at home, since he didn't look at all fragile. He shot me a sour kind of glance, and hauled himself aboard, saying nothing, just giving a brief wave to his parents as I started up and turned the nose back down the beach. He remained silent until long after we were airborne and climbing westward up Loch Carron, while I messed about getting the wheels down and tearing the map on the central lever. He held the two pieces together with one hand and the index finger of the other rather heavily described "You are here" motions, encompassing a diameter of about forty miles. I fell in with him by looking startled and darting anxious glances through the side window, so he put the map away and pointed straight ahead with a bent finger, and I acknowledged his guidance by inclining my head graciously. It's very pleasant to have your mood suited, and I reached behind for the headsets and plugged them in, so that we could talk in reasonable quiet and use the radio later on. He surprised me then.

"Today," he said, "I am a humbled man. I represent an investment of hundreds of thousands of pounds by HMG. I am defined as a Master Pilot, Lord of the Skies, fearless, deadly and unyielding as carbon steel under pressure, and, would you believe it, some cheapjack cad in a tinpot flying boat actually made me wet my knickers?"

His voice had risen an octave and I was looking at him incredulously, so he emphasised the point by roaring through the earphones: "I PISSED MY PANTS, YOU BASTARD!"

Now that he'd got it off his chest, I'm sure he expected to pay for it by having to listen to me gurgling with laughter, because his hand went out to remove my microphone jack. Instead I looked at him with interest and a little surprise while he stared grimly ahead. Eventually, hearing no audible reaction, he turned to look at me and there was gratitude in his eyes.

"Won't tell anyone, will you?" he asked, half-smiling and rueful.

"Well, look, as they say in the Mafia, I own you now. Let's just leave it that you keep your promise."

"What promise?"

"Phantom."

"I never promised. Anyway, you have to be fully vetted through Fighter Command, that takes weeks, then we have to give you a proper medical, then half-drown you in the local baths for ditching procedure and spend hours showing you what you mustn't touch. You're not even supposed to know what goes on in those things. Anyway, who would you tell?"

"All your mates, especially the juniors. And Cleodie, maybe. Anyway, I've done most of that stuff a few years back, in the RAF. I went through basic training."

He digested that and then said, "Actually, I was wondering whether I should report it, since I had a total collapse under fright."

"Don't be so daft, it was completely out of context. You were relaxed and on holiday. If something similar happened in the air or even on standby, you'd react the way you want to because you're trained for it and your whole system is higher tuned. Think of the number of times you've been practice-jumped in the air – I bet it was never that unexpected, and you must have reacted properly or you'd be the man who changes the plugs long ago. Do they still discharge rattled pilots with a big rubber stamp marked 'Lack of moral fibre', by the way?"

"No, that was a rather harsh wartime practice, although they got rid of it only a short while ago. Some headshrink discovered that more pilots got rattled at the thought of going LMF than actually got the squits in action."

"Sounds thoroughly permissive. Anyway, I shouldn't worry about a thing. I'd have thought that for a man in your lofty position, it's quite cheering to discover you have human traits, just once in a while. Tell you what, I'll let you relax for a bit and enjoy the view, and when you least expect it, I'll shout 'Bandit!' in your ear. If you crawl under the panel with your hands over your ears, then I'll agree you should report for a new brainwashing, OK?"

He grinned and nodded, then glanced up ahead. There was some cloud, but it was quite high, and I decided that once we had enough height, we could turn due east for Inverness, instead of following the glen as I had to do in thicker weather. As we climbed out of Glen Carron, the morning sun came blinding over the nearer mountains, and we both hauled out dark glasses. The day was very clear after the previous night's blow, and there was nothing much over 3,500 feet between us and Ness. When the visibility is good, it's nowhere better than in North-west Scotland, except perhaps in the Western Isles themselves. Every prospect contains such an eyeful of beauty and contrast that a feeling of slow elation always creeps over you, and that morning trouble and violence were suddenly far removed. Also it seemed there was a new dimension to my life which for a moment I couldn't pinpoint but wanted very much to continue. The question rose almost unbidden, and Jack's open honesty had removed any need for hedging between us. For all his lechery, I didn't see him as a rival.

"Jack," I asked, "is a man in love more prone to fear for his skin or less, do you know?"

"Dunno." His look implied that it was a silly question, and he raised a questioning eyebrow at me. "There are stories about chaps continuing to transmit while they're going down in flames, and mostly they're short, sharp obscenities, not usually soliloquies about gathering rosebuds while ye may. A man's gotta do what a man's gotta do, and all that gobbledegook."

"Bloody hell, what's that?"

The Teal had lurched violently, and there was a lot of buffeting all of a sudden, accompanied by the bleeping of the stall-warning horn. Jack checked his instinctive reach for the stick, remembering he wasn't supposed to be instructing, but I was shortly to be glad of his presence. We both scanned the instrument panel for an indication of the trouble, and the main factor was a sink rate of nearly a thousand feet per minute. The airspeed had fallen off, though not severely, and the needle was flickering very strangely. With the buffeting and vibration, I thought we might have lost part of the propeller blade, but the engine instruments betrayed nothing, all steady and normal. The terrain below was impossible, and I began a slow turn back to the first ridge, from where we could make a quick descent into the glen and the haven of some water to get her down safely. As we turned, with everything loose shaking like mad, my worst fears were confirmed, that we couldn't make the ridge with the present height loss. We'd only crossed it about two minutes ago, in cruise climb at about 400 feet per minute. I was just taking my eyes from the side window, when I did a double-take on a flickering shadow. I looked up sharply, and looked down again at once.

"Gremlin!" I called urgently, half aloud.

"What?" said Jack.

"Sorry, bandit," I answered, quietly, so that he'd know I meant it. I pointed straight upwards, while casting my eyes all around for something flat, hard or soft, anything. Out of the corner of my right eye, I could see Jack peering upwards through the tinted top sections of the windows, but otherwise in my vision there was only forest and rock outcrops. A stretch of water lay off to the east, but it was six or seven miles away, and I dismissed the idea of even turning towards it. Trying to hold her steady, I looked up again, at the helicopter right overhead, the two skids only a few feet above our whirling propeller. I could make out the pilot's face peering down through the glass beneath his rudder pedals.

"He's not grinning," said Jack. "Have you got any mad friends with a Bell Jet Ranger?"

"No, it's a real bandit, it must be, after all that's happened. Hold on, I'm getting out from under."

It was so close above that I was worried about hitting it with any violent manoeuvre. I tried a couple of tentative turns, and it just banked with me, and we were losing precious seconds. Even if I didn't smash our propeller on his skids, he would be able to follow a steep turn just as well. I gave her a bootful of starboard rudder and a handful of port stick, and there was a slight thump as we sideslipped violently to port. I think the starboard wing-tip must have touched him as the wing came up, but nothing seemed to have been damaged. I held it hard over for a few seconds, and merely succeeded in losing height even faster, for when I looked up again,

I confirmed what Jack was saying to me quietly, "The bastard's still there, he just held the slip with you. Try it different ways a few times."

I had the throttle wide open by this time, and slipped her this way and that, using so much rudder that she was skidding about like a saucer in a sink, but the Bell just held on like a lamprey. It appeared he was just aiming literally to fly us into the ground, and he was close to succeeding, for I judged there to be about three hundred feet left to us, no more. I racked my brains for some way to escape the paralysing downstream of the rotors, but as the Bell has a greater top speed than the Teal, nothing forwards was going to help much, we'd tried both sides for sideways, and unlike him we couldn't stop or go backwards.

With the increased speed from the application of full power, our rate of descent was slightly reduced, but there was no doubt our number was up in about half a minute or less, and then the very best that we could expect was a bill from the Forestry Commission for uprooting part of a plantation. I was furious at being unable to extract us; it was like being a ping-pong ball under a water tap, bouncing vigorously but held firmly in place.

"Any suggestions?" I asked Jack.

"Pull up and roll off the top." His voice was quite flat, like answering a question during a boring lecture.

I understood the idea, because if we could get the helicopter to sit on its tail it would stop flying and go in with no height left to play with. So might we; the Teal was no aerobat. And there was another snag.

"If we hit his skids with the prop, we'll be no better off."

"Yeah." Jack's face was without expression, his right hand hovering next to the stick, not quite touching it. Then he barked another monosyllable, sharply.

"Bunt!"

"What?"

"Bunt. Shall I do it?"

"Go ahead."

"Right, I have it. Hold on to your vicaries."

I let go the stick as he took over, and, after a quick tug at his seat belt, his left hand went up to the throttle. He made a rapid glance at the helicopter, scanned the forward horizon then eased us into a right turn. The helicopter followed suit, then we came level again, briefly. Jack repeated the turn only this time much steeper, and he held it, getting the wings almost vertical. The helicopter held the same position relative to us, banking inside our wall-of-death turn at a ridiculous angle, intent on monitoring our descent to the bitter end.

Suddenly, Jack said, "Belt!" and there was barely time to take a last tug at it before being overcome by the most horrible sensation. From our vertical turn, he rammed the stick forward smoothly but very firmly, reversing our turn into the negative sense.

The belt cut into my thighs as I came off the seat, and my vision went pink as the blood burst tiny vessels in the eyes, classic symptoms of a "red out". The high negative G-force should have buckled the wings downwards, though I didn't think of that at the time. In the cockpit there was pandemonium as the anchor and Jack's bag and various other loose articles slammed against the ceiling. After a vicious half turn, Jack reversed it and pulled the stick back, but we had lost nearly all of our remaining height and the trees were almost brushing the starboard wing-tip. The engine coughed once, cut out briefly and picked up again.

The prong on the anchor struck me with great force behind the ear as it fell back, though the bag thumped harmlessly on the floor behind us. Jack had the stick hard over towards me but she wasn't coming level quick enough, wasn't going to make it because of the slow rolling ability. There wasn't time to explain, so I slammed my left foot on the rudder to help her over the inertia, and we struck the top branch of a pine-tree just as she came level.

Off to the right, we saw the helicopter falling amid pieces of smashed rotor blade, sinking almost lazily on its side into the trees. Jack had the stick hard back and the Teal was trying to drag itself into the air, though fully stalled, the warning horn blaring insistently. The ground fell away slightly and in a moment we were flying again instead of mushing along in imitation.

Jack explained the manoeuvre to me afterwards as a deception to get your opponent to think you are trying to escape with a tight turn, then suddenly reversing it. For two fighters, it would serve to separate them and to get the one with an advantage off your neck, for even though he might follow the move a split second later, he would then be on the outside of the turn. The helicopter pilot would have tried to stay with us instinctively, but in his case the sudden reversal of force would have caused the rotors to try to "clap hands" under its belly and they would in any case have smashed into the tailboom.

We circled the spot where he had crashed to see if anything was still wriggling, but after a few moments it blew up in a black and orange whoosh.

Jack levelled up again onto an easterly heading and trimmed for climb, but neither of us said anything for quite a while until I asked him casually, "Jack, what are vicaries?"

"Things you have vicarious pleasure with."

"Oh."

"Wouldn't have got near us if you'd had a seebackroscope."

"What's that?"

"A mirror." He sounded quite full of himself and reached out to retune the transmitter.

"What are you doing?" I asked when I saw him select 121·5, the Distress Frequency.

"Better put out a Mayday for that bod."

"No," I said sharply, "it's not urgent."

"Well, a PAN then, not so urgent?"

"It's not urgent at all. I got the last two letters of the registration, it was Bravo Zulu. Did you get any more?"

"No, 'fraid not."

"His most likely fuelling point is Dalcross. Let's go in there and see if we can find out who it was, discreetly. We can fill up ourselves at the same time."

"Good idea, I could use a large Scotch."

"Fuel, I meant. Anyway, I think it's something I have to sort out myself because I have no leads yet. Someone came for me again last night but I managed to distract them. No identities though. Glad to have you along, by the way."

"I quite enjoyed that, thanks. Didn't even wet my pants, so you were quite right."

"Aha," I said, cruelly, "but suppose there'd been *two* helicopters?"

His answer was a wolfish grin which was poor repartee but answer enough, I suppose. We flew on without speaking for a while and shortly were able to see the deep blue finger of Loch Ness slowly open out its whole great length towards the north-east.

"Have you been in there?" he asked.

"Yes, but it's often quite rough, except for the little bay at Drumnadrochit"

"Can I try it, a little playtime after all that serious stuff?"

I snorted, then shrugged. "Why not? You have control."

"I have control." He took over again in the formal manner, put the nose down slightly, opened the throttle and executed a perfect barrel-roll. Even upside down, every article in the plane stayed in its place and there was no discomfort beyond a certain alarmed surprise. He straightened up, grinning, and I pointed to the placard on the panel which said, "Aerobatics Prohibited, including spins."

He feigned a guilty look and grinned again. "A barrel isn't really aerobatics, if you do it properly. Should pull One-G all the way round. I must say she side-slips well, a little joy that flaps have deprived us of. OK, what's the rigmarole?"

By this time we were heading up the loch at reduced height. I said, "First decide where the wind's coming from, then raise the landing gear. That's about it. Very shallow approach. I'll go through with you. Sixty-five knots on finals, prop in fine pitch, fourteen inches manifold."

"How can you tell wind direction?"

"Waves make slight crescents, the outer curve on the downwind side. Otherwise look for a sail-boat if there's no smoke anywhere. Or a seagull, they always sit head to wind. Or look there, a gust spreading a dark line on the water, from the north-west roughly; you can go straight into the bay."

"OK, but what about getting out again, there's high ground beyond?"

"Downwind take-off, or a running start. No problem."

He settled on his approach and then asked, "What happens if you leave the gear down?"

"Disaster. Tell you in a minute."

"OK ... Whoops!"

He came in too fast, realised it, held off for too long and eventually thumped her down very hard. As if to make amends, he tried to stop her by bringing the stick back but it was too soon, she took off again briefly and rewarded us with another spine-jarring wallop.

When we finally came to a stop, his mouth, which had been a tight line of concentration, turned down apologetically.

"Sorry. Must have been something I ate."

63

He was irrepressible and chuckling. I showed him the tight-spot take-off, starting downwind and turning hard in the opposite direction at nearly forty knots, the force pressing his body against my arm on the overhead throttle. Airborne, we flew up the northern half of the loch about one foot above the water, getting the occasional thump from a wave top. He enjoyed it all and told me that the Navy used Loch Ness to practise low flying over water because of its twenty-two mile length.

"We have to hold it six feet off, at 500 knots, so one twitch and you've had it. Hangovers are definitely out."

"Well, I reckon I have more fun because it lasts longer. Would only take you about two minutes at that speed."

When we climbed out over Inverness to join the airfield circuit, I said, "If anyone saw the accident, it would have been reported by now and on the wires. It's quite likely they didn't, since we were so low and it's mostly forest there. Anyway, when we get to the control tower, I'll sneak a look in the movements book while you distract them. Think you can manage that?"

We got Air Traffic clearance straight in and I pulled off a lovely, greasy three-pointer. Most people remember their war-books where such miracles were commonplace, but nowadays they're almost a thing of the past as tail-wheel aircraft have become the exception. I can never get big-headed about it because I recall vividly and with chagrin my very first tail-wheeler landing at Gatwick when bringing the aircraft from Le Havre, sufficient description of which was contained in the dry words of the ATC; after what seemed like the twenty-fifth bounce, he drawled, "Golf Alpha X-ray Zulu November, this is NOT a water runway." Under the rather sweaty circumstances, I confess I was lost even for a predictable reply, let alone any smart banter in return. I really thought I was going to write the machine off, and that was fairly common in wartime, too.

We bounded up the steps of the control tower and in a few moments Jack had the controller by the window pointing out the wreckage of a recent short landing. I skimmed the open movements book and quickly found a — BZ Jet Ranger had visited Dalcross only the previous day. Casually, I asked the controller if I could look at his UK registration list, which he produced for me at once. Now that I had the remaining letters, it was a simple matter to establish that the helicopter belonged to Highland and Lowland Offshore Services, which made me smile grimly. Halos, that was sweetly inappropriate. Offices in London and Aberdeen. I jotted down the addresses, signed for my landing fee and we left without further ceremony. We had the aircraft refuelled and went into the airport lounge.

We waited in the queue for coffee and a bun and when Jack finally wrenched his eyes away from the incredible variety of knickers and parted thighs in the magazine racks, he said, "I ought to call Lossie first and get us a clearance, otherwise they'll have us circling for half an hour while the controller consults his elders. Be back in a shake."

He drank his coffee quickly and went off to find a telephone. He had a stocky, purposeful walk, and kept his head well up, as if looking for the lighter side of things. I wondered if that was why broody people keep their heads down or whether the angle at which they're built makes them broody. Jack's training would tend to make him wide-eyed and exceptionally observant, not to mention the rubber neck developed from constantly searching the horizon. Conversely, I'm sure that the man in the street naturally develops tunnel-vision, enclosed as he is by buildings, his daily journey and the confines of his workplace and home, as well as the unending pressure of "civilised" stresses. The conditioning makes him unconscious of it, of course, and it's only if you are fortunate enough to cast off these cares for some reason and get a chance really to look about you that your perception takes on a vastly multiplied dimension. An exact simile in the physical sense is the way clear weather in the Hebrides literally opens your eyes, and much of what was only peripheral vision seems to become actual.

I had stood up during this musing, and was given the perfect example of how detail can distract one from the whole, when I found my eyes tugged towards a luscious figure on a magazine cover, stark naked and with her legs in the air, both hands clamped over her crutch; I realised as I turned away that I hadn't even looked at her face.

In the immortal words of one Abraham Schlink, "Und vot vas she selling, eh?"

Search me, pal.

Six

Kinloss and Lossiemouth are only a few miles apart, and when both stations are active the air is pretty full over the bleak southern edge of the Moray Firth. RAF and Navy stations respectively, they are situated there because the area is supposed to have the best all-round weather factor in Europe. Somehow one associates the North Sea with a never-ending cycle of storm winds and rolling fog-banks, but by all accounts the incidence of unflyable weather is comparatively low.

Nimrods of the RAF operate from Kinloss, and in their basic shape are more than reminiscent of the old De Havilland Comet, Sir Geoffrey's masterpiece. It is in fact the same design with the wings and the top of the fuselage easily recognised as the first and certainly the most handsome of the early jet airliners, with the four engines beautifully faired into the wings close to the roots. Below, the Nimrod differs externally with a broadened and flattened lower fuselage and the nose has grown an out-thrust jaw underneath it. The great endurance of this machine and the fabulous array of electronic gadgetry packed into the bulbous body combine to make it a sort of bloodhound of the ocean, or so they tell us, for the security is very tight and only the people who actually handle the equipment ever get to see it. When a member of the Press is allowed aboard, perhaps to spend up to ten cramped hours circling the grey Icelandic seas in the hope of one brief glimpse of a gunboat hassling a trawler, the antisubmarine equipment is all covered up with drapes, and if it had to be used he wouldn't be allowed to watch.

To get clearance through his zone, we called up the Kinloss

controller and were asked to hold our position for one aircraft on two mile final. A Nimrod was approaching from the east, landing lights blazing even on such a bright day, so I replied that we had his Number One visual and he cleared us through with the frequency change for Lossiemouth. As it was Sunday, there was little routine activity and because of Jack's call before we took off there was no query of our identity. In no time at all, we completed the pattern and landed, were directed crisply to a parking spot and immediately surrounded by four ratings with sub-machine guns held downwards across their thighs. I didn't know whether to grin ingratiatingly or put my hands up, so feeling a bit sheepish, I contrived to make an ambiguous gesture by using both hands to close off the overhead mixture control and stop the engine. Jack ignored the whole business and reached round for his baggage, so I concluded it was routine and not an arrest on one of two possible charges of assisting in the demise of persons unknown.

As we got out, a security officer strode up and two of the men were detailed to search the Teal, which worried me a little because a fair part of the structure is semi-sealed compartments. My concern was obviously noted for he spoke reassuringly.

"Don't worry, sir. It's standing orders to check on everything that comes in here. But we won't be using tin-openers. Just a quick look so I can say we've done it. Pretty little machine, I must say – wasn't it on the cover of *Flight* some time ago?"

"Yes, it was. Very complimentary, cutaway drawing, the lot."

"I remember. Now would you like to come this way, please? I suppose it was a change for you to be travelling so slowly, Commander Plumley?"

"Yes indeed, you actually see people on the ground and they're up to all *sorts* of things. Should be stopped, what?"

The Security man drove us over to the Officers' Mess and Jack asked me to stick around while he checked in. I looked around and there were several men lounging about quietly with the Sunday papers so I did the same for a few minutes while I waited. In spite of the cancelled leaves and Full Alert status, the atmosphere was one of deliberate calm.

Jack returned and said, "Nothing doing for now, we've got three flights up and one on standby so I shouldn't be called for two or three hours. You've got to see the Security Officer, Briggs, haven't you? I'll take you over."

A chilly breeze had sprung up from the east, but the sky was still bright and clear. Over the northern skyline, two swift and silent black shapes, plan-profile, showed their swept wings in a steep turn as they curved round for the eastbound runway, and the muted roar I expected to hear never came because they kept turning towards us. I stopped to watch them make a deft formation landing, and it was only as they passed that the howl from their tail-pipes became apparent. They touched, rolled and took off again.

Jack had walked on and when I caught him up, I said, "I suppose it's all old hat to you and they're only subsonic after all."

"I'm not keen on the Jaguar, not many people are. Feel it's a camel, no flair, committee job. Lot of bloody rubbish, this Anglo-French co-operation. You couldn't imagine two races less suited to getting along together."

"In a year or two you'll be considered a stuffy anachronism. Anyway, Concorde got off the ground."

"Sure, but at what *cost*! The logistics involved are beyond belief. But let's skip it. I've had this argument too often to get steamed up about it any more. I've made a resolution that no politician is ever going to make me angry again. Life's too short. Here we are, in here."

As he led me inside, I remarked that no cars seemed to be parked near any of the buildings, although there were many hundreds in rows in one huge central area. He told me it was a rigid security measure, for if anyone did manage to get inside with a bootful of gelignite it would only be effective next to a building or an aircraft where it would be highly conspicuous.

"It's only just moving into top gear, this flap. Quite a job rounding people up. I was supposed to have a week's leave. I'm really grateful for the lift, by the way, that's a terrible journey without a car, bad enough with. On the way down I got a lift to Fort Augustus and had to hitch the rest of the way."

As I followed him down a long corridor, I asked if he had a car?

"Had one till last week, but it fell over at three o'clock in the morning. Missed my date and had to walk about eight miles."

He sounded slightly bitter about it, but I refrained from making the obvious enquiry since it invited the obvious retort: "That's a bloody silly question!" I kept to an amused grunt, thinking how immediately one associates the early hours of the morning with drunkenness or questionable behaviour or both. I felt sure that if

68

Jack wanted to correct any such impression he would do so, but he remained silent. In the air, however, he wasn't at all the haphazard character he affected on the ground.

He stopped and knocked at an open door marked Cdr E.Briggs. After a moment or two a sepulchral voice bade us enter. Jack held the door for me, speaking round it.

"Hello, Teddy. Brought someone to see you. Mr Squire."

As I spoke his name in reply, he stood up to shake hands and I gazed at the tallest, boniest cadaver I had ever seen. He looked at me unsmiling from under great shaggy eyebrows, from eyes so deep set that they were in shadow and quite unfathomable. Grey skin stretched over his skull and jaw without a trace of flesh underneath. He would have made a fortune in the horror movies, especially as he had the voice to match. I was to learn that he had a brain of very devious capacity coupled with a murderous, dead-pan wit. He looked at Jack silently, with one threatening eyebrow hoisted.

Jack coughed and said, "Would you like me to leave?"

Briggs nodded, so Jack turned, stopped and came back. There was a very quizzical look on his face.

"I've just thought of something," he said archly.

"That's just possible, but unlikely," answered Briggs.

"It's rather delicate."

"That's not possible." Briggs' expression hadn't changed.

"Well, actually it is, if you see what I mean."

"No, I don't."

"Oh. I rather hoped that you would."

"Well, what is it, come on?"

"Teddy, I believe you are a patient man, an understanding, gentle, fatherly sort of man, in spite of what everyone says."

"Are you going to get to the point or have lunch first?"

"Yes, yes. But it's just occurred to me, and I do really believe it's rather delicate."

"So you said. Proceed."

"Well, it's more delicate than that, Teddy."

Briggs looked less like a Teddy than anyone I ever met. He barked out, "Well, how do I know until you've asked it?"

Jack decided to get to the point. "Have Security been trying to kill this man, or anything?"

"What for?"

"Could he have found out something he shouldn't and they've sent the boys in?"

"What makes you think that?"

"Well, someone tried to kill us this morning, possibly him rather than me, and he wants to find out who it was."

"What for?"

"Er . . . so's he can tell him to stop it, I suppose. After all, it's not the first time, you know."

"No," said Briggs with finality, after a moment's thought.

"Sorry?"

"No, we haven't been trying to kill him. If we had he wouldn't be standing there, would he?"

"You mean you'd have offered him a chair instead?"

"Oh, my dear fellow, I'm so sorry. Do sit down," he said to me, suddenly brimful of deference. I was still taken aback by the conversation and stayed where I was. They didn't notice and plunged straight in again, both starting at once. The telephone interrupted them.

Briggs answered, grunted once with an exasperated sigh, lifted the scrambler out of the drawer and waved us out of the room. The door was completely sound-proof.

Outside in the corridor, I said, "He's right, you know. They'd have succeeded. Also, they wouldn't have endangered you, that would make it an expensive way to get me off the payroll."

"I suppose so, but tread carefully; I'm always suspicious of that lot. This must be a hell of a thing, he looks as though he hasn't slept for a week, not that he'd look any better if he _had_ slept for a week."

"Is he intelligent?"

"Like a knife – a chain-saw rather, if you ever hear him laugh. He's got two brains, one carries on a completely abnormal conversation and the other is miles away on a different problem. We got him smashed again last week, always the same pattern: stands there sharp, aggressive, cynical, absolutely the same for hours, then he actually smiles and goes benign. That lasts for five or six minutes, then he just keels over unconscious. Quite normal in the morning, looks so awful you can't tell the difference. Oh good, char."

An orderly came by with a tea-trolley. We helped ourselves and stopped the man in the act of knocking on Briggs' door. Jack drained his cup quickly.

"You wait here and give him a mug when he's finished. I'll go and check the form and see you later."

He hurried off and a moment afterwards the door was wrenched open and the death's head jutted out and said, "Bloody hell," as the tea-trolley vanished round a distant corner. I held the extra cup under his nose and he took it without a word, then slunk back inside sniffing with suspicion. He reminded me of Fergus.

"I'm sorry," I said, "seem to have picked a bad moment."

"I should apologise for being uncivil to a civilian, but I'm sick and tired of panic phone calls, being chewed out for nothing and told to sit on my arse and wait for further orders and when I'm not doing that I'm supposed to screen everyone from the station commander downwards about eight times a week. Now then, the Lord High Admiral Sir Poofy tells me you're one of his boys, one who probably had more detailed knowledge of the whole Security set-up than anyone else. He's looking for a scapegoat so it could mean remarkably bad news for you if this disaster with UNS1 is the result of sabotage. Any comments?"

"Only that I had a comprehensive range of surveillance throughout the latter construction stages, but once the sea-trials began and she was effectively out of reach, my part was finished. As you may know, everything checked out on trials, the computers approved all the evaluations and she went operational immediately, since there were no domestic problems like faulty fridges and blocked loos. She hasn't got any."

"So you'd prefer to think that if anything was planted, it was during trials?"

"Naturally." I smiled. "It's quite possible. I had no look-in at that stage except that those on board were largely boffins who had worked on her throughout and had therefore been thoroughly screened; there were also about ten seamen brought in for the handling work, but I had no directive regarding them."

He thought for a moment, then said, "All right. The carrier's on station now and we've been asked to get you out there. Plumley's going to organise that. I understand you've flown in jets some time ago so you'll know most of the procedural stuff, but rules require a medical."

"What on earth for? Anyway, I've got one for my Private Licence."

"The Navy's version is more stringent. Anyhow, it's rules and regs."

I thought of my limited travel neck, a knee that played up sometimes, even the double vision which had taken eighteen months to clear after my accident. Outwardly, I gave a careless shrug.

"Regarding what Jack was saying, could you run a check for me?"

"If it's to do with your personal business, Poofy says you've to sort it out yourself, we've got enough to do. He says you'll be quite safe in our hands and you can park your plane here in the meantime."

"Thanks," I said wryly. "Two requests then. I need an Identikit and a telephone."

"Very well. I'll arrange the first now and you can use this phone. Don't be too long, we've got to get you on your way."

He went out and I put a call through to Scotland Yard. My usual contact wasn't there, being senior enough to have Sundays off, but the fact that I had someone to ask for procured co-operation. They promised to send someone round to Companies House first thing in the morning. I told them to leave a message with Briggs.

He came back shortly afterwards and led me off to another office where they had a comprehensive Identikit all prepared. I thanked him and set to work. After half an hour, I had put together a reasonable facsimile of the first intruder and then my memory was triggered. I had seen him in the pub in Lochcarron, and then I recalled seeing him at another time, many months before. A plump little secretary with a pleasing, brisk manner made some photocopies for me and put them in an envelope.

I went back to Briggs and handed him the envelope. "Can you send one of these to Security in Glasgow. Tell them I think it was someone to do with McGilvray's yard. If you send a copy to the police sergeant at Lochcarron you might get a name. Better send one to London as well, rogues gallery. Feller had a big shooter. Tell the Sergeant he's the one who drowned, by the way."

"Listen," said Briggs, "I told you we had enough to do."

"Maybe, but suppose there's some connection? Why should I get bounced by a helicopter which apparently belongs to an oil-rig service company? The Yard are going to call tomorrow and leave a message with you as to who the real owner is."

He started to expostulate but I held up my hand. "It's OK, you can leave the rest to me. Don't forget all those nice things Plumley said about you."

I let a smile crease my face; he glared at me and finally relented into his idea of a grin which better resembled an axe-wound.

"All right," he said finally. "Now, your taxi's laid on and God help you 'cos Plumley's driving. You have to go and be fitted over in D, you need a 12G jock-strap and stuff like that, it's all tailor-made these days."

"Why, what are we going in?"

"F-4."

"What? Special trip?"

"Sort of, and we're an observer short. Plumley's a senior pilot so he's allowed to go without."

The prospect was exciting but I began to wish I'd never played that prank on Plumley.

"Off you go, then. Medical first. I'll show you where on the plan. You are here, MO is there and fitting is there, got it? If anyone stops you, show them this pass."

He gave me a plastic card like a ski-pass with my photograph press-stamped into it. Judging by the tiny piece of background, someone had taken it the moment I stepped out of the Teal. I looked wryly at Briggs, who gave nothing away and gratefully dismissed me.

I went out feeling slightly bemused and made my way to another block for my appointment with one Dr Acheson. I was slightly nervous.

When I entered the ante-room, a detached voice from behind a partly open door told me to take a seat. I was left for a long time in complete silence, so inevitably I began to ponder again.

There'd been three intrusions against me, plainly lethal if the last one was anything to go by, we had a crippled submarine and there was a General Alert in the Navy. My attempt to link them together in order to gain some co-operation and protection had more or less failed, and in Briggs' shoes I'd probably have done the same. The irony was that they didn't seem to mind me getting killed, but they minded very much whether I was healthy enough to fly in one of their aeroplanes. The humour of it lifted my spirits and I sat there for a long while, musing. Meanwhile, there was no sign of activity beyond the open door. I coughed pointedly once or twice and distinctly heard a sigh followed by the sound of a book being abruptly shut.

"Come in Mr ... er ... er ..."

"Squire," I filled in for him as I stepped in front of his desk trying to look fit and healthy. He was bun-faced and myopic.

"Indeed. How do you feel?"

"Fine, thank you."

"Good." To my puzzlement, he scratched his name on the bottom of a form and handed it to me. I noticed a large book on the desk entitled *Tropical Butterflies* which he had half-heartedly covered with his sleeve.

"Off you go, then, I've got work to do."

"Is that it?" I asked in surprise.

"Is what it? I suggest you confine yourself to your own field of expertise."

"Don't you even want to take my blood pressure?"

"Are you going to insist?" he asked wearily. "You look all right to me."

"I am, thank you, you must be psychic." I hurried out with a clean bill of health.

After my fitting with G-suit and helmet, thermal underwear, gloves, life-jacket and breathing apparatus, Jack came and took me to the simulator block. As we walked over, a giant shadow was cast by a Shackleton in the circuit, and two Jaguars took off together with a brain-throbbing roar. As the sound faded he said, "Some of the gumph will be familiar to you but I'd better go through it anyway. First of all you must look and listen for everything. You've got to rubberneck the whole horizon non-stop. On a training flight you almost always get a friendly bounce, and they do it sometimes on Ops as well. The old man gets a kick out of it when he's bored. The search radar only looks forward and sensing of an attack is mainly visual, in daylight. You look behind, both above and below unless we've really got the old boot down in which case we're not likely to be caught, from behind anyway, and it'll come from abeam or on the quarter. Ahead is my business. If I tell you to take a powder, just reach up and pull, no thoughts, remarks, nothing, just get out at once.

"Formally, I'm supposed to say, Eject! Eject! Eject! but you should have gone before I've finished since you have to go first otherwise you catch all the crap flying out of my cockpit. If we're pulling too much G to get your arms up, there's a lever between your legs which you pull upwards, but it's very hard, takes about eighty pounds jerk. Panic makes it easy. Leave your legs where they are or the acceleration can break your thighs. Keep them on the seat with your feet out – they trail in automatically when you go. Just don't hesitate, always think that she's going to blow you away in half a second.

"I bounced a deck recovery in the States and missed the wires so I told my Obs to hop it, but then I thought I might make it as there was a good breeze and I'd come in a bit fast. The wheels made two furrows in the water, but she just, only just, managed to get up again and a voice from the back said, 'Eh, sorry, what did you say?' Another one I heard of, it was over the Channel Islands, Obs was dozing and didn't hear the pilot's order. When he woke up there was no one to talk to. They took about twelve hours to find him after he'd finally summed up the situation and taken to his brolly. He said the bus started to flutter and broke up a couple of seconds after he left."

"You wouldn't," I enquired speculatively, "ask me to go for a swim while you carry on, as a sort of revenge for yesterday, would you?"

He laughed and said probably not, the seats were a bit expensive.

The next couple of hours was spent going over the complexities of the Phantom's surveillance and interception radar and Jack's method of teaching by tease, banter and anecdote were remarkably effective, aided by his natural enthusiasm. It was also very generous of him because he could in fact have treated me merely as a passenger. Afterwards, we collected our kit and gathered at the briefing.

One of the observers had a black eye and a deep scratch on his forehead, and while we were chatting someone asked him what had happened. The wits were all ribbing him and there were the usual jokes like had her husband come home and so on.

"No, it was that silly sod Acheson. I was taking a stroll through the trees when our moronic medic switched on that great ultraviolet lamp to catch his bloody moths, it makes you completely disoriented and I walked straight into a tree trunk. He even had the gall to be annoyed with me and grumbled all the way to the sick-bay saying it was just the right conditions for catching a lesser-spotted spud nosher or something. Do I smell of formaldehyde?"

"I wouldn't change him," said another. "At least we don't have to worry ourselves sick about whether we're going to pass the medicals. Besides, they should only send the weak and infirm to land on carriers, it's a dangerous business." He turned to me confidentially and said, "There was a carrier off Iceland which had fifteen aircraft up on an exercise and they had a sudden freak storm and only one got back on board. He was the fifteenth, too, quite true this, and he had to watch all the others go in the drink before he could have a bash at it."

"Oh, belt up Henry," said Jack. "That was back in forty-eight, and they hadn't got ejector seats."

"Wouldn't have helped if they had. Never have picked them up in those seas. Could easily happen again. Point is, I bet those Kamikaze boys didn't have to pass out A1 Medical."

He was being extra gloomy for my benefit and everybody laughed except one man, who sat in a corner by himself looking distinctly anaemic. Jack went over and spoke to him, shaking his shoulder but receiving only a nod in reply.

The briefing itself was quite short, dealing with route, height and radio frequencies. As far as it went, it was precise and detailed but also left the leader with certain latitudes. In essence, it seemed to be providing him with all the required information and leaving the rest to his initiative. I mentioned this to Jack afterwards and he remarked that experience could only be best utilised by taxing the pilot fully whilst leaving him free to enjoy his job and sustain the interest.

"The difference is very marked with Americans," he added. "We sometimes get them transferred to our training units and it can take a year to get them out of their regimented habits. Their flights are regulated to the last foot so they might as well be driving a bus. I'm not saying they can't fly, but it does sap their initiative and removes most of the interest and enjoyment. It's also a pain in the arse for us."

"You mean they're not allowed to beat up motorists and fly under bridges?"

"Well, yes I suppose so. But it makes a hell of a difference to a chap's flying if his CO says, 'Look, lad, take off, find yourself a nice open space, preferably not in an airway, a danger area or a gunnery range, and enjoy yourself for an hour.' My guess is that most of us scare ourselves rigid on a spree, I know I did, and afterwards you treat it all with a bit more respect."

Silently I was able to acknowledge the truth of this from personal experience, when I lost most of my enthusiasm for aerobatics in the early days. My instructor had shown me complex manoeuvres on the blackboard and I went off to try a few by myself and promptly lost 4500 feet in a screaming vertical dive, well over the aircraft's VNE (Velocity Never Exceed). Pulling out, once I'd established which way I was pointing, should have torn the wings off. Fortune and gravity had smiled and relented respectively, since I'd started the exercise at 4600 feet.

The episode sent me meekly back to school, to discover that all I'd done was to pull the stick back while upside-down instead of pushing it forwards.

The trouble with being ignorant is that you don't know how ignorant you are.

Seven

McDonnell Douglas F4K, Phantom, Royal Navy squadron designate 002. No place for a claustrophobe. Over the heavy thermal underwear, worn in case of ditching, I'm burdened with a bulky G-suit, varicosed with multiple air-bladders at calf, thigh and stomach, all overlaid with straps. The helmet is unfamiliar, and I get a taste of rubberised air as I test the oxygen mask. The intercom comes to life and I hear Jack running through the pre-flight checks with an external telephone to the ground crew, being told whether the jet intake ramps are closed, whether control surfaces move in response to the controls, and so on. There have been several minutes of just removing pins, including the ones from my ejector seat. I am told it is now 'armed' and that it cost a quarter of a million pounds. I wonder if that is supposed to make me reluctant to use it, and remember reading actuarial figures for insurance claims; the average Englishman costs about five thousand pounds, while the average American costs one hundred thousand dollars, that's if you write him off. People like Jack are worth many times this in terms of training cost, and presumably justify such an expensive seat, but did that go for me?

The observer's seat, behind the pilot, is surrounded by a jumbled display of switches and dials, bewildering even though Jack has been through everything twice with me, showing added glee for the ones that are supposed to be secret.

The muttering up front continues, then to me he says, "Radar to standby." I select the switch and acknowledge, adjust my altimeter to the QFE, or airfield elevation, and check my harness for the third time.

Beneath me crouches a black-snouted monster sixteen feet high and nearly sixty feet long. To our left, three other Phantoms are lined up, the canopies still open, but otherwise deadly sinister. The noses seem to be held low, extended like bloodhounds at the ready, and the inverted-V tail-planes hang down at a most unlikely angle. In contrast, the ends of the wings are tilted upwards, the only sign that this beast is capable of raising itself into the upper atmosphere. Otherwise, its attitude from every aspect is of scything, vicious attack, a powerful wing forward stretched taut in a low tackle, the huge air-intakes on each side like hunched and massive shoulders.

There are various whines and buzzes, some which continue, others which stop. Jack looks up and the marshal waiting outside down below sees the glance and waves his finger in a circular motion – the signal to start, which Jack acknowledges with a half-salute. A humming noise begins, accelerating very rapidly to a high whine. This is the starter turbine, and when it reaches a peak of around 25,000 rpm, a low and ominous murmur creeps into consciousness, building up slowly and steadily. The beast is waking. Warning lights go out and instruments flicker their signs of life. The low hum swells to a muted roar, turning too fast for vibration, gradually becoming dominated by the whistle of rushing air, compelling the acknowledgement of its stupefying power. The marshal crosses to the other side of the aircraft and rotates his finger again, and Jack repeats the procedure to start the second engine. The canopy closes and the enveloping roar becomes more remote as does contact with normality. The air-conditioning comes on, which accentuates the feeling. Gradually, everything steadies down, and Jack's voice cuts cheerfully into my thoughts. His head is lower than mine, and slightly to my left.

"All OK back there?"

"Check."

"Radar to test."

"Check."

"Straps tight?"

"Yep."

"Radio channel Two."

"Channel Two."

"Got all the makings of a rollicking good evening."

"What have you in mind?"

"Wait and see."

In reply, I can only sigh. Our destination is a carrier, codenamed Alpha, her real name secret, but as she was the last one in commission, a guess was hardly needed. On board we would find, as in most of our Naval establishments, a horde of Jack's cronies.

He looks out to his left and exchanges thumbs-up with his Number Two, who repeats the gesture to his left. Jack transmits an order, and the replies come back instantly, in sequence.

"Blue check-in."

"Blue Two."

"Three."

"Four."

"Roger, all loud and clear. Channel One – Go."

"Blue Two."

"Three."

"Four." The replies on the new channel are staccato, crisp, eager, for eight men a little extra pulse of adrenalin. The roaring swish behind has become background and secondary.

"Tower, this is Blue formation, Taxi."

"Roger, Blue formation, you are clear taxi to the holding point runway Two-Niner, QNH 1020, QFE 1019."

The brakes are released and at once we move forward, stopping briefly to test. The three to our left move with us as we swing out and begin to trundle. The beast, rumbling and grumbling, nods and shudders like a heavy road tanker, not feeling even remotely like a lighter-than-air machine. Grouching, heaving, it has to be held in check down the taxi-way. Eventually, we stop at the holding point but the controller doesn't wait for our request.

"Blue formation, Tower, you are clear line up and take off. Channel Two when airborne, Upschool."

The last is an instruction to turn north fifteen degrees after take-off so as not to overfly Gordonstoun.

We are lined up in pairs and Jack looks across at our Number Two, index finger held vertical. He waves the finger, at the same time advancing the throttle up to eighty per cent power. The beast sits down and gathers itself, quivering in every fastening. Jack spreads his hand, then drops it and the two aircraft release brakes together, forcing us back in our seats as full power is applied. Because of over twenty tons of inertia, the initial movement seems tentative, but then the acceleration becomes numbing, terrifying, yet there is more to come for at eighty knots he pushes the throttle

80

through the gate, right forward, and lights the after-burners. The brain relegates action into an electrifying slow-motion where only the vital actions penetrate consciousness to a background sequence of blurred movement. The nose comes up, and at 140 knots the rumbling stops abruptly as we become airborne. Slight changes in attitude and resistance are apparent as the wheels retract, the flaps are raised and the leading edge droops fair into the wings. We complete the small right turn, Upschool, and at 200 knots we sit on our tail-pipes and aim at the blue, the beast sleek and "clean", all appendages tucked away, the real awakening. In a little under four seconds we are at 2000 feet, and the rate of climb eases to around 10,000 feet per minute as the after-burner is cut off. At full power and reheat, the fuel consumption is phenomenal – as is the rate of climb, initially around 72,000 feet per minute.

"Blue airborne, Channel Two – Go."

"Blue Two."

"Three."

"Four."

"Lossie radar, Blue formation on Channel Two, passing 290 for 360, en route Alpha."

"Roger, Blue formation, you are identified squawking Bravo Three, squawk to standby."

Our wingman, or Number Two, has been abreast of us but now slips back and out some five hundred yards, and a mile away Three and Four adopt the same battle formation. I have a few moments to take stock and try to pretend to myself it's all normal. Jack tells me to switch the radar first to On, then to Pulse. I change the altimeter setting to standard atmosphere 1013·2 and take a long careful look round the horizon, and then we level off – incredibly, at 36,000 feet. We are still at full military power, the Mach meter shows ·94 and a digital readout gives our true airspeed at 570 knots, or nine and a half miles a minute. Estimated flight time remaining, thirty-six minutes. In accordance with our Met. briefing, clear weather is holding, and soon the West Coast of Scotland slips steadily by. The sun is no longer setting, nor would it if we could keep going. Even with the visors down, forward visibility is difficult and I keep a close watch on the radar in between painfully cranking my head round the horizon, conscious that my neck doesn't doesn't turn as freely as it should, the result of my first beating up.

I saw something on the screen and said, "Jack – " but he cut in on me immediately.

"Lossie radar, Blue, contact four bogeys, our twelve o'clock level, eighteen miles, do you have?"

"Affirmative Blue leader, that is Red formation returning from Alpha at Flight Level 350, maintain VFR at 360 and advise any change in flight conditions."

"Roger, VFR maintain 360," responded Jack, and then did nothing of the sort. "OK Blue, coat of paint, through the gate let's . . . GO!"

Maintain Visual Flight Rules means to stay clear of cloud and able to see five miles, but our convergence has to be instrumented. My next glance at the screen sees four dots at the upper edge dropping at a remarkable rate. As the slick, "Two," "Three," "Four," acknowledgements come through, the crushing power forces me back into my seat once more. We breach the sound barrier with no apparent change since the adjustment in trim is performed by the on-board computer. During this crucial transition, vital changes have to be made to the trim to counteract the rapid movement aft of the centre of pressure, much faster and finer than the pilot can perform by feel. Seat-of-the-pants methods in an aircraft like this result in a rapid see-saw motion which breaks off the wings in under two seconds, although the terrible induced forces have killed the occupants, in terms of milli-seconds, ages before.

The dots are moving across the screen nearly as fast as the ball on one of those electronic ping-pong machines. Red formation might have heard Jack's order to increase speed, anyway they must have done the same. Our Mach meter shows 1·4, and we are in a very shallow dive to take off most of our thousand-foot advantage. The dots move across the screen's three-mile rings every six seconds, or thirty miles a minute or eighteen hundred miles an hour, anyway pretty damn quick and still increasing rapidly. At four miles, I look up from the screen and try to get them visual. Slow motion again, but I am only shown two frames of the film, four black specks apparently in line abreast, then a single blob slap in front of us, a loud bang and then nothing but clear air. It seemed they passed about thirty feet below us.

"Whaw, whaw. Ease off Blue, maintain 360, ninety-five per cent, Go." Then to me on the intercom, "Well, Seamus, did you see that evil bastard McGuinness grinning at us?"

"Frankly, no. Did you?"

"*Cer*tainly. Looked as though he had a shocking hangover!"

"Seriously, though, can you shoot someone at that speed?"

"Only by getting shot yourself. The trick is to fly at each other in great loops, but just missing and all the time manoeuvring for position. If you're equally matched, it usually ends up in a slow flying competition, sitting on your tail with everything hanging out, full power. If you muff it and spin out, then you get shot, otherwise it's the first one to run out of juice. Doesn't take long."

I thought it an extraordinary paradox that a dogfight between two high-speed interceptors should end up in a duel to see which one can fly the slowest and still stay in the air.

Our flight time has been shortened by the added speed and we are busy with calculations once more. The islands are far behind us and the setting sun has actually risen slightly, for previously its lower edge was just touching the bottom of my visor and now it's a fraction above. We're really borrowing time, but I'm not going to spoil it by musing on days of reckoning and so forth. This is a rare treat, to be doing something intense and exciting in a relaxed manner while someone else deals with the precisions and decisions. We continue blithely on our way without further interference and the treat is all too short.

Presently I hear Jack transmit again, calling Lossiemouth to say he has radar contact with Alpha and is changing frequency.

"Blue leader to Blue, start descent, Channel Ten – Go."

Again the responses come in crisp and alert, and I find myself anticipating, excited. I'd always wondered what a night deck-landing would be like, the sheer knife-edge impossibility of it, but to the uninitiated I imagine it would be little more than a graunching thud in pitch darkness. I'm delighted that my first one is in daylight so that I can see what's going on.

"Alpha, this is Blue formation, do you read?"

"Roger, Blue, this is Alpha, go ahead."

"Blue formation descending from 360, heading 250, we have you at sixteen miles, ETA one minute fifty-five. Four aircraft."

"Roger, Blue, we have radar contact your position. For identification squawk Bravo Two."

Jack complies using the transponder, which makes an identifying flash on the radar screen tuned to receive it.

"Roger, you are identified twelve miles, clear to five thousand feet."

In the dive we are just below the speed of sound, the Mach meter reading ·98. The radar screen shows a large blip and two smaller ones nearby, the carrier and her escorts. I look up and see they are real, distant but distinguishable, nothing else in sight.

"Blue formation, Alpha, we have you visual, change to Mother on Channel Six."

"Channel Six Blue, Go."

"Blue Two. Three. Four."

"Blue formation, this is Mother. Join from the north-east, QNH 1018. You are clear to the wait."

Now that we have a point of reference again, things start to happen very quickly and, glancing at our minute destination, I am a little horrified at the bland confidence on both sides that presumes an ability to plant this howling twenty-ton monster on a pitching ruler at something close to a hundred and eighty miles an hour. Whoever first thought of it must have been under some influence.

"Mother, this is Blue leader, Charlie time zero five, Chicken plus, zero eight." Jack gives these rather mystifying pieces of information denoting time to landing and fuel remaining for further attempts before diversion becomes necessary. He had mentioned "Chicken" and "Lamb" to me earlier, the first denoting sufficient fuel, the second a lack of it.

At three miles, Jack rocks our wings, the signal to the others to echelon starboard. The speed is coming off quickly, and I see the waves are capped with white but there is no great swell. All in the same high-speed blur, we turn into the ship's wake and then begin making wide circles off her port quarter at 2000 feet. The carrier still looks tiny, and a bend appears in her wake as she turns fully into wind. There are neat groups of aircraft packed tightly on her bows, but we have to get down on the angled deck, which is there so that the launch deck can remain cluttered and active and so that aircraft can land and take off at the same time – not as used to be thought, so that pilots who cock up their landing can drown with decorum instead of being chewed up as well by the ship's propellers as she passes over.

"Blue – Slot."

We ease out of the turn and pass to starboard of the carrier into our final landing circuit. Jack is muttering to himself continuously

... 400 knots, hook down ... eighty per cent ... hang a left ... 250 knots, gear down, half flap ...

"Blue leader, downwind."

"Roger, Blue leader you are Number One to final, continue."

The ship's stern passes our port beam as we stream in the opposite direction to her. We start our final turn and, in spite of the precise, high-speed activity, Jack has a word for me, in a casual drawl.

"Buttocks together. Straps tight, tight. Radar to standby."

He calls the ship again. "Mother, this is Blue leader. 2380 pounds, four greens."

"Roger, Blue leader, clear to recovery. Deck wind forty-five knots, call on ball."

Four greens is the indicator check, one for each wheel locked down plus one for the hook. The ball, or "meatball", is the centre of the projector sight on the carrier which, as long as he can see it, shows the pilot that he is on the approach or glidepath of three degrees. We are hardly gliding but making a nose-up approach at eighty-five per cent power with every slow-flying aid hanging out grasping for lift. 2380 pounds is fuel remaining.

"Ball," calls Jack sharply as we are lined up over the wake, and from this angle our target is more intimidating than ever, foreshortened into a windswept tennis court. We pitch a little as he gets too high and makes an immediate correction, but otherwise we are on line, "on the ball", and the touch and confidence of a master pilot is clear and reassuring. I can see the wires, five of them stretched across the deck as we aim for the third, and the deck is rushing up to meet us. Again the slow-motion confusion as we sway and buck in the turbulence and I take a final tug at my straps which are already painfully tight. There is a bang as the hook hits the deck, followed instantly by the wheels, then the hook takes a wire and I try to stop my arms flying forward. The beast is suddenly tethered in its headlong rush from 180 miles an hour, the nose dips in reluctant submission and my eye-balls make a determined effort to go it alone until forced behind the brow as my head jerks forward and down. Then it slams back on the headrest in reaction to the complete stoppage of movement, one and a half seconds after the first thump. The brakes are not used and must be off for the aircraft to move back a foot, enough for the hook to be released from the taut wire. As soon as it's free, the aircraft-handler makes a T-sign.

We fold the wings promptly and crewmen materialise from the deck to minister to us as we taxi very slowly up to the foredeck and stop on signal. The aircraft-handler gives the order to cut and gradually the Rolls-Royce Speys murmur down into silence. I sit for a moment completely drained and a little startled by the absence of background roar, then the canopy opens and someone immediately leans in to pin and disarm my seat. That done, he helps me disengage myself from the harness, intercom and oxygen tube. The huge noise recurs as our wingman noses up alongside us, then it too dies away.

As we step down the ladders, Jack grins smugly at me and asks if I enjoyed it.

"You bet. Can I buy you a drink now or is this an American ship?"

"Only if they've sold it recently. I know one CPO's mess that would never stand for it. First let's go and see if there's anything laid on for tonight."

He stops just before going through the hatchway and we watch our last two aircraft make their approach. Number Three comes in smoothly and expertly, but Number Four is wobbling and swaying a few hundred yards out, nose high, and we hear the roar of extra power being applied. I glance at Jack, who has contrived to narrow his eyes and arch his eyebrows at the same time, a perfect mixture of surprised worry and amusement.

"What the hell have they been doing out there? The correct recovery interval is ninety seconds, but we have had it down to eighty. More oxygen, Froggy," he adds darkly.

"Why oxygen?" I ask.

"You saw him at the briefing, Froggart. He looked shocking. Been on leave for a fortnight, I asked him if he enjoyed himself and he couldn't speak."

The extra power had taken him too high and abruptly the nose pitched down and immediately see-sawed up again in a series of badly anticipated corrections. Finally, he hit the deck with a terrible impact, bounced and hooked the last wire. He had full power on for a possible go-round and I couldn't believe the wire would stand it, but at last the aircraft came to rest as the nose settled with great reluctance. We turned away and went into the bridgeworks through a steel door, Jack chuckling merrily.

"He sounded crisp enough on the radio," I said.

"Certainly. He'd have been dragging on his oxygen. That was

my point. "Whee-ee-yup!" he called loudly, showing me how the Navy goes down ladders, facing forward and without touching steps with the feet.

"How do I check in?" I asked as we went down a darkened corridor.

"House-phone, at the end there."

He dialled the operations centre for me and I was told that Admiral Feather would not be arriving till later and they had no instructions for me as yet. They suggested I remain with aircrew until called.

I told Jack about it and asked, "What happens if you're sent up again for some reason?"

He just shrugged in answer.

"Surely you'd need a pro in the back seat if you get a live call?" I persisted.

"We'll bumble through, I expect."

"You don't strike me as being a very bumbly sort of pilot."

"That's why I'm a senior, frankly. I really like to be in charge of my own fate as far as possible, so I do as much of the whole job as I can, and treat the Obs as a sort of back-up. They have it cushy with me because I never rely on them, though you mustn't tell them that. I was on Lightnings before and rather prefer the single-seaters."

"But they'd order you to take someone else, wouldn't they?"

"Well, we'll see. It may not happen anyway. Wouldn't you want to come?"

"Of course I would, it's fascinating."

"So relax then. If there's any problem, I'll tell them you're brilliant."

We went straight to debriefing then and because of the straightforwardness of our flight, it only took a few moments. We were told to keep our kit on, have a quick meal and report back in an hour. I looked at Jack who merely shrugged and smiled.

We went first to Wardroom 2 on a lower level and about 300 feet aft where we had a good meal, cafeteria style, but I noticed that Froggart was sitting by himself in silence with just a cup of coffee and his observer was studiously ignoring him.

"Do they," I asked cautiously, "ever switch crews round?"

Jack followed my glance and laughed. "No, not usually, the teamwork's important. Trouble with oxygen, it's fine while you have it on but afterwards you feel worse, if anything."

Aircrew in flying kit were strictly excluded from Wardroom 1, but Plumley marched in there anyway and no one seemed to object to it. I wondered if there was a feeling of élitism for the aircrews, but the atmosphere was very easy. I glanced questioningly at the bar, but Jack shook his head. "Not if there's a chance of being sent up. Doesn't work."

I noticed there were a number of framed caricatures round the bar, and feeling a complete new-boy I peered for a closer look. They were beautifully drawn and I spotted a familiar face. It was Jack Plumley, spelt above a quotation as Plolmondeley. He was leaning against a mantelpiece, glass in hand, his trousers round his ankles, and the enlarged head was complete with moustache and World War One leather flying helmet, Gosport tubes connected and goggles on the forehead. The eyes had been drawn slightly divergent over a beatific smile and underneath was printed:

"For though from out our bourne of Time and Place,
    The flood may bear me far,
I hope to see my Pilot face to face,
    When I have crost the Bar."

Alfred, Lord Tennyson 1809-1892

I glanced round and he was surrounded by several officers trying to force a drink on him, and although he was protesting, I thought he showed signs of weakening under the barrage, and needed moral support.

"Gentlemen," I interposed, "will you stop trying to corrupt and influence my driver?"

One of the group turned and fixed me with a glassy stare, then spoke with heavy emphasis.

"You, sah, what is your rank, um?"

I gazed steadily back at him. Jack said, "He's a . . ." and stopped when I held up my hand.

"Supposing I put my tongue out at you," I said, "what would you do?"

He gave this a few moments' thought and glanced down at his own two and a half stripes. "I should be forced to assume you outrank me . . . sir."

"So will everybody else if you don't mind your manners, Archie," said another. "You'd better buy him a drink before it's too late."

This prompted Archie to make an instinctive gesture of invitation, which I accepted, but for later.

Jack beckoned to me as it was time for our briefing. Outside the wardroom he chuckled.

"I was going to say, 'Don't mind Archie,' but actually most people mind him very much. That was good, I think we might have some fun with it later."

"Is your name really spelt Plolmondeley?"

"*Cer*-tainly, what did you think it was?"

"It's been a peculiar day for dialogue, have you noticed?"

"No, what?"

"Like the chap who asked the Jesuit why Jesuits always answer a question with another question?"

He looked at me, waited and then asked, "Well, what did he answer?"

"Why not?"

Eight

All the ship's gangways we used after our supper were bathed in red light, as was the briefing-room, to preserve our night vision. It lent a great air of quiet suspense.

The briefing itself was more terse and seemingly more professional than the last one, but the information merely covered the overall picture. No flights were actually scheduled.

It seemed that none of the crews had till then any but the scantiest information about the new submarine, and most believed it was an advanced Polaris-carrier whose crew had been secretly trained and kept in purdah.

The briefing officer, Lieutenant Scoresby, had obviously been told to clarify the situation so that the airmen properly understood their role. My own presence there caused a query, and Scoresby had to refer to control before proceeding.

We were told that forty miles nearer the coast wallowed a stricken submarine. The Navy was gathering its resources to effect a rescue, and the carrier and its escorts were standing sentinel mainly as a counter-intelligence measure. Against massive interference from land- and sea-based aircraft, and despite elaborate early-warning systems, the Soviets persisted in attempts to overfly the area. Shipping of every description was kept to a minimum radius of a hundred miles, and it was emphasised that this meant *all* shipping, including our own. The carrier and her escorts were the sole exceptions.

The Air Traffic Controllers were having a protracted nightmare since the circumference of the area was being patrolled continuously by Nimrods and Sea-King helicopters as an anti-submarine measure. Through the diplomatic channels, an emergency had been declared with the enjoinder that an approach within defined limits would be considered a hostile act and dealt with accordingly. Since the diplomats had not been in a position to explain the reasons for such stringent measures, considerable curiosity had been aroused with the result that swarms of foreign aircraft were being sent in from every direction in an attempt to find out. The Navy and the RAF were active to prevent any aircraft from photographing the area, or dropping sonar buoys or parachutists.

Although the role of the carrier-based aircraft was the prevention of penetration by reconnaissance planes, we were also informed that until further notice any craft of any description must be reported promptly if seen steaming inside fifty miles of Point X, the submarine's position, and immediately destroyed if there was any danger of an approach inside a crucial twenty-mile radius.

In answer to a question, Scoresby answered, "Then we have all been wasting our time. Unidentified or hostile propeller signatures, surface or air, within a twenty-mile radius will cause UNS 1 to self-destruct. Because this is bound to raise other questions in your minds, like why are there no British ships or tugs standing by, the answer is that there has probably been an explosion on board and UNS 1 is not responding to our radioed 'clear to approach' requests."

He held up his hand as someone else began to speak. "I know what you are going to ask, and you will recall that you are all bound by the Official Secrets Act. The fact is that UNS 1 is not manned."

He wiped his brow wearily, as a murmur went round the cabin and a rather shocked voice asked, "You mean everyone on board was killed in the explosion?"

He shook his head. "No. UNS stands for Unmanned Nuclear Submarine. The ship has no personnel. It is a programmed and undetectable nuclear deterrent. Beyond that there is no call to inform you, and as far as this operation is concerned, you have no Need to Know anything else. Right, Blue formation F4s may expect high altitude or very high speed intercepts, and will be on standby throughout the night; I also want those on Immediate to be actually in their cockpits, not down here. Blue One is Immediate from 2100 to 2300, Number Two on standby in that time, coming to Immediate if there is a launch, otherwise on Immediate from 2300 to 0100 tomorrow, and so on. Any questions? Buccaneers are for shipping strikes and have a good half-hour's notice. Confine questions to your operational roles, please, and study carefully this photograph of the submarine's sail, so you don't do anything hasty."

He pinned up a large glossy which showed mostly sea with a very thin black fin in the middle, much slimmer and smaller than the conning-tower, now known as a "sail", of a nuclear or Polaris submarine. I suppose the adjective "conventional" will soon be applied to these, since evasion and detection in submarine cold-warfare, in spite of the rapid advance in electronics, have more or less kept pace with each other, and there is still plenty of scope for the natural cunning and skill of man. The denial of this human factor by the Grand Masters of the computer age strategic games was embodied in the almost submerged hull of UNS 1. Now their brainchild, a lethal monster, had blown a few transistors and called for help, but, like a wounded buffalo, was highly dangerous to anyone approaching.

No questions were asked and we filed out, Jack and I back up to 002 now in a position to be swung into the catapult at a moment's notice. The sky was dark without even a faint blur in the west, but the flight deck was just slightly illuminated and small lamps marked deck and maintenance crews going about their duties. Our own cockpit lighting was a faint red glow assisted by the pale luminescence of the instruments. We strapped in and adjusted ourselves and chatted quietly on the intercom in a tingling sort of tense calm. A warm breeze flowed steadily over the deck and into our open canopies, and our conversation was occasionally interrupted by crisp commands and acknowledgements for other air-traffic on the radio.

"What are they planning to do about the sub, do you know?" I asked.

"I think they've been frantically hoping for some response or clearance from its radio so they can go straight in and bring it home manually, with the aid of tugs and so on. Right now, they're preparing a commando unit to fly out here with sailing dinghies, would you believe it, so that they can make a silent approach."

"Why don't they drop parachutists?"

"Well, they can't fly very near, so a drop would have to be made from a very high altitude with a good chance of missing by a mile or so. Point is, a freefaller wouldn't be able to see the sail from above, and if he couldn't swim the distance, there would be no means of rescuing him. Anyway, that's their problem. Incredible box of tricks, that sub. Do you know anything about it?"

I said I didn't and he proceeded to ignore the Official Secrets Act.

"Not having any need for accommodation space," he said, "they've packed it stiff with reactors, machinery and electronics, plus, of course, the missiles. Normally it just skulks around apparently at random, and keeps out of the way of other shipping, but if necessary it's capable of immense speed, at least half again as fast as any other existing submarine. I don't know the figures, they haven't been revealed. Propulsion is by multiple turbines in water tunnels which can be directed aft on the quarter. This is so it can use its detection gear straight aft, normally the one way you can creep up on a moving sub because the sonar won't work through the propeller turbulence. It can go about as deep as a bathysphere, and about the only way it could be attacked successfully would be with a bombardment of aerial torpedoes in sufficient numbers to use up all its decoys, pretty unlikely when you consider how difficult it is to find. It's even got a method of destroying sonar buoys dropped in its vicinity. Since it can travel at the speed of a torpedo itself, it makes it a pretty difficult proposition."

I let the silence weigh for a while and then said slowly, "Jack, how the hell did you come to know all that stuff? It's absolutely Classified!"

"Um, feller who gave me a lift the other day. Had my uniform on, see, and he was trying to pump me. He wasn't getting anywhere, you understand, so he gave me a big carrot like that to try to lead me on."

"Can you tell me when, where and a name?"

"What'll you do; have him shot?"

"Just you, if you don't tell me."

"Shit, OK. Black Morris 1100, last forty miles back to Plockton. Friday morning, it was. No name, big bloke with a thick neck."

"Did he say where he got his information?"

"Sort of. Said he worked at Mac-somethings for a while, got laid off a year ago and was hoping to get in on a new oil platform. The pay's very good."

"Was it McGilvray's?"

"Think that was it, yes."

"Jack, this is very important. I didn't tell you that my job was specifically a counter-snoop at McGilvray's. Why would a chap with that knowledge be pumping a flier?"

"I don't know, but he was quite eager. Said he lived in Kyle."

"Can you describe him fully?"

His description was of a man crudely similar to the one who drowned.

"What else can you remember about him?"

"Now I come to think of it, he asked me if I'd ever been in a flying boat. He said he'd seen a little one round Kishorn way and – hey, where's this leading?"

"Never mind, go on."

"I said I'd heard about it from my old man, that it was owned by a chap who arrived here not long ago, quiet, reticent sort of bloke, I gathered. He asked a bit more about you, but I didn't know anything except that you read a lot and the old man had lent you books and maps, but mostly you kept to yourself. I reckon I misinformed him, the way Cleodie was looking at you. What were you doing having breakfast there, anyway?"

"Making sure *you* weren't, what d'you think?"

"Greasy bastard." He shook his head and we lapsed into silence. There was some radio traffic, then someone said "Ball" in a bored sort of voice and a few seconds later a Buccaneer landed on the angled deck. Jack gave it a cursory glance and continued his musing. Presently he began to hum rather tunelessly and then to the obvious melody, or rather an attempt at it, sang, "Who dreams of Cleodie with the dark bro-own hair?"

I smiled to myself but my mind was elsewhere. To have answered "touché" might have indicated the truth of the matter, but I wasn't going to give him any leverage. On the spur of the moment, I came back with, "Hit the road, Jack, and doncha come back . . . " and realised that the cad had pressed the transmit button when, like a rasp, the Flyco cut in, saying, "Who the hell's that?" I actually felt myself blushing like a naughty schoolboy, while Jack whaw-whawed merrily in front.

"Intercept standby . . . Blue One, was that you?"

"No, sir, it sounded like a civilian station," said Jack innocently, but the reply was curt and unamused.

"Balls. Behave yourself, Plumley."

Jack wasn't in the least put out by this and the minutes sped by

94

filled with more of his anecdotes, starting with flying an ancient Twin back to Mombasa after a party in Nairobi. The aircraft had a transmit button without a spring return, and he'd blocked all the air traffic control on that frequency for twenty minutes while he roared and sang and barrelled his way round the sky. It was only when he came to sign off that he realised what he'd done and the response was understandably icy.

With his stories, he was back on what he obviously loved best, and then he explained about the armament we were carrying: four Sparrows and four Sidewinders. Although the design was quite old, he told me, the Phantom was still the fastest operational fighter in the West, the Spey engines being more powerful than their American counterparts. The main thing about the aircraft was that she could perform so well in many different roles, being capable of 1500 miles per hour yet able to fly slowly enough to be carrier-based for the Navy. Because of the enormous power, the payload was exceptional with about 15,000 pounds of "ordnance" as well as over 1700 gallons of fuel carried internally. It could also carry three disposable tanks under the belly and wings if range rather then strike-power was needed. Furthermore, the search radar and radar-directed Fire Control mechanisms were very highly advanced.

I asked him if he'd ever had to kill anyone.

"Yes, we were sent to shoot up an encampment in the desert, supposed to be full of Ayrabs who were being revolting."

"Did it bother you?"

"Yes and no. You see, we're trained and practised in that sort of thing until the actuality seems little more than an exercise. I was in a Vixen and we just came over the hill, let go with a fast ripple and shoved off. I think the bothersome thing is that it *is* so impersonal, almost too remote to touch you. That was the only time – until this morning that is, though that was different. Do unto others what they would do unto you, but do it first, as they say."

He explained about the rockets, how, by selection on the control, you could fire singles, or a slow ripple, described as "Whoosh ... whoosh ... whoosh", or a fast ripple, his tongue thriddling on the roof of his mouth as the whole load of 144 rockets leaves the aircraft almost simultaneously. We weren't carrying them at the moment, not being in the ground attack role, and also the rocket pods reduced the maximum speed to about Mach 1·4.

The Sidewinder missiles were equipped with heat-seeking devices, while the Sparrow was aimed in conjunction with the aircraft's radar. I asked him what was the most difficult part of his flying.

"Keeping my licence, whaw, whaw. No, it's the night carrier-landing, without any doubt. After your first one, for a few days you walk around like John Wayne after cleaning up Dodge City. You've really made it then, believe me."

"In other words, you've got to be good?"

He caught the inflexion in my voice and said, "*Certainly*, they wouldn't let you do it otherwise."

"But how do you know until you've done it?"

"Aha. A licence is but a formal permission to be lethal. How about you, anyway?"

"Well, it's nothing like this, though I was asked to do something nearly as absurd. I refused, the odds weren't good and there was no point. I was using the Teal in a film a while ago, as a police plane; I did quite a lot of flying round Plockton and Skye and they shot thousands of feet of film, flying in and out of cloud, over mountains, crofters and illicit whisky stills, always wanting me about three inches above the peaks and never mind the turbulence. I did about a dozen circular take-offs in Stranraer harbour as well, but they hardly used any of it, perhaps three minutes in all, and most of it running through the titles. You must have heard about it, because that's when I met your father. He'd refused to be an extra."

"Oh, yes, I heard about it. Didn't see the film, though."

"You didn't miss much. The shots of the plane were the best part of it except for a detailed close-up of some gorgeous starlet's nether regions. I've since wondered how many 'takes' that required, considering that the cop getting out of the plane took sixteen. Anyway, the real lulu was when they carefully selected a tarn surrounded by mountains and asked me to land in it at night with the engine switched off. It was less than a mile long."

"So you said no?"

"I said yes, on condition that the starlet sat in the passenger seat so that I would have something to entertain me in the happy hunting grounds. They seemed to understand that. If I'd given them a straight no, I think they'd have stopped my cheque for cowardice."

Jack whistled through his teeth. "Phew, an engine-out night landing on a limited space, invisible at that. What on earth for?"

"Dunno, realism I suppose. But they're in another world, these guys. The assistant director used to wear a yellow feather boa and call everyone 'Lovey' in a high-pitched voice, irrespective of sex, and make the most awful obscenities sound like polite conversation by his benign tone of voice. It was a laugh, really, because the scripted piece was supposed to have occurred in the spring, but they got their schedules mixed up. It meant that the props men had to fix about half a million plastic blossoms to the trees."

"Huh. Well, I wouldn't try it if I had the whole Mediterranean, unless the engine stopped and I had to. Even then I'd do my best to think of something else!"

"Well, it'd be like your carrier-landing – you don't know you can do it until you've done it. The main thing is not to practise when anyone's looking."

He laughed and was about to answer when a transmitter was switched on, on our frequency. No one spoke for a moment, but you can tell it's there; the silence seems to acquire a larger dimension.

Presently, a voice said, "Sorry, they were just checking co-ordinates for height. Blue One, I think we have something for you, very high level. Stay as you are, it's a long way off yet." He clicked off. I thought it was a bit informal and said so.

"He was distracted, probably," Jack answered. "The tea machine keeps eating their twopenny pieces up there. I'm surprised they haven't kicked it to death." There was something about his voice that didn't quite match the levity of the remark, and I felt he was about to get back in the air. He was quiet a moment, then said, "It'll be one of those spy-planes, I expect. They're not very fast so there's no urgency. They have a terrific wingspan and float along at about ten or twelve miles up."

"Can you get up there?"

"Well, sort of, but it's scrabbling a bit. Our combat ceiling, official, is 71,000 or something, though that's not the height record. This is an F4K, but in an earlier F4B they got up to 30,000 metres, that's about 98,000 feet. It took just over six minutes, which is knocking on, you must admit. I don't suppose he'll come in much further, anyway. If it was for real and he did come, we wouldn't bother, of course, just whack up a surface-to-air missile. The Spey is a more powerful engine but doesn't have the same altitude capability. This is all rather a silly business, pretending to be friendly in a nasty sort of way. They send the long-range Bears over frequently, and we have to tell them to bugger off. Expensive chap like me blasting off in a six-million-dollar kite to mouth a few obscenities in passing at 500 miles an hour, and the Russkies lean out of the doors waving and smiling as they turn away, and we know they're saying "Piss off, you pommy bastards" – in Russian, of course. Then we each go home and report Mission Accomplished, sah. What they really need is a bloody good scare, but we're supposed to take it easy for the sake of good relations. But you know what would happen if we flew into their airspace."

We lapsed into silence again, and I became increasingly aware of the great air of mystery which enclosed the entire ship at the beginning of night. The smell of kerosene, or paraffin, was all-pervading since it was used by all the military aircraft whether turbine or jet-powered, and as the ship was keeping station, we were subjected to wafts of her own funnel smoke from time to time as she turned downwind; on deck there were continuing signs of controlled activity even though it was impossible to make out individual figures. We were isolated as well as enclosed, but the salty tang was a constant reminder despite the other smells.

I was really enjoying the soporific effect and my thoughts had begun to wander into other realms when the Tannoy and the radio crackled out simultaneously, the Tannoy being shut out as the canopies closed a second later.

"Blue One ... Standby Launch!"

Sudden activity on deck, already accompanied by the whine of the starters' rapid build-up, while Jack's voice in laconic contrast goes through his muttering routine. As soon as he has sufficient power, he begins to taxi over to the catapult, guided by the slow and distinct movements of the marshal's lighted batons. The halting, braking trundle again, this time with figures scurrying beneath our wings, and after careful adjustment we are hooked onto the steam-launcher. Next they bring out a carefully wrapped ring of stainless steel which must be free of mark or blemish, and they fit it over the restraining hook between the main wheels. At the predesigned pressure of optimum combined thrust of both steam catapult and jet engines, the ring must burst apart to release the captive predator.

Huge curved-steel barriers grow out of the deck behind us, the water-cooled jet-blast deflectors, and at the same time the Phantom begins to crouch as the nose-wheel is pumped up hydraulically, haunching down ready to spring away in a pre-determined attitude of flight. The one incongruity is the application of full flap, the landing configuration, a little reminder that a carrier launch is always a tentative business, needing every available ounce of lift. Jack has answered the marshal's signals with his navigation lights, and now they remain on steadily, cockpit checks complete. He gives me instructions for the radar in the same matter-of-fact voice and tells me to make sure my head is hard back on the headrest.

Outside, the marshal looks at the lights on the catapult, notes the steam at full pressure, interlocks on the green, speaks to the Flyco, gets the word and slowly rotates a lighted green wand. All the night signals are made very slowly and distinctly, in massive contrast to the desperate shudder and howl of the aircraft as Jack pushes the throttle right through the gate and lights the afterburners. The green wand continues its slow circling, and then, as if trying to pretend there's no drama, comes slowly, vertically down.

For a brief moment of raging tension the steel ring resists the combined onslaught of massive forces, then suddenly shatters apart. Involuntarily, my body groans aloud in acknowledgement of the real meaning of inertia as it is propelled from a standstill to a hundred and eighty miles an hour in one and a half seconds. Even then, as we pass still in shock over the bows of the carrier, we are not really flying, but progressing in a controlled but comparative waddle, sinking initially towards the water while Jack tries to bring the nose up to more advantage, raising the gear and progressively reducing flaps and slots. That slow-motion impression again, as I sense the beast hauling itself from the wrong to the right side of the drag curve, pure feeling since I do not have a full set of flight instruments and there is no visual reference beyond the cockpit where all is pitch blackness. Now we are "clean" and flying, the beast has girt all its appendages and makes like a rocket as within five seconds of leaving the carrier it is hoisted into a maximum-rate climb. Imagine being in an underground train with the speed building up to disaster level, out of control and all the lights fused, before the screaming takes over from the initial bewilderment and then quite clearly a calm voice tells you everything is going to plan.

"Blue One, continue climb initially to Flight Level 350. We have trade for you at 64,000, unidentified bogey heading 165, forty-five miles."

Amidst the pandemonium of sensations, Jack's voice answers levelly as if he were ordering his breakfast.

"Blue One, Roger, passing 23,000."

Staggered, I glance at the altimeter to verify this remark, but I've already missed it as it continues its rapid cycling like a watch with a broken flyspring, and then I feel the weight coming off my seat as he eases the angle of climb and then levels off. There is no abatement of thrust, as he calls the ship.

"Blue One to Mother, 35,000 level, heading 345, Mach One Decimal Two, increasing."

"Roger, Blue One, wind her up and go. Bogey heading steady, you are on course intercept. Standby." A pause, then, "Confirming bogey must be diverted, show your teeth if you have to, avoid actual strike. Advise contact, Over."

"Blue One conforming, Mach One Decimal Niner, pulling . . . Now."

The sequence has been fascinating so far and I hate to miss any of it, but it is literally forced on me as he brings up the nose with a steady pressure at almost twice the speed of sound; nearly four times my normal weight tries to get out through the base of the fuselage as we go into an "Energy Zoom Climb". I can feel the strange pressure of the expanding air-bladders on my legs and stomach preventing the downward blood-flow, but still my thoughts slow maddeningly almost to a crawl in the beginnings of "grey-out".

Consciousness and sight return after what seems an age, judging by the increase in height during the interval. We are passing 53,000 feet and the altimeter is still notching up another thousand every second or so as we begin to use up the precious speed gained while we were straight and level. Outside the cockpit, the sky is black but clear and sprinkled with stars, seeming more like tiny pinpricks as there is less diffusion from the atmosphere; inside we are encapsulated in an artificial world of pressure suits, pressurised pod and now breathing pure oxygen. Many of the stars are actually visible *below* us, due to our great height, but there is no sign yet of the old moon rising. The rubber taste from the tubes is distinct and vaguely unpleasant, and the mask and helmet and various other accoutrements would be thoroughly claustrophobic if you're that way inclined. Solution, as always – think about something else. How? when my teeth are bared in a manic rictus as I recover from the effects of the zoom, remember I forgot to shout as it came on, that's supposed to help, though Jack didn't bother, he's used to it. Something easeful like waterfalls, or clouds, cloudy, Cleodie ... relaxing, then suddenly suspicious of the reason for relaxing, smile in spite of it for long golden limbs, flat water, devil-may-care smile.

"Radar switch to pulse. Operate scan." Jack's voice seeming a thousand miles away – Observer art thou sleeping there below, no, I'm on my back, heading for the sky, like a young bride with booted feet raised (not kinky, my actual position in relation to the earth) wondering whether to submit in passive terror or enter into the business wholeheartedly. Now I've got something to do, which is a kick in the right direction. To continue the simile a moment, there's not much point in her coming down to earth not knowing what's occurred, though it must happen. Quite a lot to be said for a good briefing ... for Jack this is business, so go easy on the facetious remarks.

Operate scan.

"Contact!" I call, my voice almost over-ridden as Jack transmits simultaneously, "Mother, Blue One, 62,000, contact one bogey, high, bearing 355."

"Roger, Blue One, you are fifteen miles. Bogey steady at 65,000, continue."

By now our rate of climb has fallen considerably in the thinner air, the jets gasping for oxygen. Jack begins to ease the nose down from the absurd angle of the earlier stages. Outside, the temperature is some fifty degrees below zero, in the beginnings of space, the air desperately thin and insubstantial for supporting a machine without the assistance of great speed or an enormous wingspan; but unlike the arrow aimed upwards and ultimately compelled to fall back, we can alter our trajectory as we lose momentum, hoping to find our target somewhere near the top of a huge, dying parabola. Our groundspeed would still be very high, but airspeed measured in the rapidly diminishing particles of air in the pitot head shows us close to the stall.

"Blue One this is Mother, we have you nine miles from bogey, you are one thousand feet below. Show lights now and position alongside at your discretion."

We are still climbing but much more slowly and the Phantom feels sluggish. Jack's hands on the controls are tentative and coaxing as he starts a wide turn hopefully to bring us in line with the oncoming intruder. I assume our landing lights are switched on but I cannot see them in the air too rarefied to reflect a beam. The blip on the screen is dead ahead and seems to be unwavering. I raise the scan as it fades, getting it back for a moment for he is still just above us, then it moves to the side against our turn to port. It's an eerie game of cat-and-mouse because he is still invisible to the eye unassisted by electronics. In front of me, Jack is working hard, sometimes silent, sometimes muttering in a low, calm voice. We continue our great wide turn and the blip disappears from the screen. Like a centenarian, we gasp up the final few steps to our target height without any encouragement from below.

A long moment of silence extends itself beyond reasonable limits. Hopefully, I lower the scan, since no one is telling me what's happening, and in a moment I pick up a blip close by to port.

"Gotcher!" says Jack, as if he'd just performed the unpardonable in a rugger scrum, and then transmits, matter-of-factly.

"Blue One has bogey alongside, level and steady."

"Roger, Blue One, maintain. Confirm you have shown yourself."

"Blue One confirming."

During the pause, I strain my eyes out of the cockpit, but only imagine I can see a black shape half a mile away to port, wondering if the radar can lie, wondering why he hasn't turned away.

"Blue One, this is Mother, put one across target and maintain surveillance."

"Mother, Blue One, will you confirm I am to fire one missile ahead of target?"

"Roger, Blue One, that is confirmed. Expedite."

Jack has already reached up and armed the Fire Control panel, for he turns slightly towards the intruder and there is a threatening Whoosh as a Sidewinder tears itself out from under our wings followed instantly by the faint bang as it goes supersonic. We resume our heading and wait, but there is no change in our relative positions. He *must* have seen the trailing flash streak across in front of him.

Quietly to me on the intercom, Jack says, "Someone isn't playing the game." He waits a few more moments and calls the carrier.

"Mother, Blue One. Your order complied, bogey maintaining height and heading."

"Roger, Blue One, standby."

I realise the situation has acquired a measure of gravity, and far down below in the black void a red-hot buck is being passed quickly up the ladder of command. Very quickly, for in a moment the order comes up in a tense voice, up through twelve miles of atmosphere.

"Blue One, bogey is assumed latest unmanned reconnaissance aircraft. It is now closing the prohibited zone. Destroy bogey, repeat, destroy bogey, expedite. Mother over."

With a touch of air-brake, he eases back slightly, at the same time re-arming the panel and locking the radar to the target. Each move is precise and swift, borne of long practice, and glancing at the screen I see he has completed the slight turn needed to bring the target dead ahead. There's no pause in the series of movements as he lets go a Sparrow without so much as a "Tally-Ho", and in front of us there is a searing gout of yellow flame rapidly falling away.

"Mother, this is Blue One, bogey picked, over."

"Roger, Blue One, suspect that was possible decoy. More trade for you twelve miles north, two hundred feet, intercept, Go!"

With the most sickening, sinking feeling imaginable, he puts the stick forward and points us straight towards the earth. Even with the throttle reduced, the altimeter begins to unwind the hard-won height at a speed too fast for the eye to follow. Nose vertically down into the inky black void with no other reference than the gently glowing instruments, how the hell will he know when to stop? I can just about follow the inner needle registering in tens of thousands. Jack feigns a vomiting noise into the intercom, follows it with a brief "whaw, whaw", then there's concentrated silence again. Somewhere down there another interloper is trying to get in under the distraction of our high-altitude antics, and I wonder with what intent? He's too low for any effective pictures with an infra-red camera, even for general information gathering – does he know that too close a proximity to UNS 1 could cause it to self-destruct, and is that the intention, or is he a distraction for yet someone else? Is it worth the risk of being blown out of the sky? I suppose it's our job to force the issue and find out, and it's a lot quicker for us to do it than to launch another interceptor, even though our Number Two would have come to immediate standby to replace us.

"All right, dear, I'll be down in a couple of minutes," comes Jack's voice on the intercom, to be interrupted at once by the radio.

"Blue One, Mother, suggest incline west at sixty degrees. At five thousand feet turn to 110 to intercept. Bogey is now one hundred feet, heading 165 steady, eight miles."

At about 15,000 feet we pass through some scattered cloud, the first indication of reality for several minutes. Seconds later, after a vertical half-roll, the downward pressure comes on my seat again, but this time he really means it. A strangled bellowing noise comes through the intercom; I remember now and join in, roaring as loud as I can. The bladders in my G-suit clamp hard on my legs and body and my buttocks seem to groan into the padding as nearly ten times my weight actually flattens them. Even my eyelids are forced down and for a second or two my brain ceases entirely to function, just dimly aware that we are coming retchingly out of our plummeting dive, level on an easterly heading. During the dive, the radar showed only clutter, but now it clears and I begin the scan again. The carrier confirms the pressure setting, adjusts our heading for interception by a couple of degrees and the foreign blip appears on the left of the screen, converging at high speed. The altimeter reads one hundred feet, and unseen just below us the Atlantic waits hungrily for the slightest pilot error, just a quarter of a second to instant disintegration . . . Four miles to intercept . . . three . . . Jack arms the panel once more. At two miles the blip is no longer converging but moving parallel, then gradually turning away. On instruction we turn to shadow, to make sure the intruder has left the scene for good; after four minutes and some thirty miles we are recalled and then I remember what comes next, the hard part for heaven's sake, the Recovery, as the Navy always calls a landing. If it wasn't vital, I feel I could just about manage without it. The last encounter has passed without comment, for we are like an electronic watch-dog patrolling the perimeter with not so much as a woof or a whoosh of rockets, its very presence deterrent enough once spotted on the intruder's radar screen. Had it been an exercise, one might have had the chance to say, "Rat-a-tat-tat, you're dead," but when it's for real, there's no word spoken, just a hundred pairs of watchful eyes fixed on pale green screens all around us, trying to keep a cold war from melting point. One down, one gone home tail between legs. How many others?

"Mother to Blue One, you are thirteen miles, steer 185, clear to the Wait."

"Blue One inbound, 185."

Jack starts his muttering sequence again, little of it intelligible except for a brief bark of "Straps", which I hardly need telling since my apprehension is more, not less, than the first time. His checks are completed before we have entered the holding pattern, and hopefully he calls, "Blue, Slot?" since we are alone in the area and they might let us skip the formal circling at the Wait. As we swing left to pass down the port side of the carrier steaming towards us, the answer comes back crisply, "Affirmative."

In precise and very rapid sequence, he reduces power, puts the hook down, calls, "Downwind," applies air-brakes to reduce speed enough to extend gear and half flap, completes the turn into the ship's unseen wake, working the whole process only with reference to the radar; full flap, slots, then he calls, "Four Greens," applies power, steadies up with the trim, calls his fuel state at 1250 pounds and then pauses briefly.

It is awkward for me to see past him, especially as we are at a high nose-up angle and the ship is showing hardly any lights. Suddenly he calls, "Ball," and, craning my neck with great difficulty and looking for where it ought to be, I see one bright light pointing up at us. Another one below it, smaller, shows for a moment as we slip below the glidepath, but it goes out at once as Jack makes the slight correction, and in spite of all the confidence and precision, it still seems to me like leaping off a building in the dark and hoping that the boys below haven't walked away with the safety net.

As we sink decisively in this enormous act of faith, I hear the twin jets whine up to full power, and over the roar comes the distinct bang of the hook hitting the deck. Suddenly, I am again a reluctant believer as the straps try to dismember me into five or six large pieces, my head goes forward and then snaps immediately back as we come to a shocking halt, the jets subsiding to a comparative murmur.

As the deck crew manoeuvre the captured beast off the landing area, I sigh involuntarily in disbelief at the numbing speed of events, for we were airborne just over fifteen minutes, the bulk of that time taken in the latter part of the climb to high altitude.

The experience is still trying to find a compartment in a scrambled brain, and then there's Jack's voice on the intercom.

"Very interesting that, my first 'kill'; talk about a sitting duck, though."

"Second. You got a chopper this morning."

"Ri-ight, different though. Anyway, I think a little celebration is on the cards, don't you, after all our efforts? Put out the old fire-in-the-belly, what?"

"Well, I felt about as much use as a one-legged man at an arse-kicking party."

"Nonsense. Anyway, you can drink, can't you?"

"Oh, yes, and if you're buying I'll even tell the others how terrific you were. Nice to have someone to show off to, isn't it?"

"*Cer*tainly, essential. Right, come on, then."

Nine

The bar was filled with a growing buzz premonitory of worse to come. Jack's tale of our exploit became more involved by the minute with a nonsense about computerised evasive tactics by the pilotless spy-plane. His infectious manner created so much enthusiasm that you couldn't tell whether the others believed him or not.

At the debriefing, of course, he'd told the truth and we weren't kept very long, although left in no doubt that outside the ship the incident had never occurred. The Reds could not admit they'd kicked a ball over the wall let alone ask for it back, and from the combined tactic it was clear that the spy-plane had been expendable. Scoresby complimented Jack on what had been almost a solo sortie, and finished with a slight reproof on his hasty landing technique. Feeling he was on safe ground, Jack explained that he'd been thirsty, sorry sir, and Scoresby dismissed us with a resigned smile. Even though junior, the briefing officer is always called "sir".

The news was ahead of us and many of the others wanted to buy us a drink since it was the first bit of real "trade" to be knocked down for ages. Jack said I was terrific and I said he was terrific, and everybody drank to it, then he spotted the ill-mannered Archie hanging back and said, "Your round, old boy," in a loud voice and the cry was taken up with enthusiasm. It was plain that Archie did not fancy buying a large one for about twenty-five people, though at ship's prices it wouldn't have broken him, and he did so with a marked lack of grace.

For a short while we had an interesting discussion on the idea of war where nobody got killed, pilotless machines of every description being sent out to do battle while the real antagonists watched the moves on remote screens; rather like the armies of Biblical times watching their champions decide the issue in single combat.

The ideas were beginning to lose coherence when I was summoned to The Presence. Admiral Feather was seated in a spacious cabin looking stern, slim and dapper, beautifully manicured and making the usual rather limpwristed gestures which had earned him his nickname. He was polishing rimless glasses with an immaculate white silk handkerchief, and eyed me rheumily for a moment before replacing them.

"What I call a negative job, this," he said. "It goes well and there's no bitchiness, no pats on the back either, but when the old faeces hits the fan, who gets smacked? All we know for sure is that we don't know yet what the trouble is, only that our baby has stopped and surfaced. Either sabotage or malfunction, no one to tell us which, and we daren't approach with anything mechanical.

"Now then, Squire. You had a roving brief. Can you think of anything unusual, anything at all that might have occurred between the conclusion of sea-trials and actual departure?"

"Yes, sir, I can: the fact that I was excluded from the sea-trials and had no opportunity to vet those on board. I mentioned it at the time."

"I know, I know," he answered impatiently, "but the scientists you had already screened to their knickers and the seamen were largely leading ABs drawn at random."

"Yes, sir, but who drew them and were any of them allowed below? Were they all searched, were they all accounted for, and are they all locked up at the moment?"

He was jotting steadily on a pad and I noticed him hesitate for a moment. Then his hand floated gracefully to the telephone and he asked for a call by radio-link.

Replacing the receiver, he looked quizzically at me again. "Anything else?"

"Yes. I discovered tonight that the sub's various systems are not all that secret." I told him about Jack Plumley's information. "Also, it's just possible that he described the man who came to get me and drowned. The only motive I can ascribe to this is that the man may have thought I recognised him, which was in fact the

108

case, but only with hindsight. Did Briggs tell you that there were two further attempts against me before I got to Lossiemouth after I spoke to your stand-in? Right. In the first I saw no one, and for the second I'm getting a make on a burnt-out helicopter. Until this evening I confess that I was merely taking it personally, since your office wasn't interested, or to be fair, they had other things on their minds."

"I don't believe there's any possible connection. In an operation this size, that's a hopelessly tenuous link, more likely some bolshie Highlander doesn't like your aeroplane, noisy little beast anyway. Right, I want you to stay here with me and keep a random check on all the ongoings. Work under Captain Lucas, all right?"

"No, sir. I'd like to play a hunch. You don't have any leads whatever, unless you haven't told me something."

"Why would I do that? The answer is no, the order stands."

"Order?" I said quietly. "I'm only under your orders if I choose to be. My part in this operation is technically concluded."

He sniffed with annoyance while I was speaking, and then went very still and icy. "You are aboard a Naval vessel, subject to Naval discipline and you will do as you're told. Or else," he added pettishly.

"My commission came from the Admiralty in London. When this is over there'll be an enquiry and it will come out that you have prevented me from turning over every stone and refused co-operation for my particular brief."

The icy look continued in silence for a while and the thought that he might smack me on the wrist nearly made me grin. He took off his glasses, polished them again, replaced them and said, "Seamus, would you like a drink?"

"Yes, please. Scotch."

He poured two stiff ones and said with a slight smile, "What this country needs is a few more bolshie, single-minded pricks like you. All right, I can get those leads of yours checked out at once."

"There's no need, it's all in process, but I think it would be tighter if I did it myself."

"Very well. How long?"

"Twenty-four hours should do it. What's the schedule out here?"

"God knows. You've never seen such a quandary. I bet those

Reds are guffawing into their vodka – it makes me squirm, it really does."

"Will you authorise transport back to Lossie for me?"

"OK, first light. Get some kip first."

"Very good, sir. Dismissed?" I couldn't hide the grin and he responded, waving me out with a floppy gesture.

It was easy to get lost in the seaborne labyrinth, but the last part was easy since the noise from the bar had reached the proportions of a Maori war-dance.

Because of the racket it took at least five minutes for someone to explain to me why Jack was upside-down on a chair, on a table on top of another table, purple in the face with his trousers round his ankles and his buttocks pressed hard against the deckhead. I was told that he had once been at a very posh but very boring Mayfair cocktail party and had asked an acquaintance if he could think of any mischief to liven things up a bit. The other was also apparently bored and probably rich, for he ventured to bet Jack fifty quid he couldn't perform something quite unthinkable on the ceiling. My informant said that by all accounts the ceiling had been a good twenty-five feet and although Jack had made posterior contact of sorts and duly shocked the entire company, he had failed in the final analysis. He was awarded the fifty quid for trying, but was still piqued at his failure, which he looked like repeating. Personally, I am convinced it is humanly impossible to pass an irregular motion over the heads of the assembly when they are throwing cold beer at your exposed undercarriage and you yourself are roaring with laughter and close to apoplexy. This time the matter was quickly settled for him when the ship gave a slight lurch co-incident with his taking a deep breath and, with insufficient contact at the apex, the whole edifice tumbled. Everyone but Archie managed to get out of the way and there was a lot of beer on the floor for him to slither into, breaking Jack's fall in the process. The company was too convulsed to help him up, and certainly showed no great concern. Archie left us then in rather low spirits, but I have little recollection of the rest of the evening and I can't think of anyone there who might be able to remind me what happened, certainly not the upside-down aerobat himself, whom I was not to see for a while. My second pint of beer tasted different from the first and I can only conclude that someone had tipped about half a bottle of vodka into it.

I was shaken awake at some ungodly hour in a cabin I had never seen before, given a strong cup of tea and told there was a lift back to Lossie in half an hour, but that Jack's Blue Section had been ordered to stay on board.

I had a trip back in a Vixen with lots of oxygen as a temporary respite from the constant slow ripple being fired off inside my skull. Self-respect usually returns with a little dose of laughter, but on this occasion my pilot was a rather dour Lancastrian, who obviously felt that people who spoke the Queen's English and behaved like baboons should be sent away – to the colonies, perhaps? Anyhow, I was in no state to argue, since to one in my condition he would have sounded convincing enough.

It's strange how a hangover makes you feel guilty even if you don't know what you've done, and I felt murderous towards whoever had spiked my drink.

Back at Lossiemouth Briggs looked no better than the day before and matched my mood, commenting acidly on my appearance.

"Where can I get coffee?" I rasped at him. "I feel like an umbrella that's been blown inside out and tossed under a bus."

"Just a typical Plumley Monday," he cackled. "Most reliable feller, very regular habits. Anyway, there's nothing in for you yet, why don't you go along to the Mess? Stick a large brandy in your coffee, usually does the trick."

Half an hour later, my system all shot up with caffeine, I went back to his office and there were three messages. The Kyle police had found a body washed up on Skye, confirming Plumley senior's prediction, and it was complete with shoulder-holster but no identification. Sergeant McFadzean was on his way over to have a look. McGilvray's yard reported that a man similar to my Identikit photo had been sacked more than a year before, for reasons unstated as they could find no file on him. He was named as Roy Metcalfe. Finally, the Yard gave as the main beneficiary of HALOS one Torben McHarg of Dunnachan House, Carrondale, Wester Ross.

Briggs left me alone while I sorted it out, then I telephoned Cleodie and asked her to come and meet me in a couple of hours in Loch Coultrie, which was more of a mountain tarn a mile or two up behind my cottage. I used it sometimes in bad weather when Kishorn was too rough for the Teal. Cleodie asked me what was the matter with my voice and I told her that Plumley had tried to poison me.

Carrondale was on my route back but I avoided it with a wide detour and sneaked into Loch Coultrie low from the north. It has a very narrow waist in the middle, and I saw Cleodie's car waiting on the road as I creamed through the gap. The merest breeze puckered the surface and the peace was awesome once I'd switched off. I'd sunk an old engine block up there for a mooring, with another tripping line arrangement; although there was no tide to worry about, the edge was heavily bouldered.

She walked down to meet me and feathery feelings stirred my insides. I felt I ought to suppress them but I didn't want to. She stood with her hands on her hips.

"Why don't you get a boat, it's much more restful? Safer too."

"Same reason you haven't got a bicycle. I knew a chap once who was starting to get fat so I suggested a few games of squash. He said playing squash was too uncomfortable. Anyway, thanks for coming."

"Por nada, señor. Hop in."

I winced as she switched on the engine and she responded with a smile for the little red Elan had seen better days and the exhaust sounded like a leaky bassoon. There was nothing wrong with its performance, however, and Cleodie wasn't inclined to hang about.

She looked across at me and said, "Where to, your honour?"

"Can you spare an hour or two? We could have a sandwich in a pub and then I'd like to be dropped off to see someone, a little way up Glen Carron."

"Fine. I want to have a look at what you've done to your cottage sometime."

"Not today. There's something I have to do and I want to avoid McFadzean in case there's any red tape. They've found the body on Skye."

"Oh? He was looking for you yesterday. Must be the worst crime in the last fifty years, he was being really heavy about it. Seething with threats and irony, says you're not supposed to have gone away, he hasnae funished hus investergeshions."

"That's him. Cheerful soul, isn't he?"

"And big with it. Thinks this chosen land shouldn't be settled by over-privileged show-offs. He didn't mention my nakedness in front of Carruthers but he's got it in for you all right."

"Did you spring to my defence?"

112

"How could I? I hardly know you. Actually, I egged him on, thought it might give me a sense of balance. Takes a man to know a man."

"He doesn't know me."

"Does anyone?"

We were speeding down towards the head of Loch Kishorn, Cleodie's movements light and precise, just finger and thumb on the gear-lever, the fingers of her right hand merely resting on the wheel. I looked across at her, knowing she would be aware of it but too busy with the winding narrow road to look back at me. She flushed a little and smiled.

"Well?" she asked, after a moment.

"Yes. I was thinking about a friend at university after we'd seen a movie with Grace Kelly in it. He was absolutely moonstruck and kept saying, "Damnit, there's nothing *wrong* with that woman!""

She gave a little laugh. "Rather negative viewpoint."

"Sensible though, trying to establish the bad points first."

"I suppose so, if you want to stay a bachelor. What do you see with your jaundiced eye?"

She was distracted by a few friendly waves as we drove through Achintraid, which was as well, because I had no answer, not one that I was prepared to give. I was trying to tell myself that she wasn't an eyeful of perfection, a better hangover cure than lungfuls of pure oxygen, failing in her attempt to look boyish and unfeminine. As we climbed up through the woods on her side of the loch, she hummed a little tune, the inkling of a smile at the corner of her mouth. After a while, she asked me why I didn't look very well and if Jack had taken me flying, so I told her about it, leaving out the classified bits which I judged to include Jack's circus act in the wardroom. I did tell her that he had been very shocked when we buzzed him in the speedboat but without betraying his awful secret.

We went briskly through Lochcarron village and swept up the glen for three or four miles, the railway converging from our right and then crossing to our left as we reached Loch Dhughaill. She was going quite fast when a car, which had been parked on the nearside, suddenly pulled out in front of us as if starting a U-turn. I suppose we might have stopped in time, but it would have been a long howling slide. Otherwise, there was the loch, forty feet down to our right, or else a steep bank up to the railway on our left. For my part, some notion took over and put my feet on the

113

dashboard and my arms over my head, but Cleodie, who had been telling me something, merely stopped speaking, swung over to the right and *accelerated*. The other car, a heavy sports job, was stopped across the road and its driver's door, which had been opening, suddenly shut. Still with her foot down, Cleodie swerved the Lotus towards the left bank, swept along it as if on a banked circuit and slithered back onto the road beyond the obstruction. I was quite startled at the prompt, cool reaction, knowing that without the extra speed and the centrifugal effect of the angle made towards it, we would have fallen off the bank.

I put my feet down again and said, "Have you jilted anyone lately?"

"I've never jilted anyone." She looked a bit white and then I saw her eyes narrow at the mirror.

"He's coming after us. What the hell *is* this? Shall I stop so you can beat him up, or is your hangover too much?"

I looked back to see a green Jensen or Aston Martin growing larger, although Cleodie hadn't slowed down much. She watched him a few moments longer, then grabbed a handful of third and took the revs right into the red sector. He was still gaining on us, though more slowly, but he didn't pull out to overtake when he could have done, just slammed hard into the back of us.

Cleodie said something indistinct but venomous, correcting as the rear wheels leapt sideways, and glanced across at me looking bewildered and a bit scared. He hit us again then, and the boot-lid sprung open to be torn off a moment later by the slipstream. The light glass-fibre panel struck the windscreen of the Jensen and stayed there for a moment, which made me hopeful as he dropped back, but then it spun off into the road.

By this time we were doing about a hundred and ten. The road ahead swept round in a long curve to our left, but I knew that the slightest off-centre nudge at that speed would probably be fatal. Lumbering along in the same direction was a mammoth articulated truck, four or five hundred yards ahead, and Cleodie began to ease the speed down. As she did so, the Jensen hit us again, though perfectly straight. Half a mile ahead, where the road bent back to the right, I saw another truck approaching, and Cleodie must have seen it too for she began to slow up in earnest.

"Keep going," I said.

"But there's a . . . "

114

"I know. Keep going. Flat out. Overtake him, I've got an idea."

We raced up on the big truck, the Jensen repeatedly nudging the splintered and shredded rear of the Lotus. The curve continued to the left as Cleodie pulled out to overtake and her face looked desperately strained as we came alongside. We both knew there was another truck coming and my one hope was that the driver of the Jensen hadn't seen it yet. I had seen his square features set in a composed mask, expressionless.

It's a questionable assumption that if you stick close to an overtaking car, you will get by as well because of the slight margin the leader has to leave, and the higher the speed, the greater the margin, allowing for normal judgement. I didn't mean her to leave any margin, even for ourselves.

I glanced quickly at the Jensen which moved slightly to the right, seizing a perfect opportunity to shunt us under the rear wheels of the big truck. There was a terrible bedlam of noise and I had to shout, emphasising with a sliced movement of my hand towards the centre section of the trailer.

"Go under!"

It must have been a great relief for her and she didn't hesitate an instant, braking very sharply and slipping the low-slung Elan under the open centre part of the trailer, with no more than a couple of inches to spare overhead. There was another thump as the Jensen driver made his move at the same moment, but we were already going in the same direction and most of the impact was absorbed by his windscreen pillar against the trailer. This had all happened very fast, and I saw again the cold ruthless face of a killer, watching, certain of himself, then the whole tableau disintegrated.

The driver of our sheltering truck must have reacted instinctively to a crisis of which he'd only just become aware, touching his brakes for an instant. The front of our car clunked once against the fixed steel parking struts, but mercifully he must have realised the futility of it and the rig's brake lights went off at once. Simultaneously, the Jensen driver became aware of the oncoming truck, too late for him to pull back behind the trailer, and he wrenched his car towards his one remaining option – the loch. I didn't see him go in because the second truck screamed past in a locked and smoking skid. Our driver eased down to a controlled

115

halt, and we slipped quietly out and over on to the left-hand verge, stopping alongside him.

Cleodie was looking at me, her hands gripping the wheel with a quivering force. I reached out and switched off the ignition, then gently prised her hands away and held them between mine. Suddenly she flung both arms around me and buried her face in my neck, shaking and making soft mewing noises.

From outside, I heard running footsteps. I touched one of the switches for the electric windows and lowered the one on the driver's side a few inches. Under the truck, I could see legs slowing from a run, then heard the sound of another man jumping down and a cab door slam. The truck's engine had been switched off and the two men must have stood without speaking for a few moments, I imagine looking down at the water. The silence was absolute except for the occasional tick of cooling contraction from under the car's bonnet. At the sound of voices, Cleodie stiffened and raised her head, but I rather liked it where it was and pushed it back. She didn't resist.

A broad Glasgow accent said, "Di' ye see tha'?"

There was a long, long pause, then another voice, like gravel, simply said, "No."

"Och, come on man, ye must o' seen it! An' where's the other car, the red jorb? Ah seen them from way ba', comin' up on ye, hell for lither."

A match was thrown to the ground and a second pair of legs approached the first. The gravelly voice said, "Ye'll no help 'em whither ye saw them or no, so I say no."

There was again a long meditative silence and some uncomfortable shuffling by the first pair of legs, then a resigned: "Aye, a' right."

He walked off back to his truck, and we heard him start up and drive slowly away. The other driver stood for several minutes, his feet pointing away from us, presumably smoking and gazing at the water, and presently he too got back in his cab and drove off. As he pulled away, we must have come within the vision of his near-side mirror, for he braked suddenly, then changed his mind and ground steadily up the road. A light breeze ruffled the loch's surface, but off to the right there was a spreading patch of oil. I was a bit surprised that he hadn't managed to get out, but if you go in nose first and the windscreen shatters, you can be too badly impaired by the force of the water, especially if a seat belt has

116

prevented you from ducking under it. Judging by the steepness of the hills, the loch was probably very deep. I remembered our mid-Channel plunge in the Cessna very vividly.

I said to Cleodie, "You can come out now, everyone's gone."

She had stopped shaking, and raised her head. "Didn't you say something about a pub, earlier on?"

"Yes. Would you like me to drive?"

She nodded and we both got out and walked round. At one point she stopped to look at the loch and the oil, shuddered briefly and got into the passenger seat. I turned the car round, explaining that I was going back for the boot lid. After about a mile and a half we came up to the second truck, which was stopped, and saw the driver standing on the other side of the road examining a battered piece of red plastic in his hands.

Stopping the car next to him, I said, "Can we have it back, please?"

He was a short bow-legged man with curly ginger hair, and he looked puzzled and upset. He must have been longing to chew over a good post-mortem with somebody, and was torn between this and his implied pact of silence with the other driver. I got out and took the lid from him, put it into the shattered opening and got back in before he could say anything. I thanked him, said it was a lovely day for a drive, shut the door and moved off. When I glanced back, he was still standing there looking dejected, but when we found a pub, feeling sympathetic towards ourselves and ordering large ones, I was relieved to see him roar past. I'd parked the Lotus right round the back where it couldn't be seen from the road.

Cleodie looked a little brighter after making heavy inroads into her drink, and leant towards me across the table.

"Do I have to go through things like that every time I want a cuddle?"

"Well, you deserved one, I must say. Didn't put a wheel wrong."

"It was horrible. Do you realise how much blind faith I had to put in you, when you said you had an idea? An *idea*! You sounded all crisp and authoritative and made me go against the absolute certainty of a head-on crash . . . I suppose that's how they got the troops to go 'over the top', plus the threat of a bullet in the back."

"We'd have got it in the back from the other guy if you hadn't."

"That was incredible. Do you know who it was, jilted lovers eliminated?"

"I think it's got a lot to do with where I was going. I hadn't meant for you to come, just to drop me in the area. I'm really sorry you had such a scare, I had no reason to expect it."

"Oh, well, these little things bring us closer together." She twinkled slightly, then turned her mouth down. "My little car's a ruin ... somehow, I don't seem to be able to take this seriously. That's the second death I've more or less witnessed in a few days. Won't you tell me what's going on? It's all sort of ridiculous and unreal."

"I know it is, and I can't answer you. I don't know, but I was on my way to try to find out. Look, we'll have another one of these and a sandwich, then I want to take you home. Will you lend me your car, what's left of it? I'll see to that, by the way, in case you were worrying. Mind you, it was time it had a refit anyway."

"Nonsense. Anyway, why can't I come with you?"

"No. But there's something you can do for me. If I'm not back in, say, two hours, call the cops and send them up to where I'm going. It's Dunnachan House, Carrondale."

She looked defiant but I glossed over it by going to the bar and ordering a couple of sandwiches. When I came back, she was staring into her drink and without looking up she spoke quietly.

"You haven't been straight with me, have you? You're not what you say you are, I'm sure. You can't be that ice-cold and detached about terror and death unless you're conditioned to it. And another thing, it's unnatural for a healthy man to isolate himself in a remote cottage in the Highlands, unless he's hiding or running away from something. After all, you're not anti-social, you seemed quite pleased to be with us the other evening, and you resisted my advances out of policy, not inclination. And in case you're wondering about that, I don't believe in playing hard to get – I do and say what I feel, unless it's unkind. I don't believe in giving oneself a fictional value by teasing or coquetry."

"Admirable," I said, smiling, "but the trouble with being forward is it makes other people hold back. It's an instinct I'm trying to overcome."

"Nonsense, you're old enough to know better than that. You've got a reason, and a very strong one, for avoiding involvement, but it might be unkind to badger you about it, um?"

"Well, it's just caution. But you are teasing, you know, by making out that you're 'easy', which I don't believe you are."

"And you're the red-blooded male who wants to respond to a challenge, to pursue and ensnare, to strut and show off his feathers and impress me into a swoon? If I let you do that, you'd only show me your good side and it could take months to discover the truth! I've learnt much more about you my way."

"So what am I supposed to do now – recognise defeat and surrender my honour, with of course a suitable show of resistance, a few half-hearted 'stop-its' thrown in?"

The way she smiled over her glass was quite enchanting and I couldn't stop myself returning it. We kept that up for a long time and must have looked very foolish, but the three or four people in the bar were engaged in a heated fishing conversation. I recalled the touch and feel of her when she had held me in the car, her hair soft and thick, no make-up, no perfume. Suddenly I knew for certain that I wanted more, and more, and that there could never be enough. The stall-warning horn went off in my head, too late, not enough height left for recovery. I was aware of having failed to find something wrong with her.

I thought back to another time when I had fallen for a poised and perfect creature, it seemed years ago, who didn't always meet my eyes, and I'd put it down to being demure and shy ... I suspect that the attraction for me had been that she was unusual, which is some men's vanity. The loss of her at that time had been so excruciating that I'd refused to dwell on it at all. It had stayed numb and buried, and only now did it occur to me that Old Man Shriver might have actually done me a favour.

Cleodie interrupted my thoughts. We were still grinning at each other.

"What were you thinking then?"

"About a fair-weather sailor."

"Well, I thought you were planning how to turn the tables on me."

"No, because in your cunning way, that's probably what you're working towards."

"Yes, dear," she said and laughed gaily. Some heads turned and regarded us with suspicion. Fishing is a serious matter to a Highlander. When they resumed their talk, Cleodie continued the banter.

"I don't think you were a flying instructor at all, there's

something shady you haven't told me. I know, I'm going to guess
... a sleuth, that's it. Divorce work, is it, tell no tales?"

"'Sright."

"And sometimes you have to force a party to commit an
indiscretion, and some of them resist, or some just don't like you
around, so every now and again you get a few lumps cut out of your
hide?"

I nodded.

"And you've just pulled off a big one, so you're resting, or else
you're just building up to THE big one? Shouldn't be much action
round here, but still someone's got it in for you. I suppose if the
party won't co-operate, you knock him or her off, which saves a
lot of aggro and lawyers' fees?"

"Wrong. I opted out when they tried to draft me into the
contracts department, so now I work freelance, when I feel like
it."

"Oh, the little sleuth has a conscience about knocking people
off, has he?"

"Yessir, except in self-defence. And I cost more than a lawyer
because saving face comes expensive."

"Have you got lots of juicy files on people?"

"No, I keep it all in my head."

"I'll get you to talk in your sleep, don't worry." She put her hand
on mine and said, "Where's that other drink, sleuth?"

As I got up from the table, she leaned over and said, "Are you
going to tell our children that's what you do for a living? They're
bound to ask, you know."

"I expect you'll think of something. When's the first one due,
by the way?"

She ignored that with a calculating look and said, "Have you got
a middle name?"

"No."

"Well, if we give him the middle name Oscar or something, his
initials would be SOS, which stands for Son of Sleuth. I'll bring
him up without a conscience and he'll make more money than his
old man. So there."

When I came back with the drinks, her eyes were alight with
mischief and something else, and a man can't help enjoying being
looked at that way. Apparently, one of the body signals to which
we respond unconsciously is the involuntary dilation of the pupils
of the interested party, and Cleodie's eyes were wide and bright,

120

despite the gloom inside the bar. I made a deliberate effort to close mine, and the result was immediate and startling.

"What happened then?" she asked in alarm, and then dejectedly, "I blew it, didn't I? Going too far, too fast."

"Look again," I said, relaxing.

She frowned, unable to work it out. "I think that's beastly, just switching off like that. What did you do, think about Grace Kelly or someone?"

"My Nannie. She always said I mustn't court, that was her word, anyone I hadn't seen in church. She was Irish."

"Oh, that's all right. I've joined lots of churches in my time. Were you in love with her?"

"Yes, until she got into trouble with an agnostic postman. She was replaced by a huge ugly dyke and it affected my emotional development."

"So you're not . . . like other men are?"

"I don't know. I've never looked."

She laughed. "Well at least that's easily solved. I met a bloke once who said he wished he was a Lesbian and when I asked him why, he explained that he was absolutely nuts about women but didn't understand them!"

"That's an interesting approach. Did it work?"

"No fear. He had big soft eyes like a randy spaniel. Carruthers said you looked haunted by something."

"Is she all right? I noticed her flinch a couple of times."

"No, she isn't. I've finally persuaded her to go for a check-up. Seriously, though, you're not up to anything illegal, are you?"

"Of course not. Mustn't get put away when I've a wife and family to support."

She continued gazing at me with her chin still partly hidden in her hand. She had broad, generous hands. I went to the bar and paid, and she was still in the same attitude when I came back. I had to take her arm and ease her, trance-like, from her seat and back to the car, and she bumped into things because she was turning round to look at me all the time. Her hair bobbed with the spring in her step, and she ignored my laughter which was in fact a cover-up. My solar-plexus was in trauma, and I felt like a fifteen-year-old on his first assignation.

We hardly spoke on the way back, and she insisted on being left at the end of her road.

She said, "Take care, see you later safe and sound," and made to get out of the car.

I put my hand on her arm, and very, very slowly she turned and leaned towards me. Her kiss, finally, was of chiffon and champagne and then velvet, delicate but firm, lingering, perfect. I closed my eyes and flew for a while on instruments.

Disorientated, my brain went into a power dive, pulled up into a loop, tried to roll off the top, stalled and began a dizzying, inverted spin with no chance of recovery. The engine began to scream and then suddenly died, and then I came to, realising that I'd put my foot hard on the car's accelerator until finally Cleodie had reached out and switched off the ignition.

Very gently, she touched my face and said, "Bye. Be very careful," then slipped out and ran off down the road, but I was still in a coma and couldn't answer.

Ten

As she ran, I noticed, she didn't throw her feet out to the side in the way that most women do when the action is unfamiliar. I sat for a moment watching her retreating figure, and began to see the situation with an awful clarity.

As we had just been shown, my contact with her put her in a distinctly dangerous position. Unless someone had the mountain road staked out, they could not have known that I was with her in the car until the attempt was made to stop her on the road, so whoever was trying to "influence" me was quite prepared to use her for this purpose. I could hardly ask Cleodie to go off and hide somewhere with her mother, but how else could I get the heat off them short of flying myself into a mountain where everyone could see? I had to shut off the heat at source.

The tail-pipe fell off as I wrenched the car round in a furious burst of acceleration, and sounding like a heavy machine-gun tore off back towards Carrondale. I was really very angry, and this dispelled any notion I had of a quiet approach to case the place.

When I found it, Dunnachan House appeared tall and forbidding, approached by a single track and surrounded by a high wall, which was topped with broken glass and barbed-wire running through insulators. The gate was shut and heavily padlocked, but after repeated blasts on the horn, a heavy-set character appeared from a tiny lodge joined to the right-hand gatepost. He glowered at me questioningly for some moments, and getting no response started to unlock the gate. When he'd opened it to come through, I flapped the car door and made as if to get out, which had the desired effect of persuading him he didn't have to lock it up again, but as he walked towards me, I slipped back in and drove past him in a spurt of gravel, nudging the gate fully open as I went through. He shouted, of course, and in the mirror I saw him running into the lodge as I roared up the drive, but the exhaust's fractured racket was as effective in announcing my arrival.

As I stopped by the front steps in a scatter of gravel, one half of a tall double door opened and a man appeared, looking at first suspicious then startled and wary as an alarm went off somewhere and dogs started barking round the side of the house. Suddenly from behind the man an eager and somewhat athletic youth charged out of the porch, leapt down the five steps and turned a shotgun on me, all in one movement. It looked rather practised.

I got out of the car, to much jerking from the shotgun muzzle. The one on the steps spoke first, looking relaxed, confident and very hard.

"Who are you and what do you want?"

"I want to see if he's got the safety catch on."

The youth stood hunched over the barrel with the stock in his elbow, so that if he'd fired, his right arm would have wrapped itself back round his head. He stood still, glaring at me, as I went to him and peered over the barrel, which was now against my stomach. The catch was off.

"It should be on 'safe' unless you're going to fire it," I said quietly, and took hold of the barrel, pulled it aside and towards me and kicked him sharply in the slats. He let go of the gun and sat down.

The man on the steps watched impassively as I broke the gun open, walked up and handed it to him.

"Does the milkman get that sort of treatment every day?" I asked him mildly, although the little gesture had done nothing to dispel my anger. He ignored the question, and said, "Your business, Mr . . . ?"

"My name is Squire, and I've come to discuss with Mr McHarg a matter concerning some of his property which may be missing."

I could tell he was about to come out with the usual patter about the master not being home, but then he thought better of it and ushered me inside. He signalled me to wait in the entrance hall, which was the usual Highland clutter of glass-eyed stagsheads, claymores, and those enormous, ancient fowling pieces which you stuff with bent nails and rusty bits of ironmongery and preferably get someone else to fire for you. Whoever was responsible for the décor had about as much sense of taste as a carrion crow.

From beyond the glass panelled doors came a distant voice raised in anger, then after a couple of minutes my dour and silent usher came back and beckoned me through into a wide corridor hung with gloomy paintings. He led me to a room at the far end, opened the heavy oak door and was dismissed with a nod by the figure seated behind a huge desk. A telex machine was rattling away on one side of the room, which was strewn with reams of paper, most of it still attached to the machine. I suppose it could have been running since breakfast, or else nobody bothered much about filing.

"Mr Torben McHarg?" I asked politely, and he nodded again curtly, without getting up. He was immensely broad-shouldered, really filling his large jacket, with a thick neck trying to burst an eighteen-inch collar. His head and neck were very red as if suffused with anger, his eyes bulged, his ears stuck out slightly, and black hair lay flat on his head supported by greying sideburns with still quite a lot of red in them. The general appearance was of extreme aggression, tight-bunched, explosive and rather wicked-looking, like a dum-dum bullet.

The telex stopped as if to order, and McHarg spoke with a clipped rasping voice.

"What the hell do you mean by charging in here like that, and what's this about some property of mine?"

I pointed to the chair facing him and he nodded again savagely, as if bidding me not to interrupt. There was a copy of the *Financial Times* on the chair, which I picked up before sitting and placed on my lap.

"Well?" he said, impatiently.

"Yes, I believe you've lost a helicopter?"

"So?"

"I can tell you where it is."

"Then do so."

"And a Jensen?"

His eyes narrowed a fraction, but he shook his head.

"The car's not missing."

"Where do you think it is, then?"

"Look, if you've got something to tell me, get on with it, otherwise you can piss off."

I gave him a pained look as if he'd offended my sensibilities.

125

Mild manners are like red rags to a bully, so I kept my voice soft whilst nervously rolling up the newspaper.

"First I would like you to tell *me* something, like why I am being constantly interfered with by people connected with you, and in a manner which suggests a permanent solution. I'm sure you know who I am?"

"Yes, but I don't know what you're talking about."

"Don't you? Well, first there was Roy Metcalfe, who unfortunately decided to drown himself, but the driver of the Jensen is a most informative character."

"Rubbish, he wouldn't say a . . . " McHarg stopped in confusion, and suddenly realised that the die was cast.

"Where is he?" he barked at me.

I just shook my head slowly because I could see his dilemma; he didn't know how much I knew, but he must have realised I was taking shots in the dark otherwise he would have been arrested already. Now that I'd met the man, it suddenly occurred to me that pretending to hold the driver as a hostage would probably carry no weight at all. Instinctively, I decided to rattle him.

"Didn't you find the helicopter?" I asked.

"No, where is it?"

"I'm surprised no one saw the smoke. Yesterday morning, it sort of fell out of the sky. I have a placard on my instrument panel which reads: 'Ignore thine Altimeter at thy Peril, for the Earth shall rise up and smite thee.' I suppose he was gunning for me but he came up against a sort of airborne Billy the Kid and got himself creamed."

The light banter was making him livid. He put one foot on his chair and bunched two powerful hairy fists. I've seen this sort before, and they usually rely on sheer aggression to force a cowed opponent to submit. A lot of the time it works, but if it doesn't, they're so angry at that stage that they come out with their fists flailing and all the mechanical advantage packed into a short muscular frame is very difficult to stop. He looked as though he was about to leap at me across the desk. He was bristling with gathered fury as he spoke.

"You're a dead man, that's for sure."

Using his chair as a starting block, he leapt at me across the desk. The normal reaction is to step back hurriedly and get clobbered all the same, so instead I came forward fast out of my chair and rammed upwards under his chin with the tightly rolled newspaper. The soft flesh just behind the jaw-bone is very vulnerable and he spat a gout of blood onto my trousers as he went down heavily, scrambling immediately onto one knee. I chopped him hard across the neck, but it was like hammering dried meat. He stayed where he was, so I did it again and slowly he subsided to the floor, looking vacant.

I turned to the door and locked it, not wanting any interference from the hard, confident-looking man who had shown me in. I had enough to deal with in McHarg, but I'd underestimated him. As I turned back from the door, his hand jerked savagely at my left foot and I fell heavily onto my right hip. I bounced to my feet but he was ahead of me and a sledgehammer blow connected perfectly about two inches below my heart. A solid one there is as good as a knock-out, except that there's a curious delayed reaction of about two seconds during which I tried to smash his nose and missed by a whisker. Then the reaction came and all the air went out of me like a wide-necked balloon. The fist that swung up was aimed at my jaw which would have sprung out on each side in separate sections but by then I had bent in the middle and my head came down. The blow that smacked me on the forehead was the most powerful I had ever felt, and I slithered over the desk and went down in a flaccid heap on the other side, the chair tilting and sliding underneath. Semiconscious, I scrabbled to my feet and then gasped with agony as the desk slammed across my pelvic bones and crushed me against the wall.

I was braying for my breath like a senile donkey and through the groggy mist of pain, I saw McHarg nursing his right hand, his hip jammed against the desk and one foot planted on the far wall to hold me in position.

One of the telephones rang, and I was surprised they were still on the desk. Everything else was thoroughly scattered. McHarg picked up one of the receivers and grunted into the mouthpiece. He was breathing hard and still dribbling blood as he listened, and when he spoke it was with difficulty.

" ... No, bring her over, we may need her yet. I'm not going to waste much time on him, so if he doesn't tell me in about five minutes, he's all yours ... just what he knows, that's all. And keep Trigger away, he's too kill-happy, at least until we've got it all ... No, Muir, forget it, we don't know the dose. Anyway, the old method works well enough. Just give me a few minutes, I'll manage."

He looked over at me with narrowed eyes. I couldn't reach him with my arms, the desk was too wide.

"I suppose you got the gist of that? You might as well start talking."

I didn't answer, and thought I *had* got the gist of it. Only the last part, though – I hadn't yet connected the first part with Cleodie ...

The telex clattered into life and McHarg glanced towards it, very briefly, and in that split second I straightened my legs and moved the desk enough to slide out sideways before he could thrust it back at me. He spread his legs and waited for me to come to him but instead I strode diagonally across in front of him, towards the telex. The move must have puzzled him since I wasn't even looking his way, and when I was almost past him as he stood on my left, I pivoted on that foot and swung the right away from him through 270 degrees. You connect with a lot of momentum and with the most powerful muscles in your body and it doesn't even hurt unless you fall badly in the follow-through. The heel of my right shoe clicked smartly on the side of his jaw and he went down like two hundredweight of wet mud.

I got up slowly from the floor, watching him all the time, but he didn't move. His right hand was clearly broken, the middle knuckle bent upwards and back. I wasn't surprised as there was already a half duck-egg swelling out of my forehead, but the grogginess was going.

The telex rattled to a halt and I went over and glanced at some of the typescript. It seemed to be linked to the Aberdeen offices because neither of the answerbacks tallied with this machine, and I assume McHarg liked to monitor all the business that was going on. Most of the messages referred to rigs and supply vessels, dates, numbers, quantities and so forth, but a few were typed in black to show they were outgoing from this station, and rather typically these were terse and dictatorial, mostly starting "I want" or "You will" and spattered with strong words. Definitely not the lovable type of employer.

My searches among the papers and drawers revealed no clue as to what else was involved, not at any rate which involved me. And if it was important enough to warrant killing, why had they not succeeded? Perhaps because people were being deputised for the job and it's not that easy if your heart isn't in it. Also it seemed that McHarg was too angry and unstable to be masterminding anything except hard business, since the successful man of intrigue needs to be cool and precise, even detached.

In his diary there was an entry for the next day, 16 May, just a phone number, Husinish 381, and next to it a very heavily printed letter B in a circle. Because there was a similar reference on one of the telex outgoings, I went over and checked, finding the same number ... "call me tomorrow evening sixteenth at Husinish 381 at exactly 7.00 p.m."

In the desk drawer I found a bottle of Dabitoff, so I prised out the padded cork and splashed some on his face, which made him start to come round. The rest I emptied over his clothes.

His first sight when he opened his eyes was of me bending over him holding a box of matches, one ready to strike. Carbon tetrachloride isn't flammable, quite the opposite, but it's so volatile it smells as though it must be.

His hand went straight up to his chin, where the pain must have been intense, and his look was scared and demoralised. Keeping clear of the reach of his powerful arms, I bent over him and spoke tersely.

"What's so important that you've just lost three men in trying to get rid of me?"

He shook his head slightly and gagged. "Metcalfe recognised you from Glasgow and reckoned you were investigating him."

"Metcalfe's dead. Why the others?"

"Dunno. Maybe they thought the same. You've flown over this house about four times."

"That's all bull. It was your helicopter and your Jensen. Tell me what you're afraid I'll find out, otherwise we're going to have a little burn-up."

He must have had more to fear from telling me since he managed to shake his head adamantly. There was alarm in his eyes as I struck a match, moving it slowly towards him as it burnt down, but he still refused to answer. The telephone rang, but he didn't take his eyes off the match and I used the distraction to put him out again. The least I could do was to give him cause to resent me.

There were two telephones on the desk, and I picked up the internal one. I gave a nondescript grunt and recognised the voice of the big, quiet man who'd shown me in.

"Mr McHarg, Murray's arrived with the girl. Where do you want her?"

That's when I blew it, Cleodie. Everything followed from that moment. I thought I knew all about fear, but I knew nothing about fear for you.

I tried to sound like McHarg, but I simply hadn't had enough time to assimilate his gruff, machine-gun speech. I told him to wait, I'd be along in a minute, but I could tell from the silence that I hadn't fooled him. If he'd been smart and pretended to have been taken in, he'd have had us together.

I cast around for some distraction or a weapon of some kind, but there was nothing, and in a moment there was the sound of rattling at the doorknob and the thump of a heavy shoulder. I knew that our only chance was to make myself inaccessible: if I was taken it would be the end for both of us.

I opened the window and looked out to a seven- or eight-foot drop, so I climbed through and hung for a moment, letting go as the deep, bass BOONT! of a shotgun shattered the lock.

The short drop to the ground seemed endless, because it gave way and I was falling, sliding into blackness with a searing pain all down one side. When you hit your head really hard, the bright-lit explosion in front of your brain seems to go on for ages, and I recall thinking as I went away: they'll let her go now, I'm out of it all.

I woke rigid with cold and in pitch blackness. My head hurt abominably and my hair was matted with, presumably, dried blood. There was a lot of dust and gritty particles and I began to realise I must be in some sort of coal cellar. I remembered uselessly that there were matches on McHarg's desk, and gradually other things started to come back. For several minutes I strained to catch some sound but there was none, so I began to feel around me. Eventually, I came up against what felt like a steel chute, and I concluded that I must have fallen through the hatch and gone down the way the coal is supposed to. It was inclined at about forty-five degrees with its edges curled upwards.

I groped around further and found some steps with a door at the top but it was firmly locked and opened inwards. I couldn't move it, so I went back to the chute and started to crawl up it, but the edges dug brutally into my hands. It was slippery with coal dust so I slid back down several times. I tried climbing up the structure that supported it, but was faced with the same problem once I was high enough to try to climb on top of it. Heaving with exertion and pain, I tried another tack, sliding up the chute by putting my arms

130

round it and grasping the structure, with the upturned edges digging fiercely into the front of my shoulders. I didn't have much choice, since I could hardly take a run at it in the dark, and I struggled up until I came to where the chute passed between the brick edges of the opening. Here the space was too small to allow my arms to squeeze in between the chute and the walls and by that stage I was getting ready to slide down again into a grovelling heap. Action: sublimate the pain and self-pity, imagine you're sitting at a desk trying to solve a theoretical problem, and get angry. Taking one hand away from the underneath support, I put it into the space and made a fist which effectively jammed it. Doing the same with the other, I was able to start inching my way upwards again until finally coming up against a vertical wall. I took one hand off and felt above me, but there was nothing to get hold of within reach. At this point, I lost my grip with the other fist and poured down the chute again like a greasy fried egg. This time I was conscious, so it hurt more but did less damage as I was able to protect my head with my arms.

By now, the particular exercise was really getting desperately, frenziedly aggravating. By the time I reached the top again, my anger and pain had each increased to an alarming degree and I began to feel dizzy with the total output. Once up against the wall, I drew up one foot carefully and shoved the toe into the space, and then did the same with the other. I've never been in such an awkward position, my feet bent outwards and down, and I gingerly unclenched my fists and spread them against the side walls. Coming up into a crouch from there, my head came against the hatch at about three feet above the top of the chute, presumably to allow it space to swing open. I groped around the underside of the hatch for some time before realising that it was a double door held closed by powerful springs, by which time my feet and legs were really screaming at me. I pulled down on one of the sprung levers and managed to open one of the halves sufficiently to get my fingers into the gap, but pulling down on it just lowered the door without lifting me up – which was fortunate, I suppose, otherwise I wouldn't have been able to open it. Eventually, I was able to twist round and brace myself between the lowered hatch and the wall underneath and wriggle out that way. It was quite dark outside.

I lay on the ground for some time waiting for the gasping to subside. There were no lights showing in the house, at least on that, the rear side, and after a while I got up and did a complete circuit. No sign of life at all, and Cleodie's car had gone. I went down to the lodge, but that too was deserted and the gate padlocked.

It only began to dawn on me then, I was still a bit confused. Somehow, it's hard to think that falling down a coal-hole and knocking yourself unconscious can be a lucky thing to happen, but the mere fact that no one had come down to deliver the coup de grâce must mean that they thought I had got clean away, which left them with no choice but to evacuate.

It was Square One again, with a vengeance. I smashed a window to get back into the house and the alarm went off, so I switched the lights on, found the fuse-box eventually in the entrance hall and pulled out fuses in turn until the noise stopped. No one was likely to hear it anyway.

My watch was still going, though the glass was cracked. It said 10.30 which checked with the clock in the hall. I picked up the phone and called Carruthers, who sounded her usual placid self until I couldn't tell her where Cleodie was. I had to make sure I wasn't mistaken, since she hadn't been named by McHarg.

"I thought she was with you, didn't she go out to meet you this morning?"

I had to bend the truth to reduce her anxiety. "Yes, but she had to go off somewhere. I was going to meet her later, but don't worry. Must have been a misunderstanding."

She sounded content with that and rang off, but it did nothing for my peace of mind. It was the worst confirmation, and I had no illusions about calling for police help. I just struggled to quell those frantic feelings which are worse than useless at a time like that, and then turned them into bitter fury.

Moving at a run, I virtually ransacked the house, which showed all the signs of hurried evacuation, but there were absolutely no papers to be found anywhere.

All the time something kept niggling at me, denying recall because of my turmoil and anxiety. I made an effort to compose myself, then, as a distraction, I raided the kitchen where I found bread, ham and coffee, which I laced with some very expensive Cognac. On the way back, I caught sight of myself in a tall mirror and got a bad shock thinking it was someone else. My clothes were torn, one of my shoes had burst and I was absolutely caked in coal-dust.

132

It came at last, suddenly, when I was thinking of something else. Husinish. I picked up the telephone and spoke to the local operator.

In those little communities, the operator knew everything that went on, even whether the person you were calling was in or out, and if the latter then where to find them. When I asked her where Husinish was, she told me I ought to know since I was calling from McHarg's house and he had phoned there several times.

"Can you get me an address for a number, please, this is terribly important. There's a life in danger."

"Is there noo?" She sounded sceptical. "Whose might that be?"

I could have got the information by going "through channels", but it would have taken too long. "Will you keep it entirely to yourself?" I asked, and, realising that would be too big a burden, added, "At least until I get it sorted out, then I'll tell you all about it."

The conspiratorial eagerness in her voice was quite patent as she agreed.

"Thanks," I said fervently. "It's Cleodie McNeil, but no one must know, not even her mother."

The name triggered her into quiet, efficient compliance but I had to wait while she chewed the fat with, presumably, the Husinish operator and came back to me about ten minutes later.

"I had to check back my records that you had the number right. Ye see, it's a call-box on a little island called Breac, just off the west coast of Harris. The Husinish lady says there's just three cottages on the shore facing the mainland, with a wee strip of water in between, and there's a public phone box in among them. She said the crofters have gone, then there was this hippy colony who all got arrested for drugs, and now there's some casuals, weekenders she thinks, must be very rich with a helicopter, but strange because they have no women with them and . . . "

"Thanks, honey, you've been a great help. It sounds as if she knows it well."

"Aye, she's still on the line, would you want to know anything else?"

"Yes, how wide is the strip of water?"

A pause, then, "She says it's about five or ten minutes' rowing, perhaps a quarter of a mile or a bit less. She said they had a call this evening."

"What was said?"

"Och, ye don't think she'd listen in, do ye?"

"Yes, I do."

She laughed gaily and came back after a few moments. "She said she couldn't understand, it was like a private sort of code and some of it was foreign."

"OK. Thanks. Now remember your promise, won't you? And tell the other lady not to mention that anyone's asked."

"She won't. She says she doesna like those people, impatient and no decent manners. I'd say worse than that, mysel'. I hope Miss Cleodie's going to be safe, the wee bairn?"

"Yes, I'll let you know. Can you find me a taxi?"

"I'll try. I'll ring you back."

I hurried to a big wall map in the hall and after some anxious searching in the dim light had revealed nothing, I ripped it down and took it into McHarg's office. The island of Breac when I found it was tiny and the blue of the channel no wider than a thick pencil line. It was crazy, really, but once I'd hit on the idea, I got single-minded about it, jotting down the co-ordinates that I'd need to lay off on the aeronautical chart.

By this time it was after 11.00 p.m. and the operator called back to say she couldn't raise a taxi anywhere without going through to Kyle, which would have taken another three-quarters of an hour. The summer nights are very short in the North so I told her not to bother. In a cupboard in the hall I found a big torch with a rather feeble battery, and following the drive round the back of the house I came to garages and outbuildings. The garages were all unlocked but empty, and the frantic feelings began to build up again. In one of the outbuildings was a miniature tractor, the kind that expensive people use to mow their lawns, but, with a top speed of about five miles an hour, it's quicker to walk. Finally, in a stall right at the end, I had some luck, for there was one of those ridiculous high-handle-barred bovver-bikes, or whatever they call them nowadays. I shook the machine and there was a sloshing noise from inside the tank. With the aid of the torch, I quickly examined the mechanism, and saw to my relief that it was a simple lawn-mower carburettor, which meant that I understood it but practically guaranteed that it wouldn't start. I checked that there was no ignition switch after kicking the starter fruitlessly for a couple of minutes. I checked that there was fuel coming through and there was a spark from the plug lead, but with a two-stroke

134

that doesn't mean a thing, in my experience. I did not, however, notice that there was no silencer on it, until it suddenly burst into life for reasons of its own, and the shattering noise in that confined space almost jellified my brains as the RPM went straight up to maximum before I could twist the throttle shut. The headlamp worked as well, so I put the torch in the box on the back and wheeled the machine outside.

The one remaining problem was how to get it through the front gate, and I looked everywhere for some kind of bolt-cutters or hacksaw, but without success. At last, in a lean-to garden shed at the end of the row of outbuildings, I found a ten-pound maul, which I put on the bike's saddle with the long handle sticking out at the back. Carefully I sat astride both hammer and machine, and after some fiddling eventually found a gear to engage. Thus equipped, I let out the clutch and headed off erratically down the drive. It's completely unnatural to ride anything with your hands higher than your head, and for the life of me I cannot imagine how those handle-bars ever found favour even with the most revolting.

I propped the bike by the gate and left it running so that I could see in the light of the headlamp; I smashed at the huge padlock with the maul until my arms were on fire and the sweat ran off me in black drops, and when I stopped, unable for the moment to lift it again, I realised it had hardly distorted the lock and wasn't going to work. When I'd recovered sufficiently, I turned my attention to the hinges, where I had more luck. They had cast-iron pintles, and one really hard downward smash broke off the lower one cleanly and I was able to pivot the gate between the upper hinge and the lock sufficiently to squeeze the motorbike through in the corner. I left the maul there and was soon on the road, feeling very light-headed with exhaustion. I wondered also if I had a slight concussion, but the breeze drying the perspiration off me and the fact of being at last heading somewhere was a great relief.

The hard part was quelling the frantic anxiety feelings for Cleodie because these were going to be of no use to me, or to her. I had to find her before she could be used against me, and the thought of what might be happening to her at that moment was not a bit useful in what I had to do.

I got the bike going flat out on the sweeping road passing the loch where the Jensen had gone in that morning.

The perfect distraction was to give free rein to the most sadistic feelings towards McHarg, what I was going to do to him, and how long I was going to make it last. If I'd known what was to come, I wouldn't have been able to dwell on him at all, but still it was a lot better than even the immediate prospect. Night flying in the mountains has its own set of terrors with a single engine and the clouds full of granite.

Eleven

I had nothing to tell Carruthers that wouldn't alarm her, so I pressed on past her place and round the head of Kishorn. I stopped briefly at my cottage to collect a few things and all was quiet, though there were signs of a recent going over and the front door lock was forced. The ancient double-barrelled pistol was in its drawer together with the box of cartridges, so I grabbed these and a dark blue anorak and turned to go. The torch beam fell on a piece of paper on the table and I had to peer closely at it to read the pencilled scrawl: *Go back to Dunnachan House and wait in the lodge for our call. Make no contact with anyone or you can kiss her goodbye.*

It didn't make me feel worse because I couldn't, and it was no more than I'd expected. It would also make no difference if I did as I was told – they would just be setting me up where I'd be no help to her. Being able to identify them, she'd only be kept alive as long as I was free.

There was no sign of Fergus and I hoped they hadn't harmed him. I had no idea of what equipment I might eventually need and it wasn't worth wasting time in debate, so I got the bike started again and set off up the hill towards Loch Coultrie.

The next problem was a night take-off from a short piece of water with a dangerously narrow waist in the middle of it. The gap was just visible beyond the Teal in the bike's headlight, but I couldn't be sure of starting from exactly the right place at the far end because aiming at the light wouldn't necessarily keep me clear of the converging banks. I needed a transit, but I wanted to keep the torch, so I stopped the engine and tipped the bike on its side,

137

spilling a quantity of petrol onto the heather. As far as I could judge that only left about half a cupful of petrol in the tank, which might be cutting it disastrously fine. Next I ripped up a lot more heather and piled it onto the petrol-soaked base, then re-started the bike and ran it down about thirty feet nearer the water, keeping the pile of heather, marked with the torch, in line with the bike and the gap.

After that, I only had to pull in the plane, leave the bike running on its stand so that the light would shine, and then set fire to the makeshift beacon; I still hadn't got any matches, which caused another few moments' vexation until I remembered the pistol. One cartridge did the trick and then I was scrambling into the plane to get lined up at the far end before the bike stopped or the fire died down.

The engine started at once, but as I taxied away the tailwheel caught in the mooring line because I'd used some cheap floating rope, so I had to switch off and paddle backwards until I could clear it. Precious seconds wasted, the bike still running making a great racket across the quiet water, but the tongues of flame becoming listless. Once freed, I set the gyro-compass by the magnetic one, lined the plane up on the fire and the light and took a bearing to get me through the gap. There was no question of taking off in that direction because of the steeply rising hills beyond. A reciprocal heading would not have been good enough on its own for the run back because I would only need to be a few feet out in lining up at the far end to pile up in the narrows. I didn't think the plane's landing lights would give me enough warning of a bank coming up.

When I got to the other end and turned, I couldn't see the fire at all, but the light was still there, and I was able to use it as a reference to get lined up with the gyro. Except for making certain that I was switched on to a tank with plenty of fuel in it, I ignored all the other checks and just opened the throttle. There are times when you simply don't want to know if something isn't working properly.

As the Teal surged on the step and started to pick up speed, there was a brief spurt of flame from the fire, which showed me placed exactly in transit, and a few seconds later the landing lights picked out the left bank blurring past just a few yards beyond the wing-tip; I snapped the stick back and she came off, although the stall warning blared in protest. Outside, the night was quite black and there were no reference points or lights visible, so I waited about a minute before easing the angle down to a fast cruise climb and turned just five degrees to starboard. I wanted a northerly heading, but to select it before I had climbed to a good margin would have been to challenge the invisible heights of An Sgur and Bada Chreamba on the peninsula between Kishorn and Carron, each reaching to nearly 1300 feet on one side, and Cattle Pass at 2000 on the other.

Blithe reassurances about aircraft engines not failing are all very well from the warmth and safety of the drawing-room, but it's another matter entirely to pin your faith to a snarling piece of metal in the middle of what seemed the darkest night of the year over rugged country which offered not the slightest chance of a successful forced landing. One's sensitivity to the merest change in the steady drone, although quite useless, increases to an unbearable degree, and the only way to combat the mounting tension is to continue with the flimsy act of faith and preferably think about something else.

When the altimeter showed 1500 feet, I turned gently on to 290° and promptly went into cloud. I was entirely on instruments anyway, so it didn't affect me immediately, but it posed a severe question for a little later on. In a fit of parsimony, I had not ordered an Artificial Horizon when I bought the aircraft, so the only way to tell if the wings were level was by ascertaining that she wasn't turning. The process was like getting a reasonably competent tightrope walker to make his tentative steps along the wire in pitch dark. Now there would have been a test for Blondin, across Niagara Falls *at night*. Nowadays most students learn blind-flying in a simulator, which of course has all the necessary instruments, but it has its unreality in its complete safety. Even in the air, wearing a hood so that you can't see out, you still have the instructor with you who can, but for the tyro it's a very tense, fraught exercise and one's normal responses can often go haywire. You can think you're climbing when you're not, or, more severely, you get the "leans", thinking the aircraft is in a steep bank when in fact it's straight and level. You have to trust your instruments entirely or you end up in an overwhelm of wrong information. Death follows surely, on the heels of sweat-blinding panic.

At 4000 feet, I turned on to 305°, and then spent some time trimming very carefully into cruise-climb because I had to do my map-work as well. I switched on the interior light and, as soon as

I started work, the big dreads hit me badly. I had enough experience to know that my chances of success were about as good as a poor darts player hitting the bull's eye, not after several tries, or even three, but *first* time. I'd have preferred being about to do my first solo deck landing on a carrier. At least if you cock that up, you've got a chance to eject to a friendly reception.

It was only then that I cast around for an alternative, but it was nearly 1.00 a.m. and I knew there would not be time to land elsewhere, get myself across to the Sound by some other means, find a boat and get in and out during what darkness was left in that high latitude. Yet logic and training both said that getting into the Sound of Breac unnoticed in the dark was both impossible and suicidal, especially since it meant doing it without lights *and with the engine switched off* – a once-only commitment.

The argument was clinched for me by the fact that if I succeeded, then Cleodie and I both stood a *chance* of making it out of there, whilst if I failed and wrote myself off, they might just possibly let her go. In spite of that I still wanted to have time to think about it some more but I knew that I would be giving in and "lose the name of action".

The Teal droned steadily northwards, and there was hardly any buffeting in the air, for which I was really grateful. At 6000 feet and nearly thirty-five miles out, I began to pick up a weak signal on the VOR from the Stornoway Radio Beacon, which was a considerable relief. By mistake, to verify the call-sign, I turned up the volume control not on the VOR but on the radio, which was still tuned to Lossiemouth, and I heard them calling faintly, in spite of the range. I was tiring from the instrument flying and feeling completely shredded by the previous night's poisoning and a thoroughly punishing day so I didn't realise at first whom they were calling.

" ... repeat, unidentified aircraft, height unknown, heading approximately 320 over North Minch, state identity, height, destination and flight conditions, I repeat ... "

I wasn't in controlled airspace so I had no need to answer, but I was curious as to why they wanted to know. When he had finished the next repeat of the message and paused, I pressed my transmit button and said one word.

"Why?"

"Caller, this is Lossiemouth radar. There is a security clamp-down, and all flights, controlled or otherwise, have to notify MATZ or Scottish FIR of origin and destination. Please do so."

"Lossiemouth, this is Golf Alpha X-ray Zulu November, Teal Amphibian, origin Kishorn, Destination Stornoway, Flight level unspecified, I am at 8000 feet on the QNH, in IMC."

"Roger, Zulu November, you are advised that Stornoway is closed until 0700. What is your alternate?"

"No alternate."

"Make sense, Zulu November. Do you wish to return to Lossiemouth?"

"Negative."

There was a pause, which gave us both time to think. The suffering controllers know that everything they say on the air is automatically recorded so that it can be reproduced if there is any enquiry. It would be unfair to say that this is why they tend to be most courteous and helpful, but it must be an inhibiting factor on ill-temper.

After a few moments, he came back. "Zulu November, Lossiemouth, what is your endurance, correction, endurance on fuel remaining?"

"Zulu November has approximately five hours' fuel remaining. To anticipate your question, I will land on the water and wait for Stornoway to open for breakfast."

"Roger, Zulu November," he answered drily, "goodnight."

There was good reason for my evasiveness – Cleodie's safety depended upon not alerting the opposition. I was not to know that my flight had already started a secondary alert and that a Sea-King was about to be scrambled. I had twenty-five miles to run to Stornoway and a further twenty to the point where I planned to begin my let-down. Just then the interior light packed up, which alarmed me because I didn't know how much was left of the torch batteries. At the time, I had the craven thought that it could change the whole terrifying prospect since I could not continue if the chart was invisible. Up to that point things seemed to be "all right so far", there was no appreciable cross-wind factor and my confidence had been increasing slightly, entirely without justification.

I droned on for nearly an hour, too concerned to spare a thought for the faithful Lycoming engine overhead, which kept the propeller turning without a missed beat or a murmur of complaint. At height you have to lean the fuel mixture because the air is thinner, but it is vitally important to remember to move it back to rich when you descend, otherwise the engine starves and cuts out. I'd forgotten once during a radar let-down into Glasgow. Because of the enormous responsibility resting on the approach controllers, they're not allowed to bring you right down to the runway threshold in most places and have to leave you to your own devices at one mile out. I'd just made a rapid descent in cloud from 6000 feet, and it was precisely at the one-mile point that the engine began to give up with the houses of Abbotsinch suddenly appearing just 300 feet below, shrouded in fog. You don't do it again, provided you get away with it once.

Most of the flight had been up over the North Minch, a thirty-mile stretch of water between the mainland and Lewis, and during the latter part I had also been getting a VOR response on 114·4, which put Benbecula where it was supposed to be, further south in the chain of the Outer Hebrides, and about forty miles away. It was still cuckoo-land, of course, and sitting up there in the thickest cloud of it, playing even with finely accurate cross-bearings, I knew with certainty and a terrible dread that they would be of no use to me in the end. The VOR is accurate to two degrees, but by the time I arrived over Breac the cross-bearings from Benbecula at thirty-five miles and Stornoway at twenty-odd could put me up to two miles out in any direction. The channel I had to get down in might be only two hundred yards wide, as far as I could gather from the operator's description, and in any case both beacons would be effectively shrouded by high ground once I was below about 1500 feet.

Eventually, I picked up the null over Stornoway, switched at once to Benbecula and adjusted the gyro compass. The magnetic variation for this area was twelve degrees west and I needed as much absolute accuracy as the Good Lord would allow. I was also running into patches of turbulence, and it was nerve-racking trying to peer at the chart and scribble in the margin with the chinagraph at the same time as trying to keep the aircraft straight and level.

All of a sudden, the combined tensions accumulated to the point where my overloaded brain threatened to pack up. I was shaking and sweating and convinced it was NO-GO. I would have to let down eastwards over the Stornoway beacon, come back in over a measured distance, land there on the water and think of something else. I was just about to start the turn when the wave of relief that flooded into me was so great with the immediate anxieties shed away that I knew it for what it was – pure blue funk. It made me coldly, bitterly angry with myself that the the final test had tripped me, that I had failed Cleodie. It was horrible to be there, my lip curled in unutterable scorn, and the object of it – myself, flinching under the censure. In a moment I recovered, ferociously as though I had been whiplashed back into the awful rhythm like a fainting galley-slave. I knew I had to be just a machine myself, obedient, cold, unemotional and completely precise, that my hands must stop shaking and cope only with the immediate problems.

The immediate problem was straightforward enough, its execution close to impossible: to get an accurate fix at a great height, to switch off the engine and glide to an invisible, narrow piece of water, flying all the time with an accuracy of less than half a degree. There was one major factor in my favour, that the high pressure seemed to be holding and my track over the Stornoway beacon showed no appreciable wind. Still, once I was committed to the descent, the two radio-beacons would be of no further help to me.

The chart showed a marine lighthouse about seven miles north of Breac, a very high one at 850 feet above sea-level. The snag was that I might not be able to see it from above and, more important, four miles to the south of it, on the track of my descent, the land rose sharply to nearly 1900 feet. In addition, I did not know the height of the cloudbase. With Ground Surveillance Radar, a radio altimeter and an aeroplane that could stop and go backwards, like a Harrier Jump-jet, it would have been a piece of cake.

When the cross-bearings put me ten miles west of Stornoway, I started to lose height where I should have been safely over the sea, and, after a few minutes, the picture changed somewhat for, at 3500 feet, the enveloping, oppressive cloud cleared away. I was not aware of it at first, having been so firmly orientated to the instrument panel for nearly an hour, and actually it made little difference since the night was still as black as Hades. I turned carefully through 180 degrees and almost immediately picked up the lighthouse dead ahead on the point of Great Bernera, according to the chart and a reasonable assumption. I didn't get the beam itself but was able to see the loom and the brief sweeping reflection from the land behind.

Extreme care and precision were now called for, so, keeping just under the cloudbase at an indicated 3600 feet, I adjusted my speed to ninety knots to ease the calculations. Once over the lighthouse, still faintly visible, I turned 180 back onto a westerly heading, and held it for exactly two minutes, or three miles, at which point Breac channel should lie due south, nine miles distant.

At that height, it was too far to glide with a sink rate of 2000 feet per minute, and, in order not to be heard, I would have to switch off at a greater distance than three miles and I had to be sure of clearing the high ground in between.

I turned north and climbed back into cloud at sixty knots for ten minutes, increasing throttle as required to maintain the rate of climb steady at 300 feet per minute. Because of the angle of climb, the distance over the ground would be slightly less than ten miles, so I continued for another twenty-five seconds and then made a "procedure turn", going right to 045 degrees for one minute, then banking left in a Rate One turn (three degrees per second) for one minute, holding the reciprocal heading of 225 for forty seconds and then turning due south again. After twenty seconds of flight southwards, *in theory* I should be in exactly the position where I started the procedure turn, ten miles due north (Magnetic) of a point three miles west of the Great Bernera lighthouse, at 6600 feet.

The altimeter confirmed the height, but to calculate triangles, everyone knows you need at least two data, and more for three dimensional work. If there'd been an appreciable wind factor, the problem would have been too much, considering the conditions I had to work in, a crumpled map across my knees, a protractor which kept slipping to the floor and the real need to keep most of my attention on the instrument panel.

At this point, I increased speed to ninety knots again, descending very gradually to 6000 feet, keeping a constant eye on the Air Speed, Gyro, Altimeter, Rate of Climb indicator and the dim face of my watch. I had to hold this course and speed for fifteen miles, or ten minutes, and with the speed raised by fifty per cent over the climb north, I should be abeam the lighthouse, far below and invisible, after just over six and a half minutes. The Stornoway beacon eased down to 045 degrees on the VOR as this interval came up, which was some encouragement. Something was nagging at me and I couldn't place it for a moment, until I next glanced down at the chart in the fading light of the torch and saw the dotted red Variation line running right through the islands. For one horrified moment, I thought I would have to convert all the data by subtracting twelve degrees to get True bearings, and in the pressure of the moment, I nearly blew another mental gasket. Somehow, I got it under control again, imposing the logic that although I was using a chart with True grid lines, all my ground references had been made in relation to the beacons and the lighthouse on the magnetic scale. This moment of mental torment was unlikely to occur in the cool of a classroom, but to me it had been so alarming that I almost missed the ten-minute point. Just in time, I reached up and slid the mixture control knob back to full lean.

As the engine died, every survival instinct tried to claim my attention, clamouring about the sheer lunacy of the act. I had no choice now but to suppress them, finally and completely. I cut the magneto switches, trimmed to eighty knots after raising the landing gear, and made sure that no lights were showing. Once stabilised, the ROC indicator flickered fairly steadily at a sink rate of 2000 feet per minute. Three minutes, four miles and a bit, 6000 feet to lose.

The silence was awful in the most literal and extreme sense. I thought of those terrible mid-air crashes where they morbidly record and report the stunted conversations of the air-crew plunging down from 40,000 feet, still coherent but certain of death in two or three minutes, with absolutely nothing to be done about it except perhaps a final decision about belief in God and a hereafter . . .

Two minutes. Four thousand feet. Course and speed steady, cloud dispersing, no turbulence. Sinking into blackness, should be just past the high ground. Suddenly, to my left, a tiny faint light, then another. Houses, must be Brenish, a little village on the coast, someone reading late for these parts, someone who would know these waters as his lifelong education, who could help me clear the group of tiny islets that lay under my course, some perhaps too small to be marked on the chart, right *in* my course if I was fractionally too low. I was still on the sea-level pressure setting of Kishorn, but there had been no means of establishing any difference for this area, short of wasting time to come right down to the surface before the final positioning. I began to wish I had done so, it could be a difference of two or three millibars, sixty feet, ninety feet. More?

Or less?

145

One minute . . . wanting desperately to look ahead and around, forcing myself to keep my eyes within the cockpit, firmly on the instrument panel. Altimeter unwinding steadily, the unremitting countdown, 1500 feet . . . 1000 . . . 800 . . . 500 . . . 200.

At 100 feet indicated, I began to ease back on the stick and the speed came off to seventy, sixty-five, sixty . . . Altimeter reading zero, then less than zero, the silent swishing abruptly shattered by the stall warning horn, fifty-five, where was the surface? Any slower and she'll stall and go in anyway, come on, baby, come ON!

There was a ghastly tearing noise over the continuous blaring of the horn, then a sharp jolt, and I seized up completely, knowing this was curtains, that I'd missed, whether by a foot or a mile was irrelevant.

I let go of the stick and braced myself, forearms across my face, stomach tightened against the seat belt. The aircraft checked slightly and the upper half of my body rocked forward, though with little impetus. The tearing noise was receding, the horn had stopped, and my mind was in the utmost confusion, the incoming data hopelessly jumbled.

Movement ceased and I pushed up the side window, to jump before she exploded under me, but, a few feet below, I heard the sound of water lapping quietly against the hull.

Distant now to the south, I could hear the diminishing roar of jet engines, which a few seconds earlier must have been overhead, sounding like a giant tearing whole bolts of calico, amplified a hundred times to my over-sensitive ears.

I felt rather unsteady and quite bewildered. I might have been anywhere, in silent darkness, my only reference being the slight motion of the Teal underneath me. Then I peered behind the raised canopy and saw a solitary dim light off to starboard. I checked the compass and saw that the nose was still pointing south, and it was some moments before I could persuade myself that the light was fixed and landed, was not a masthead light, and therefore I must be in a channel with an island off to the right. There was only one it could be.

Despair was gone and there was only anxiety, but the momentary relief made me feel light-headed. A voice seemed to say that if I was so surprised to have made it, it must have been madness to try. Wryly I agreed, but dismissed the voice at once. One can cope with only so much unreality.

Twelve

I searched all around, but the only visible thing in my full circle of vision was that solitary light. I took the extending paddle out of the rear compartment and, after cautiously putting the wheels down in the water so that they would touch before the hull, I began to paddle steadily over to the right. After a while, the light disappeared behind some intervening object, presumably a rock, but I was able to keep a check on my heading from the luminous lines on the magnetic compass. All the other instruments were switched off, and I began to cool rapidly as the perspiration dried on my skin.

I tried to work out the probable state of the tide, but it seemed so long ago that I had had anything to do with it, and also it had been a good fifty miles to the south. Eventually, I concluded that it must be on or just after high water, and hoped it wouldn't make any difference. The main thing was to make sure that the Teal wasn't left sitting high and dry on a rock.

After about ten minutes' very slow progress, I felt a slight check and, probing down with the paddle, found contact with hard sand. Putting the paddle away, I slipped quietly over the side carrying the anchor and line with me, making one end fast to the cleat on the nose. The water was very cold, reaching nearly to my waist, so, working quickly, I swung the nose round until it was pointing the way I had come in and then pulled her back until the tailwheel was well grounded. A few yards further in, I could now see little tell tales of white where the wavelets jostled on the sand. I took the anchor up to the beach and bedded it firmly with the line taut, then went back to the Teal for my anorak and pistol. While I was filling a pocket with cartridges, I began to think dimly in terms of diversions, and, as there was little choice of combustibles, an idea came to me quite quickly.

I got an old polythene bag out of the map-pocket and quickly filled it with petrol from one of the drain plugs on the side of the aircraft. I tied a knot in the top of the bag and, thus armed, feeling thoroughly makeshift, I waded out again and began to make my way cautiously along the beach in the direction of the light.

I didn't take the torch because it was getting rather dim, and anyway would only upset the night-sight I had acquired already. Also, it could easily give me away, and I wondered if my face was still black with coal-dust or whether the sweat had run it all away. Certainly a large rock didn't see me coming and I barked my shin painfully, dropping the bag of petrol. The stupid pistol dug into me as I groped around for the bag, and I decided it wasn't much use in my pocket, unloaded, but loaded it stood a good chance of going off by itself and removing something vital.

I wished my personal piece didn't have the silly curved hammers on it, as well. They look nice on the wall but always catch in your pockets. I slipped two cartridges into it and kept it firmly in my right hand. After some more scrambling and a short climb, I crested what must have been a rock promontory and from the top of it I was able to see a lighted window, about three hundred yards distant. I set off towards it and, after a while, the ground became more level although very mushy, presumably peat bog. Occasionally, I had to lift a foot out with a sucking noise, because I had quickened my pace and sometimes came down too hard where the surface was uneven.

When I was about two hundred yards away, a door opened in a shaft of light and I saw the dark shape of a dog bound through it, followed by a man with a torch. He whistled once or twice, but I quickly lost sight of the dog in the darkness and couldn't tell whether it came to him or not. It didn't take long to find out.

I moved on, cautiously now, but after a few steps I slipped into a hole with a soft squelching noise, down on one knee, arms spread for balance. Alsatians usually give a warning growl before they attack, not so a Labrador or a Dobermann. The latter growls usually once he's got hold of a piece of you and is trying to worry it off. All part of the scare treatment, and it's very effective.

The growling started a split second after my right wrist was seized by horribly powerful teeth, and my arm thrashed about as

148

if caught in a fly-wheel. In a trice, I was pulled off balance to one side, sprawling my length and dropping the bag of petrol again, but I managed somehow to keep my grip on the pistol. I was grateful for the thick padding of the anorak as well as the fact that the dog had been trained to keep a grip on the gun-hand, against its instincts to go for the throat.

We started a tug-of-war with my arm as the prize, and gradually I was able to pull it towards me enough to transfer the gun to my left hand. I kept tugging hard so that the dog wouldn't decide to transfer his grip, then I got one hammer cocked, shoved the muzzle between its jaws behind my wrist and pulled the trigger.

There was hardly a sound, as all of the report was absorbed inside the unfortunate beast's body, which exhaled the smell of cordite as it died. Quickly, I moved away a few yards and waited as the torch came nearer. Every few seconds, there was a sharp whistle getting more insistent. As he came closer, I could see the man was following a path and swinging the torch from side to side a little. The beam swept over the body of the dog, then came back and there was a sharp intake of breath as he hurried forward and crouched down over the prone form.

It was a cardinal error which might have saved his life for all I know, because I only had to step up behind him and put the barrels of the pistol behind his ear. He was nicely silhouetted against the pool of light from the torch and was reaching out to touch the dog. I think he sensed me because he stiffened, so I spoke before he could do anything unpredictable.

"Pass me the torch, very slowly, keep the beam down. Here." I tapped his arm with my left hand, and, after a slight hesitation, he did so. He held a shotgun in the other arm. He was still in a crouch so I pulled him off balance and shone the torch down on him; he squatted on the path with one leg hooked under, one arm flung out for balance, the other reaching into his jacket. I recognised the face of the hasty youth at Dunnachan House. His mouth was open and he looked a little scared, and because of the torch shining in his face he didn't see me slip the barrels of the pistol into his mouth until too late. He choked and moved back until his head was against the earth and his hand came away from inside his coat. I reached in myself and took out a small, flat automatic, which I pocketed.

"This is how I killed the dog," I whispered. "You can make your own silencer the same way or answer a question. Where's the girl?" He refused to answer so I put a knee in his stomach and ground away at the back of his mouth with the pistol. Eventually, he made a gargling noise and tried to speak, so I moved it to the side and twisted it so that the twin barrels were flat inside his cheek and his tongue could operate. His eyes watered vigorously.

"End housh. Upstairsh."

"Which end?"

He didn't answer and I had to saw at him a bit more, which made him gag and try to retch. When he spoke there was despair in his voice, which maddened me for the time wasted.

" ... going to kill me anyway."

"No, I'm not, but your only chance is to answer me. I'm in a hurry, man, take your chance."

"Thish end."

"How many others in there?"

"Only one."

"Another dog?"

"No."

"If you've told me any lies, I'll come back and kill you. Want to change anything?"

He only shook his head.

"OK. Where's McHarg?"

"Next house. Ashleep."

"Is the girl all right?"

He nodded once then remembered, shaking his head. "No, but it washn't me. I didn't hurt her, it was Muir."

"The big one?" He nodded again.

"Where is he? What's he done to her?"

"Same housh. Downstairsh. Broke arm ... think shoulder out."

I felt absolutely murderous, but managed to quell it.

"How long are you staying here?"

"Tomorrow morning, but ... depends."

"Depends on what? Come on, quick now."

"Whether they've got you. No need if they've got you."

"And if you haven't, how were you getting out?"

"Shubmarine."

I reached out and pressed hard on his carotid artery and he slumped down. It only lasts about a minute so I had to prop him up and sap him quickly with the pistol butt. I was getting overloaded with weapons so I tossed away the shotgun after taking

150

out the shells. There seemed to be a hint of lightening in the sky and I was getting really anxious about the time.

I was able to use the torch freely now, so I retrieved the bag of petrol and set off at a trot towards the house. I was just coming up to it when a telephone rang very loudly, some way away. The door opened wider and the huge, hard figure of Muir appeared, also carrying a torch. At the first sign of him, I had switched mine out and slipped into the deep shadow at the corner of the little building. I heard a rapid dripping noise and realised the polythene bag was leaking on my feet.

Muir went off down the path towards the insistent ringing, so I slid quickly inside the cottage. There was a tiny, smoke-blackened living-room with a fire burning, a very heavy smell of peat, centuries of it, and a paraffin pressure lamp hissing loudly on a rough, splintered table. I put the bag next to the lamp, but it was leaking steadily, so I thought better of it and put it in one of the grubby armchairs by the fire.

A door led into a stair-box with its lock shattered, and it was kept closed with a stout piece of cloth tied round the knob to a heavy nail. I ripped it off quickly and went up, keeping low, following a tiny, steep little stairway. At the top, there were three doors leading off a minuscule landing, two of them open and the rooms empty but for a couple of iron beds with sleeping-bags on them.

I tried the third door, which wouldn't move, and a high voice, strained, feminine but seething, described my person and what it might do to itself. The words were shocking and without ambiguity, but to me they were pearls.

I thrust at the door, saying, "It's me, Seamus."

"Bollocks," came the answer, and then a pause with a little sob in it. "Prove it."

I was getting anxious about Muir's return, and tried to think of a phrase she'd recognise.

"For heaven's sake, Cleodie, open up, damn it, all right, I wouldn't do it if I wasn't ... "

I heard a chair being wrenched from the door and in a moment I was inside the room. I closed my eyes and shone the torch in my face so that she would recognise me, forgetting about my appearance. She let out a gasp and I heard her backing away and the scraping of a chair against the floor.

I shone the torch in her direction, keeping it away from her eyes so as to preserve her night-sight. She was in a terrible mess, her clothes torn, ripped half-open at the breast, blood on her throat, half one leg of her jeans missing and her left arm hanging useless. The forearm was splinted roughly with a scarf to a broken chair-leg and she leaned her body sideways, favouring her left shoulder.

I spoke quietly. "It *is* me, I got a bit dirty on the way, that's all. Are you OK to walk, we must leave now?"

I went over to her and put my arm round her shoulders and she clung to me with her right hand. She said, "You're supposed to come for me on a great white charger, not a bloody coal lorry."

"Yes. Quiet now."

Keeping the torch in my left hand and the pistol in my right, I led her down the stairs, but, as we neared the bottom, I heard footsteps outside. Quickly, I put the torch out, transferred the gun to my left hand and pulled the little door closed. Heavy footsteps sounded just below us, but I didn't hear the front door shut.

Through the crack in the splintered woodwork, I could see Muir crouch in front of the fire, poking at it until the flames grew and licked up the chimney. I could just see the left side of his face, which had some deep gouges down it. He stood up, reached back for the arms of the chair and let himself into it, heavily and with a grunt. It was the last shock of his life.

With a squashy noise, the bag of petrol burst under him, squirting all over the place but mostly towards the fire. As the whole lot exploded, Muir leapt upwards with an almighty yell, struck his head hard on a ceiling beam and fell back into the chair, which was a complete inferno. He didn't get up again, whether because he'd knocked himself out or because he'd inhaled fire, I didn't need to find out. The flames were already spreading as I pushed open the door and led Cleodie out of the stairway.

I tried to hurry her past, but she saw the figure in the blazing chair and pulled me back.

"No, come on, it's Muir."

"But we can't –

"Yes, we can. There's no TIME, come on. He's had it anyway."

We hurried out of the door and I still had the image of her streaked face looking wide-eyed with horror in the light of the flames. Even though Muir had hurt her so badly, she still wanted to help him out of there. I can't say I was so concerned.

We went quickly down the path, using the torch freely, Cleodie sometimes making indrawn gasps of pain as she jolted her arm and shoulder on the uneven surface. Behind, I heard a sharp crack as a window-pane exploded and I looked back to see the lower half of the cottage brightly lit. Beyond it, I could see a light appear in the next building.

A figure was sitting in the path with its back to us, head in hands. It was the first torch-bearer coming round, so I went quickly up to him and put him out again.

Cleodie said, "How did you do that, what did you do to him?"

"Sh-sh, if I told you, you'd go round doing it to everyone. Come on, now."

There were shouts behind us, but soon the ground started to rise and in haste we climbed the rocky promontory and slithered quickly down the far side on to the beach. I got Cleodie to hold the torch while I gathered in the anchor and rope, then I carried her into the water and helped her into the right-hand seat. I slipped out the co-pilot's stick and tossed it in the back.

The water was certainly shallower than when I'd left it, and there was a distinct brightening in the sky, just enough to make out a few shapes. Distantly, I heard the sound of an aero-engine as I pushed and struggled behind the wing, trying to shove the Teal into deeper water, but I couldn't shift her beyond rocking a few inches back and forward.

The engine noise was louder now, and more distinguishable. I recognised the deep snicker of a powerful helicopter, approaching from the east over the high ground of Harris. Friend or foe, it was immaterial, I had to get out of there and quickly before anyone started a little fatalism. Much more light and the blue and white Teal would be clearly visible.

As I stood on the undercarriage leg to get in, I saw the twin rotating beacons of the helicopter descending on the far side of the channel, and then they were suddenly switched off. I started the engine, and, with full power, she came slowly out of the hole and began to move forward, so I got the wheels up and began to accelerate in a turn to the north. We'd only been going a few seconds when she crunched into a sandbank and stopped, which meant I had to switch off, get out and heave her clear. The next time, I moved further out into the channel before turning, but the same thing happened again, only she stuck much harder and it took me a couple of minutes' straining to shift her back into deeper water, and I fell headlong as she moved.

Off to the right, there was a lot of noise by this time, the helicopter clattering a few hundred feet over the cottages, and I could see figures in the light of the first one, which was well ablaze, the flames running clearly up the roof.

Just then, two magnesium flares fell from the helicopter and lit up the whole area bright as day. I was just getting back into the cockpit with water pouring out of my clothes, and we were frighteningly snapped in almost indecent exposure. As I scrabbled back into my seat, pulling the hatch closed, I saw a sandy promontory extending almost the full width of the channel, so that you could easily walk across at low tide. It must have been formed recently by tidal action, otherwise the telephone operator would certainly have mentioned it. I must have landed just over the top of it with the tide well up, in fact it could have been the cause of the jolt, but now it was effectively blocking our escape route.

Before I got the engine restarted, I heard the chatter of machine-gun fire, and I saw a couple of rockets spew out of the helicopter towards the little cluster of buildings, still brightly lit by the flares – but so was the helicopter, a Sea-King with Navy markings, and suddenly a gout of flame appeared from it, swirling in the downdraught. The firing continued as it hung there, and then it seemed to topple and sway like a huge leaf in uncertain descent.

I had the engine going by this time and I was short of options, so I turned south and opened up, in time to see the helicopter hit the ground, not very hard, and figures leaping from it. I could see the figures fall as they ran and there were a lot of muzzle flashes.

We had to pass in front of them and we gathered speed under what I hoped was an effective distraction. I was just about to lift off when I saw spurts of water being kicked up just in front of us, then there were a couple of thumps which I think must have sheared the pillar on Cleodie's side. Air rushed in and the plexiglass screen went all floppy. Cleodie gasped in the way people do when they're suddenly, badly shocked, and I felt sharp things in my hands and face and some sort of liquid on them.

I pulled the stick back enough to lift off, making no attempt to climb; I just wanted speed, more speed to hamper the deflection shooting.

I kept her down until we were safely out of range, then began to climb, but I was straining ahead uselessly into the black because the flares were behind us and had ruined our night vision. I groped around in the back for the torch and switched it on, but I still couldn't see. Clutching the torch and the stick in one hand, I tried to wipe my face with the other and, for a moment, I saw the dim red glow of the torch, through the blood that was pouring down my eyes. I called out then.

"Cleodie, can you see?"

Very quietly, she answered, "Yes, sort of."

"Can you find something to mop my face with?"

"I can't move really. There's something sticking into me."

"Where?"

"Under my ribs, on the right."

I wasn't on instruments, I wasn't on anything, and you can't fly an aeroplane just by feel. All I knew was that we were still airborne, and I tried not to move any of the controls in the slightest.

"Look, sorry, but we've got to get some safe height. Can you read this instrument here, it should say Altimeter on it?" I pointed to its familiar place on the panel.

"The big hand says eight, but it's going up towards nine."

"OK." I reached down and trimmed her so she would keep climbing at the same rate.

"Now what about this one, should say Airspeed?"

"It's not there, it's all mashed up, so are the others, most of them."

I put out my hand and felt a lot of jagged edges and the snick of broken glass on my fingertips.

"What's left, then, can you tell me?"

"The ones in front of me are all right."

"Those are all engine. What about the ones on this side?"

"There's one marked Climb, the needle's about half-past nine, ten o'clock."

Four or five hundred feet a minute. OK.

"What else?"

"Move the torch a bit to the left, yes, that one's moving, but I can't see what it says on it. It's got a sort of spirit level in it, a little black ball, and a needle above. The ball's in the middle and the needle is pointing to the right a bit."

"OK, tell me when it's in the middle, too." I banked left very gently until she called, "Now!"

"Any others?"

"Yes, in the middle under the radio."

"OK, that's fuel and pressures. Is the radio all right?"

"Seems to be, the front's not damaged." Maybe not, but they go back a long way, those expensive magic boxes.

The roar of air through the holes was very loud and I shivered heavily in my soaking clothes, but at least the draught seemed to have dried into a crust the blood that covered my face, and it seemed to have stopped running down. I put the torch on the floor and let go of the stick; hopefully she would continue to fly on her own for a bit. I used my jersey to scrape my eyes clear, then got hold of the torch again and bent across to examine Cleodie's position. I didn't look at the instrument panel, figuring I already knew the worst.

Her face had a few tiny splinters in it, little spots of red, but down on her right side, a high-velocity bullet must have hit one of the vertical alloy ribs, which had been forced into her but had at least deflected the bullet. The idea of those light projectiles is that they hit part of you at great speed, get diverted by something solid and *then* do the most awful damage as they tumble about, all mis-shapen. Unless the bullet had removed part of the metal, which seemed unlikely, there was probably a couple of inches sticking into her just under the floating rib. Any movement would give her terrible pain, but I had to get her off it somehow and I didn't have any painkillers.

I reached up to her neck and put her out, watching her face so as not to overdo it, because it's rather painful for a moment's squeeze. She looked at me wide-eyed with astonishment, then her eyes closed and she began to slump. Before she could drive the metal any deeper into her side, I let the torch fall, grasped her under the arms and lifted quickly up and towards me. The effort made the blood flow down into my right eye again, but I was able to see that she was at least pulled clear. Holding her over towards me, I got my right foot over and forced the metal back as far as it would go, then eased her carefully back into the seat. I leaned over and examined the wound, which had certainly bled but seemed to have stopped once she was slumped over it.

The shifting of my weight had caused the Teal to bank to starboard again and I had to correct this first, before removing my anorak and tying her upper body to the seat-back with the arms. I had no dressings for the wound, and I was desperately anxious to get her to proper treatment as soon as I could, so I turned my attention back to the aircraft.

By this time we were back in cloud. The interior lights weren't working and it was very cold with the air rushing through the torn panels. Fortunately this made me think of the hole next to Cleodie's wound, and I stuffed it with the corner of the jacket. I noticed the piece of metal was stained for several inches, but how much blood had run down it, I couldn't tell. The main thing was that there was no other matter clinging to it. All this time the chart had been thrashing around in the back, so I dumped the anchor on top of it and turned at last to the stricken instrument panel.

That was when I forgot the cold, the injuries and all the other discomforts, like metal splinters and pounding headaches.

The magnetic compass was still there but the gyro had gone as well as the VOR indicator. In fact, the panel was a complete shambles, and of flying instruments I was left with altimeter, Rate-of-Climb and Turn-and-Slip. I went through it again not wanting to believe it and noticed that the altimeter was creeping very slowly down, although the ROC was still showing a climb of 300 feet per minute. This meant that the airtight capsule of the altimeter must have a tiny puncture, causing the pressure to equalise, and it was therefore already useless.

Still climbing I settled shakily on a south-westerly heading by the magnetic compass. Outside there was a faint diffusion of light in the cloud, but there were no wisps, nothing to indicate that it was anything but thick and solid. I intended to head well out to sea for safety's sake, then let down through the murk as the light increased so that I could navigate visually near to the surface and find a sheltered spot for landing. After a while I made a tentative turn southwards, carefully watching the Turn-and-Slip. The full shock came when I referred back to the magnetic compass, which still showed 245° – it hadn't moved at all. Desperately I tapped at it and speared my finger on a tiny piece of shrapnel embedded in the circular base. I felt the fluid leaking out and couldn't prevent it. With great caution I turned back to starboard for about the same amount of time and steadied up again. I could only hope that it was still roughly west as shown by the compass before the fluid was all gone. If it was wrong I could easily be heading over high ground, and I had no means of telling if I was high enough to clear anything in the surrounding area.

The only remaining reference was sitting benignly above the clouds, either the fading stars or the rising sun, but even if I could get up there for a look, it would be very sticky holding a westerly course during the long descent. Still, it was the only answer.

I brought the nose up at full power until the horn started to pout at me, eased forward until it stopped and trimmed her there. The ROC showed a climb of between four and five hundred feet per minute, which would gradually diminish as height was added until our eventual ceiling was reached. I knew from my journey over that the cloud tops would probably be over 8000 feet so I settled down for a long climb.

Cleodie's head was slumped forward so I lifted it and kissed her gently on the left temple.

"Again," she said quietly like a little child. I just caught the word in the rushing of the wind, diminished now as our forward speed was down. I did so, and she repeated it, so I did it over and over again as she came back to consciousness. Then she said,

"Spoilt my dream."

"Who did?"

"McHarg, Muir, those other buggers."

"What dream?"

"Gentle Parfitte Knighte, shooting pieces off his nice white steed. And he can't see, must wipe his eyes." She winced suddenly, "Damnit, everything hurts so much."

I could just see her face now in the growing light. Her eyelids fluttered, and she turned her face towards me and kissed me accurately on the lips. After a long moment, she drew her head back and looked at me, laughed, and winced again at the pain it caused.

"Promise me something?"

"Sure," I answered, meaning it.

"Don't make me laugh, please don't make me laugh. Anything . . . reminds me of the dentist."

"OK, relax."

"No, I mean the story. Tells the woman patient she's got to have a tooth out. She says, no, anything but that, I'd rather have a baby than have a tooth out. Know what he said? He said, well make up your mind, I'll have to adjust the chair again!"

Fortunately, she only smiled wistfully to herself, then after a moment, said, "Can I?"

"Can you what?"

"Have a baby instead?"

"Yes, all right."

"Now?"

"No, I'm busy. Can you hold on a bit?"

"Um ... I'll say, NO, NO, NO! until you promise me everything, only I know I'd blow it, I wouldn't be able to wait that long, damnit. Tell me, my darling, are you any good in bed?"

"Yes and no. How about you?"

"Never tried it. Had you there, you filthy old lecher, didn't I? Oh Lord, I've just realised."

"What?"

"It'll never come to that, 'cos of what you said, you wouldn't do it if you weren't good."

"That's only for public exhibition. You're allowed to practise when no one's looking."

"*I'll* be looking."

"You certainly won't. You'll have your eyes closed, your duty to the party."

"Don't tell Carruthers, but I think I'm a Liberal. She'd murder me. Oh Lord, she'll be worried sick about me."

"No, it's OK, she knows you're out with me." Understatement.

"But it's morning almost. She knows I haven't lost my cherry yet and look at the state of me, she'll think I've been gang-banged, I nearly was, you know. It was Muir who stopped them, I thought he wanted me all for himself. I fought and fought him when he dragged me up those stairs, I scratched half his face off and kicked him where a well-bred girl should, but he levered my arm up and broke it and my shoulder came out as well. He just left me up there, I had to splint it myself. How come he was burning like that, anyway?"

"Desire, I expect."

"Gosh. Could you do the same, or half of it anyway, and warm me up? I'm so cold and sore, could we go home now please, my dirty Knight?"

"Shortly, I'm working on it."

"My ears have gone funny."

"That's because we're climbing, I want to get on top of this lot and see where we are."

"Oh. If I dared move and you weren't all wet, I'd snuggle up to you. Could you snuggle up to me, do you think?"

"I'd love to, but this is rather a strain. If I don't keep a careful watch, we could go upside down or spin and there's nothing to tell

159

me what to do about it. There's a heater in the nose, but it may be damaged and start a fire. And I think we may need the fuel."

I was flying on the right tank, which was reading almost empty, so I switched over to the centre one, which showed just over half. If the engine stopped now, it would be very difficult to get the trim right again, and a spin would be just one wrong movement away.

There was still no sign of a break in the clouds as the rate of climb diminished steadily and the engine manifold pressure dropped. This gave me an idea for working out the approximate height, except that the damn thing was calibrated in inches. How many millibars to the inch? About thirty-four, give or take a fraction. One inch was therefore about 1000 feet; the indication could only be very approximate anyway, but given that the sea-level pressure was 1020 millibars, quite high, say thirty inches, deduct four inches for carburettor suction at full throttle and the gauge was actually reading eighteen, we were round about the 8000 foot mark. Periodically the horn would beep as the engine's ability to push out power decreased with height, and each time I had to ease the nose down and trim carefully so as not to approach the stall. It was horribly fraught, this time like tightrope-walking on a soggy wire with your shoelaces undone.

It was getting lighter all the time, but the cloud persisted like a dirty blanket beyond the screen. Somewhere up above was beautiful clear sky, with the level top of the stratus to be my horizon and take the awful strain off me for a few moments at least. I knew that by now the stars would probably be invisible and the sun not actually risen, but one look at the dawn sky would be enough to orientate me for the descent.

As the Teal struggled gamely up towards her ceiling (the sales blurb boasted 13,000, so knock one off for optimism) I became as uncomfortable, cold, miserable and anxious as I had ever imagined. For Cleodie it must have been worse, trying not to shiver because of the pain of her injuries whenever she moved. Her eyes had closed, and I tried to tuck the anorak more closely round her. She mumbled something inaudible, so I put my ear close to her mouth and asked her to say it again.

"I said, thank you, dear, your slippers are by the fire, will you be coming up soon?"

I touched her cheek and reassured her. She had black round her mouth from where she had kissed me.

160

I went back to my personal tightrope, cursing the thickness of the cloud and at the same time blessing it for not being turbulent. There were occasional slight bumps, but nothing much, otherwise rapid and accurate corrections would have been impossible.

On and on we droned, and the cloud became whiter until I thought it was at last time to come out of the top. In fact, it must have been simply the strengthening light of day, for we never did emerge, never did get any kind of bearing. When the ROC settled conclusively on zero and the manifold pressure was below fifteen, the cloud was as thick as ever and I knew it was no good. At full power, we'd also been burning fuel rapidly so that the main tank was reading below a quarter. Both wing tanks were already reading empty.

I got out the headphones and switched on the radio, and was relieved to hear a crackle. I hadn't tried it before because there was no one in particular I needed to talk to, and I *had* had a plan of sorts. When you're in trouble and have to ask for help, one of the most important things is to know where you are and the question would have been a useless embarrassment. Stornoway and Benbecula were both closed, and although they had the VOR transmitters, neither of them had their own VDF, or homing equipment.

I tuned to the distress frequency, 121·5, and started calling.

"Mayday, Mayday, Mayday, all stations, Golf Zulu November, do you read?"

I repeated this solidly for fifteen minutes, hope failing each time I released the transmit button and heard precisely nothing. I switched to Lossiemouth but got no reply. Nobody else would be mucking about the Highlands at this hour, and the only other station likely to be open was Glasgow, at least 140 miles away to the south, well out of VHF range – unless we'd been flying south all the time.

I tried it, of course, and I went right round the dial, all 260 channels, and heard absolutely not one word. I thought of Carruthers and Cleodie and the stupidity of their bland confidence in me, and inside I raged with frustration. Then the engine began to stutter and I whipped the tap back to the starboard tank. After a few moments it started to pick up again, but it couldn't last long, so I put the nose down, very, very carefully, hearing the wind noise increase until it was shrieking at about the level it had been when we high-tailed out of Breac channel. I estimated that would have been close to ninety-five knots before we started to climb. I throttled back and trimmed her as best I could to a descent rate of 1500 feet per minute. The time-lag on the ROC is also confusing, since you have to lose height before it can tell you you're losing height.

We were both breathing quickly and I made all my movements very slow and precise, against the inefficiency caused by lack of oxygen. That would soon pass with our rapid descent, but it was granite and not hypoxia that was my main concern. We could just as easily be over the mountains, the devil, as over the deep blue sea, but the die was cast, nonetheless. We had to go down.

I switched back to 121·5 and tried again.

"Mayday, Mayday, Mayday, all stations, Golf Zulu November, do you read?"

Once again I repeated it time after time, for over five minutes, then briefly I opened the throttle wide to read the manifold pressure. I got twenty-two inches, round about four thousand feet left, half a minute to extinction if we were over the mountains. I was so startled when a voice suddenly answered me that I jerked the stick and had a worrying few seconds trying to steady up.

"Station calling Mayday, say again and state your position, please."

"Mayday, this is Golf Zulu November. My position and heading are unknown, I have total instrument failure. Do you have VDF?"

"Affirmative, Zulu November, Roger your Mayday. You are entering a prohibited zone, you must immediately turn One Eight Zero degrees and we will assist you to another station. Imperative you comply immediate."

"Zulu November cannot comply. Am without compass and fuel state is zero. Is my position over land or water?"

"Water. You are approximately one hundred and fifty miles west of Hebrides. Hold One, please."

Moments ticked by, then he came back. "Zulu November, do you intend ditching?"

"Zulu November is amphibian, will attempt surface touchdown. What station are you?"

"Call me Mother, Zulu November. Imperative your earliest shutdown, repeat shutdown your engine immediate." He sounded very agitated and then I understood why. Mother! The carrier – and UNS 1. It was either a preposterous coincidence or else the original heading before the compass seized up had been correct, and due to the Teal's stability, the still air and some accurate trimming, we'd managed to hold it. The submarine was obviously still in the same predicament, a thorn in their side and now a non-hostile had blundered right into the lethal area.

"Roger, Mother, I appreciate your predicament, I was your guest the other evening. What chance I reach you for deck landing?"

"Negative, we are twenty miles upwind your position. Confirm you have shutdown engine."

At this point, we emerged from cloud and I switched off the engine. The relief of having an external reference was overwhelming, although the nose dropped and the speed built up quickly in a dive until I took remedial action. Below us the sea was dirty grey, and oily in sluggish motion. You don't land small amphibians in the open sea because the long swells are killers.

"I confirm engine shutdown. Can you stand by to relieve me of injured passenger?"

"Zulu November, continue your let-down and advise." After another pause, he said, "Do not acknowledge our further transmissions unless requested, to preserve your battery, just advise touchdown."

I brought the nose up until the ROC showed 1000 feet per minute sink-rate then depressed it until the horn stopped blaring. That gave me the minimum glide speed. I turned to Cleodie.

"We're going to land in the sea and it may be very bumpy. Will you brace yourself as best you can, and put your right arm across your face and your head as far down as you can bend?"

She was well aware of what was happening and nodded in silence. I pulled her seat belt buckle as tight as I could, moved her splinted arm out of the way and hoisted up the central under-carriage lever. I estimated we were below 1000 feet at this stage, and I could see clearly the pattern of long swells approaching on our port bow. Closer still, there was a slight wind pattern on the tops, but nothing significant. I was just about to ask Mother for the surface wind when they came on again.

"Zulu November, surface wind Two Five Zero, six knots."

It all happened rather quickly then, because there was no question of using the engine to hold off. I turned right until we were parallel to the swells, the slight crosswind on our left, which I ignored. I wanted to sideslip to the right anyway, to keep pace with

163

the swell, which moves at about twenty-five knots. Finally, I picked one and kept my eye on it, pursuing it intently with touches of left rudder and right stick. I also tended to its forward side, because although the swell was moving, the water itself was not, and I would have to take all the slip off her at the last moment.

It worked well, although close-to the water looked lumpier than it had half a minute earlier. We touched on the rear slope of the swell, just right with the horn starting up again, but then we bounced and bounced, sickeningly and endlessly, Cleodie gasping all the while, and the wind chasing us over the crest and into the trough beyond. I pulled the stick back as early as I dared and stopped her just as the swell lifted us again and went purposefully on its way.

Thirteen

Cleodie was still slumped, so I helped her to an upright position. Her face was white, and a single tear had squeezed out of each eye. She managed to smile rather thinly.

"You don't want to practise that again, do you?"

"Not today. How are you feeling?"

"Terrific. I used to sleep nights before you came along, but I suppose I'll have to get used to it."

I was really choked up about her, but I tried to smile back reassuringly. I felt the blood caked on my face start to crack open, and I could tell by her response that a brown and black gargoylic sneer was the result.

I pushed up the hatch and looked round, but there was nothing to be seen except a circle of grey, sluggish ocean, the most unlikely situation imaginable after a landing. Visibility was only about two or three miles. I washed some of the encrustment from my face with sea water, then turned to the radio.

"Zulu November is down intact," I said, and the answer came at once, "Roger, well done. Listen out this frequency. Acknowledge this one transmission, do not, repeat do not, attempt to start your engine."

"Acknowledged. Listening out."

The Teal had turned head to wind naturally, and we watched the long, spaced rollers march towards us, lifting us up and down with ordered precision. Occasionally, water lapped onto the nose, but none came as far back as the screen, which was cracked right across and detached from the lower fastening strip over most of the right-hand side. With the pillar gone, I was surprised that the side-window had stayed in place, and I supposed that the air-pressure had flattened the screen out over the edge of it and prevented the wind getting behind and tearing it away.

I peered down the central well which housed the undercarriage lever, but could see no sign of water in the hull bottom. The hole in the metal on Cleodie's right side, not quite underwater, had soaked the corner of the anorak, but wasn't leaking badly. I looked at her wound and saw it wasn't bleeding much, but the whole area was bruised and swollen.

She looked down and said, "I remember now, you put me out to get me off that. Is that what you'll do when I get too demanding?"

Before I could answer, the headphones crackled. So I switched over to the loudspeaker.

" — vember, Mother here. As you know, we are here for a particular purpose. The situation is unchanged, although we expect delivery of sailing craft later this morning. Meanwhile, for the same reasons as before, we cannot effect your rescue at this time. In fact, you should have been shot down before entering the twenty-mile zone, but it would, ahum, seem that the pilot missed. Because of your throttle-back descent and slow approach, we assume vessel in question did not react as expected. We have warnings of deteriorating weather in the next three to four hours, with strong westerly winds. Please state briefly your physical condition."

"Passenger in urgent need of medical attention, pilot OK. Aircraft damaged, unlikely survive rising sea."

"Roger, Zulu November. Was your origin western Outer Hebrides?"

"Affirmative. Do you wish sitrep?"

"Go ahead, speak when on wavetops please, we lose you at times and you are faint."

"Roger. Bunch of bogeys on island called Breac. Took out Sea-King, Navy markings, this a.m. Survival of crew extremely doubtful. Bogeys due to be picked up by submarine this morning."

"Thank you, got that. Admiral Feather asks if you established any connection between them and the current problem?"

"Negative, that is not firmly established, but likely. One of them, now dead, worked in Glasgow. Their action was due to the fact that they thought they were under surveillance."

"Roger. Hold one, please. We have a request for you."

I began to get angry with them for dickering about and not organising a rapid pick-up. In my fraught and exhausted state, it took that long for me to realise it wasn't possible, and the change to fear must have shown even through my smeared features. I felt Cleodie's eyes on me and turned towards her.

"What now?" she asked quietly.

I could only shrug in reply. I was completely spent and drained, my back and legs numb from so many hours in the same position on the thin padding of the seats, but my anxiety for her outweighed both that and the wicked throbbing in my head.

I reached out to try to remove the splinters of aluminium that I could see marking her face. It seemed better than saying anything, but again she surprised me.

"Do you like tea in bed in the mornings, or straight down to breakfast?"

She winced as I pulled a sliver out of her cheek, then removed one herself from my forehead.

"Straight down to lunch, then a siesta." We smiled at one another, painfully. How I blessed her for not getting hysterical when she had every right to do so.

"Zulu November," crackled the speaker, "can you sail your machine?"

"Affirmative, but very badly. Not like a float plane, we are displacement."

"Roger. In view your own and weather situation, we see little choice but to request your direct assistance." The remark was so ludicrous that I snorted. " ... problem is approximately three and one-half miles north-east your position. We estimate that if you can bias your drift from the wind direction by approximately half a mile to the north, you should be able to rendezvous. Further instructions will follow when it is clear that this can be achieved. Over."

"To what purpose?" I asked quickly.

"You are alone in the area and at the moment we cannot assist you. If you follow our instructions, we see it as the quickest solution to both problems. Please do not refer specifically on the air to the main problem."

For me, there was only one problem, that of getting medical attention for Cleodie. I felt absolutely outraged and was about to shout at them to stuff it when I began to see the logic. However, there was one flaw in it: a throttled-back engine well inside the twenty-mile radius had failed to set off any self-destruct mechanisms. I mentioned this to them, but they dismissed at once any motorised rescue attempts as being hopelessly chancy.

I foresaw them asking me to leave the Teal, which meant leaving Cleodie, and I cast about frantically for some alternative. There was a long silence broken eventually by the carrier.

"We appreciate your dilemma, Zulu November, but it would take you at least six hours to drift out of the danger zone and there is bad weather in the offing."

"I can solve it straight away," I answered unreasonably, "just by starting my engine. If she blows, then I've solved my problem – and yours."

"No, you would contaminate many hundreds of square miles. We strongly suggest you comply."

I guess it was the plain truth and after a long pause, I acknowledged. Exhaustion was making me tremble and I felt completely mis-cast, as though woken up in the middle of a crazy, illogical dream. But there was no unreality – Cleodie's pain and our exhaustion and distress were too prevalent and overwhelming. And now there was worse to come: she would have to endure without knowing how long, and I guessed I was going to be asked to swim in the open North Atlantic, and to perform something that teams of fresh, hard, trained men were lined up and powerless to do.

I had a feeling of condemnation, ominous of disaster, as I let down the water-rudder and pressed hard with my right foot on the pedal. After long moments, the nose moved to the right a few degrees and the tip floats began to slap loudly on the water as the waves moved under us at an angle and we rocked to their motion.

Cleodie said, "Can they call Carruthers a bit later and tell her I'm all right?"

I thought it a bit unlikely, so I passed her the microphone. "You ask them, they might do it for you."

She looked surprised and held the mike hesitatingly for a moment, then cleared her throat and said, very pleasantly, "Hello, Mother, this is, er, November, can you call Mrs McNeil at Lochcarron 245 and tell her I'm all right and should be home for dinner, oh, and wait till about 8.30 otherwise you'll wake her up. Please," she added, and looked at me embarrassed. I gave her a cracked smile as she handed the mike back to me. There was a long pause.

"Zulu November, most irregular. Will do our best." Then, drily, "I hope you don't want us to play a request for you as well?"

It lifted the mood, anyway, and I sat on the ledge and started to paddle, Cleodie keeping her foot pressed on the rudder-pedal for me. The plane was moving through the water mostly sideways, but there was a slight forward element. If I could get her moving a bit quicker, the rudder would be more effective at counteracting the weather-cocking effect of the vertical tail, and the exercise began to warm me up. My clothes were still damp, but not actually wringing wet any more, and the steam began to rise from my trousers. Cleodie saw this and cocked an eye at me.

"Desire? Don't burst into flames."

She thought for a moment and said, "You know, Muir might not have meant to rape me at all."

"'Course he did."

"Sire, you flatter me. Still, I couldn't know it at the time."

"Look, Muir was a big, tough, hard man and he'd have known what he was doing when he broke your arm. He had it coming to him, and he'd have got it today anyway. There'll be a big firefight when they send the boys in to clean up, and the Navy won't be best pleased about their chaps and the helicopter."

"What was it doing there, anyway?"

"Suspicion. They picked me up on radar on my flight up to Stornoway. I expect they were sent over to investigate. I was only just in time because finding the island was rather tricky. I can't quite decide whether their coming saved us or caused us to be shot at. If they hadn't lit the place up, we might have got out unscathed, although without them there we'd have been heard mucking about on the sandbank and our wake would have been visible as we took off down the channel. Also there'd have been more guns pointing at us. Thing is, but for that mysterious sandbank, you'd be warm in bed now."

"Don't talk about it, please! You can put the heater on now, can't you?"

"No, 'fraid not. It would suck in water through the intake, even if it isn't damaged."

"All right, never mind. What have you got to do now, exactly?"

"Without going into details, there's a crippled submarine

hereabouts, and someone's got to get aboard and switch off something so that it doesn't blow itself and us to Kingdom Come."

"Zulu November," crackled the radio, "your present northward component is insufficient. However, surface wind here now increased to ten knots, will this assist you?"

"Affirmative."

"Roger, continue, we will advise progress. You have just over two and a half miles to run, Over."

I'd only been paddling for about ten minutes, so that should make an eventual difference, but I was getting tired. After a while, I could feel a little more strength in the breeze, which tended at first to swing her round into the wind more. I had to work hard with the paddle to prevent this happening, otherwise the forward component would be lost into a purely backward drift. As the wind increased a little more, it lifted the upwind wing on the top of each long roller, which had the effect of digging in the leeward tip float which in turn levered the plane back the way I wanted it. I had to keep paddling in the troughs to prevent the opposite reaction, and overall, the forward and northward component both increased. On each crest, I looked in the direction the wind was going, but visibility was poor in the grey light and I couldn't see anything. I find no romance in the dawn at sea at the best of times, whatever the poets may tell you. In a small boat it is merely a bit better than the pre-dawn watch, when you can actively hate those others who are warm and snug below. Right then it was just ghastly.

After about half an hour, Mother came on again, a different voice, rather clipped.

"Zulu November, your northings about right. Wind here fifteen knots, gusting twenty. Can you copy?"

"Negative, I'm paddling."

"Roger. Then memorise carefully, please. It will be necessary to swim the last few yards as it is imperative that aircraft does not come into contact with hull. I will pause between each instruction so that you can query if necessary, otherwise do not acknowledge.

"The hull is submerged, only the sail showing, therefore radar cannot tell us which direction hull is lying. When you get close you will be able to judge from the sail. Its after part has a ladder running up it . . .

"There is a hatch in the side of the sail which can only be opened from inside, and in any case would allow access of water. You must go to the top and unfasten the hatch there by turning the four-pronged wheel clockwise, I repeat clockwise, which is a word you must repeat to me at the end of these instructions. If you turn it the other way, she will blow . . .

"You go down the sail about twenty feet, where you will find another hatch which opens conventionally, or anti-clockwise. This hatch is safe . . . "

"What about light? I have a torch which is now rather dim, and is not waterproof." The calm in my voice surprised me.

"Good question. You will have to get this torch across without getting it wet. Below the second hatch on the port side is a bank of switches to light the ship, but we have no means of knowing what systems are out. It is felt unlikely that all the generator systems are defunct, and the failure is more likely in the communications control-room, since we have had no radio signals apart from the ELT, that is Emergency Localiser Transmitter . . .

"Note your bearings at this point, because from here you must go down and forward, repeat forward. The first compartment you enter, through a conventional upright hatch, is about forty feet long and consists only of conning and control systems for the ship's three-dimensional movement. Do NOT touch any item in this compartment, but proceed forward to the next, through another similar hatch. This is the communications and defence centre, and is of similar length. The fourth, repeat fourth, bank on the starboard side, repeat starboard, is marked SD systems, repeat Sierra Delta, and in the centre is a master-switch marked Armed and Disarmed. Move this to Disarmed, repeat Disarmed . . .

"The next bank on the starboard side is a small one marked AD, repeat Alpha Delta, for Auto-destruct. There are twenty-three switches on the top of this panel, all relating to crucial failures of one system or another. All twenty-three must be switched to OFF . . .

"You have no ship-to-shore facility, since for docking we use portable transmitters. Therefore, once you have completed the above, you must return to your aircraft and signal to us that all is clear . . .

"Please repeat to me now the essentials, as briefly as possible, and give your battery state."

"Clockwise, anticlockwise, second chamber forward, fourth bank starboard, Master to Disarmed, fifth bank, all top switches, twenty-three, to Off. Battery state unknown, I have only alternator charge rate. Over."

"Roger, Zulu November, therefore do not transmit again unless essential, you are faint. You are two miles, just under, heading is good, we will advise you further shortly. Be advised wind now eighteen knots, gusting twenty-four, slight precipitation."

That could begin to make things tricky, although it had by no means reached us yet. Mother was at least twenty miles upwind, presumably, and I estimated we had still only ten or twelve knots of breeze. But it was coming all right. Our rate of drift was about one and a half to one and three-quarter knots, just over an hour to go at the present rate.

I said to Cleodie, "Do you see what we're doing, using right rudder like a weather helm in a dinghy, to keep her from turning head to wind? If the wind gets much stronger, this wing'll lift more on the crests, driving the other one into the water. The further it goes, the more area this one exposes to the wind and it'll try to turn us right over. I know you can do it by yourself for now, if I have to climb along this wing to keep it down. Trouble is, we don't know whether the sub's broadside to the sea, or fore and aft, and we'll have to play that as it comes. I want to put this lifejacket on you now."

Because of the pain of movement, she was most reluctant, but I couldn't leave her by herself in the aircraft without means of buoyancy. If the worst came to the worst, she wouldn't be able to swim and keep herself afloat.

"If anything happens, that is if you have to get into the water, just pull this lanyard to inflate the jacket, but it shouldn't come to that. I ought to be in and out in five minutes or less, and when I wave to you, just pick up the mike, call Mother and tell them ALL CLEAR. Then they'll come and take us off, to whisky and coffee, blankets and sleep."

"What about the Teal?"

I shook my head. "No chance. Bad weather coming, you heard him."

She thought for a moment. "Will you get another one?"

"Yes, I should think so."

"Can you get a four-seater, then we can put the children in the back?" Again that bland, innocent and utterly alluring smile. Her eyes sparkled in spite of the strain showing in their darkened rims

172

and in the white face. The sight of her kept catching me like a jab in the solar-plexus.

Before I could answer, the port wing reared up, and I clambered half out on to it. It subsided gently. There was still nothing visible downwind. I untied the rope from the anchor and made one end fast to the cleat on the side of the nose. While I was coiling the rest of it, water slopped over the sill and down my back, just a little, but enough to tell me the sea was waiting for a mistake, as always.

I put a bowline round my waist with the other end of the rope and left the coil on the seat, then I unbuckled the baggage harness and looped it twice round the torch so that I could strap it on top of my head. I had to clamber out onto the wing several times after that. The wind was definitely increasing. I heard the speaker crackle while I was out there, and when I got back in Cleodie told me what they'd said. She even managed to make that funny, in a voice like a superior commentary on a silly "Man's game".

"That was Mother, believe it or not. He said, Heading is good, one mile to run, ease off the northing, if anything. Oh yes, and advise visual contact."

"What about the weather?"

"Didn't say."

"OK, that's good. You can make with a little less rudder, but keep her on the wind. Whoops . . . " I dived out of the hatch again onto the wing as it began to lift severely. I thought then that I'd better stay up there on the shoulder, to be a quicker remedy. The gusts were definitely stronger. I leaned through the side-window and spoke to her.

"When we get there, you'll be able to leave her head to wind, so she won't do this any more, but the nose might start to dip into the waves. Do you think you could use your right arm to stuff the anorak under the screen to stop the water coming in, or would you rather I did it before I get off?"

"No, I'll manage. Warm now, pain later, hah hah."

I gazed at her, astonished by her resilience and aching for her pain. I wished desperately there was a quicker way to make it stop. I swept my eyes along the eastern horizon and, on the third sweep, in between hand-and-bottoming along the wing, I saw a thin black shape. It was quite high but very narrow. I remembered the profile pictures they'd shown us on the carrier and realised that I had a fore-and-aft view, and that the submarine was end-on to the wind and sea. That at least eliminated the impossible demand on the Teal's "sailing" ability, of rounding up under its lee if it was broadside, but I wondered how I was going to be able to tie the aircraft to it if the hull was underwater, even using a long line to keep them from touching.

"Head to wind, now," I called, and, as we slowly rounded up, I climbed back in to the cockpit. The drift increased noticeably once the lateral resistance of the hull was removed. The wind began to flick water onto the screen.

I picked up the microphone. "Mother, this is Zulu November, have visual contact, approximately one half mile."

"Zulu November, this is Mother, did you call, you are almost unreadable? Be advised we have you closing target, less than half a mile, confirm if you have visual contact."

"That is confirmed, I repeat, that is confirmed."

"Roger, Zulu November. Continue, do not attempt further contact unless mission completed or aborted, your transmissions are exhausting your battery. If you are clear to continue, do not acknowledge."

I stood up and peered under the engine pylon at the approaching silhouette. I watched it for some time without saying anything, because the sight was confirming a niggling fear that had been growing. Wind-rode, we were going to pass reasonably clear of the hull, which we were approaching slightly on the angle, but in between the swells, which continued sedately on their way, the black hull was sometimes visible both fore and aft of the sail, the water sliding off it in a smooth dark sheen as it rose and fell. The ship was more than 350 feet long, the sail just about central, and I had only fifteen fathoms of rope, ninety feet. I couldn't attach it to the sail, because the hull would come up underneath and strike the Teal, but neither could I attach it to the ends, which would have been submerging at least twenty feet between swells.

When I went over it later, it was supreme torture to me that there might have been an alternative, but one never occurred to me nor was suggested by anyone else. I simply had to let the Teal drift on past, whilst I got into the sub and out again as quickly as possible, before it drifted out of sight. There *was* one alternative, and that was to ignore the submarine and continue on with the Teal. Because of Cleodie, I might possibly have opted for that if I'd thought of it seriously, but in retrospect the rising wind offered no chance of survival to the perimeter of the twenty-mile danger limit, where we could be picked up.

And that blithe smile made me an optimist.

I said, "It's not far off now, you'll be able to see it out of your side-window. I leave it to your judgement to go as close as you can without hitting it. I'm going to stay with you till the last possible moment and sit on the nose with the paddle in case I can help. Thing is, I want to close my hatch before I go, to stop the water coming in."

I took the bowline off my waist and off the cleat, and tossed the coil in the back. She saw that and looked at me directly and levelly, and we both knew at once that there was no need to discuss it.

"Funny expression, that," she said, "'Worse things happen at sea'."

I remember nodding very shortly, but she just nodded back in imitation and smiled serenely. I wanted to stay and say nice things to her, very badly I wanted to do that, but it was time to go. I began to smile back but it felt wry, so I climbed quickly out onto the nose and shut down the side-window, taking the torch and the paddle with me. The shift of weight made the water swirl up the nose alarmingly, but with legs astride I stopped most of it from rolling under the damaged screen. Our course seemed as though it would take us fifty to a hundred yards from the sail, which seemed about right, so I put the torch on my head and tightened the strap-buckle under my chin until it dug in tightly. Once it was clear I had no need of the paddle, and I slid up the window two inches and pushed it back inside. After that, we made silly faces at each other through the screen until I was abreast a point between the after end of the submarine and the sail. It lay stern-on to wind, monstrously shrugging off hundreds of tons of water as the ends rose and fell.

I gave a peremptory wave and slid off, whilst Cleodie gave me an encouraging smile and blew a kiss. From absolute sea-level, the Teal looked tiny and low and terribly vulnerable, and the rate of drift alarmingly high in the rising wind. For a stark moment, I thought of the swimmer back in Loch Kishorn, and knew it was impossible to catch it, even keep up with it. The feeling of decision and commitment was heavy on me, so I thrashed at the water for action and distraction. Fortunately, I remembered the torch before I put my head down, and generally I was too concerned to think about the cold, which was intense.

My clothes, especially my jersey, made me sluggish, but I got across the gap well enough. The problem arose when I reached the side of the submarine. It was so big it was more like a half-tide rock, unmoving while the seas rolled over it in deep, powerful swirls, and each time I strove to get near the ladder behind the sail, the water would roll me back again in a huge cascade. Once I nearly made it, then the sea swept me right over the casing on the other side. All the time, I struggled to keep my head and the torch above water and I was absolutely done in, especially when a big sea hadn't yet cleared the hull before it was reinforced by another, and in combination they lifted half way up the sail. That gave me one single chance, however, for there was a brief relapse straight afterwards. With the last of my strength and with the real shock and horror of the cold penetrating the marrow, I got one hand on the slimy ladder and a foot on the casing, but the foot slipped as I tried to stand and I fell heavily. I thought my forearm was going to burst with the effort of keeping the fingers curled round the ladder and I glanced round to see another relentless monster surging up the casing towards me. Desperately, I clawed with the other hand and managed to get a grip just above the first, on the same side. As the sea lifted me, I made my hands go up, one over the other, but the sea rolled over my head as I did so, and I felt something thump into me softly from below. At that stage the torch was secondary to the problem of sheer survival, and when the water subsided again, I was left clinging to one side of the ladder, my feet hanging loosely until I could hitch them round onto the rungs.

As I looked down the ladder, I saw what had bumped into me as I climbed the first rungs. Black in the swirling water a single, wet-suited frogman floated face down, his legs streaming over the port-side casing, and his wrist and hand were caught and jammed between the lowest part of the ladder and the steel edge of the sail. Taking my eyes away, I shinned unsteadily up the ladder as fast as I could before another sea came for me.

At the top I had to rest a few moments, and, looking out across the water, I saw the Teal's starboard wing rear up into the air, to be quickly corrected as Cleodie brought the nose to wind again. She must have been trying to sail her, otherwise she'd be sitting quietly head to wind. She was obviously doing all she could to minimise the downwind drift. Just in time, I resisted the urge to wave to her, which she would have interpreted as the all-clear.

As I bent down to the hatch-lock there was spattering of rain, and I looked quickly to see a thin squall approaching. There was enough to think about, and the lock wouldn't move. I sat down and pressed against it with my heel, remembering to take it clockwise, but still it wouldn't move until I had kicked at it frantically and got the rotation started. After that, it spun quickly all the way by hand and lifted open without any trouble. I took another quick glance to leeward and saw the Teal back on the other tack, bravely trying to hold against the wind. The curtain of rain made it indistinct and a gust of wind lifted the port wing briskly. The only way I could help her was by getting on with the job, so I spared it no more than a glance before letting myself down into the darkness on narrow, slippery rungs, my teeth chattering uncontrollably.

Ignoring the torch, I opened the second hatch by feel, frankly not wanting to know if the torch would work or not. Ten rungs down the next ladder, my feet reached a platform and I felt around with my left hand until, at full stretch, I could feel a'panel with plastic projections. With a scrabbling motion, I swept down every switch and at last a powerful light came on in my own compartment. Dazzled for a moment, I checked that they were all down, then made my way quickly to the hatch behind the ladder. There were eight clips but they all moved well enough, and in a moment I was through into the huge, brightly lit control-room.

There was no concession to human habitation whatsoever, no seats or even places where you could comfortably stand watching instruments, just endless banks of boxes with millions of miles of wiring showing under the crude alloy channel-plates that supported them. There'd been no attempt to "pretty" anything up. I rushed through to the far end without pausing and set about the next hatch.

When I got it open, a really unpleasant, noxious smell came through, but there was no light beyond. Because of the haste, the torch was still on my head, so I unbuckled it quickly, tearing skin where the buckle had dug into the bristle on my chin. I unscrewed it frantically and shook the water out, but I was still soaking wet and had nothing to dry the batteries and terminals, where normally in a ship you'd have no trouble in laying hands on a piece of cloth. The clock ticking away in my head was tugging at me, and I just screwed the thing together again, missing the threads once and jamming it.

To my intense relief, it lit up, though dimly, and as I went through the hatch I could see very little in its sorry glow after the glaring striplight brightness of the control-room. After a moment, I could at least make out that the compartment was a complete shambles, largely on the port side. Smashed boxes and tangled wires lay among bent tubing, and I moved over to the starboard side so as not to trip over anything. Even so, there was more wreckage in the way and my foot caught briefly in a heavy cable as I twisted my body through. I went rigid as a great sizzling flash lit up the whole compartment, and there was a horrible smell of electrical burning. I stepped over the virulent black snake, but then my trousers caught on a jagged edge of metal. I ripped myself away and fell heavily over another obstacle, without trying to break my fall as I was clinging tightly to the torch to protect it. Pain rocketed through my left arm as something penetrated the skin and it seemed to take forever coming out as I got to my feet again. The whole organism was at fever pitch by this stage, like the front runner in a long-distance race, stretched to the limit because the rest of the pack is breathing down his neck.

The torch was still alight and dimly I made out the bank marked SD Systems. Self-defence? I didn't know. The master was there clearly in the centre and I snapped it up quickly and moved on to the next bank. I ran the torch along the top row, clicking switches and counting. One of them was already up, which I ignored at the time, but I recalled its marking: "RadCom". I finished quickly and scrabbled back through the wreckage, which I was able to see better against the light showing through the hatchway.

Panting, I took the length of the control-room at a run, and almost threw myself up the ladder, my feet slipping at times on the greasy rungs. I was already waving as I came up out of the hatch at the top and looked out over the slimy guardrail.

There was nothing there. The visibility was sharply reduced in heavy driving rain, and white caps were showing where the Atlantic rollers lifted their smaller brothers and exposed them to the increasing wind.

Straining my eyes downwind into the murk, imagining I could see the diminutive Teal still bravely tacking, yet hoping she wasn't because of the wind getting under a wing and driving it over, I found myself reaching out with both arms as if pleading with the squall to clear and to let me tell her all was well.

But it was no squall, the wind continued to freshen and the rain pelted down in increasing malevolent frenzy. All we needed was

178

the briefest sight of one another, oh God, please just let me see her, she has suffered enough, I shouted and screamed at the weather and the heavens, pounding my hands on the coaming till the blood thumped behind my eyes and I became dizzy in a final paroxysm of grief, rage and exhaustion.

Slowly I sank down next to the hatch and the uncontrollable shivering took me over into jibbering incoherence. My sheer powerlessness to help her overwhelmed me. I was marooned but safe in this huge, ridiculous, grey monster, but somewhere out there Cleodie would be sitting patiently, trusting, while the frail amphibian, damaged and leaking, tossed and dipped in waves much higher than it was designed to ride. Unfairly, perhaps, I ranted at the controllers on the carrier, who must have understated the worsening weather, but they had only us to lose and much to gain. I wondered how many swimmers they'd lost already in their desperate attempts to get someone aboard. I looked down the outside ladder again, but there was no sign of the frogman. The sea had taken him, who knew the risks, who played the game and had lost a round. You only have to lose one.

Somewhere out there, the sea would be playing out a heedless, uncaring round with Cleodie, the sledgehammer and the nut, a pointless, ruthless exhibition of overpowering might, unbridled in its fury that we dare defy it. But she had not come in defiance or even adventure. If she was still afloat, she would be huddled and mystified in her pain and imminent death, and the last contact she'd had with another human being was to blow him a kiss as he cast her adrift . . .

I brightened for a moment at the thought that she still had the radio, but I knew she wouldn't use it without a signal from me. If they called her and she told them the situation, she might ask for help, but one thing was quite certain – she wouldn't get it. Her only hope lay in staying afloat for a twenty-mile drift and *I* could hope for that until I burst, but I knew there was no chance. The wind was up around thirty knots, and had backed slightly, setting up a confused cross-sea, which slashed at the sail in petulant ill-temper.

Feeling utterly defeated, blue and shivering, I made my way back down the interior ladder. It seemed absurd that this electronic super-marvel didn't carry such a relatively stone-age implement as a basic two-way radio. I might have tried sending something by simple on-off switching in Morse, but the communications centre

179

was well and truly wrecked. I went into the control-room, remembering their enjoinder not to touch anything in there, and I grew bitterly angry again. TO HELL WITH THEM, I shouted, if I could make it fly, I would! If it blew up, they'd come looking all right.

I walked quickly along the banks, casting my eyes over the myriad switches, dials, screens, test buttons, amongst mysterious labels saying things like Computer Interlinks, Secondary and Tertiary Back-up, Sonic Analysis Read-out, Reactor Thermal Efficiency Monitor, and so on, endless gobbledegook, total bafflement, until there in the centre I came to an extra-wide bank which rang the layman's bell.

Manual Override, said the legend, and above it dangled a microphone, presumably just for bridge communication when docking. Below, an endless array of touch-button controls, small dials and miniature wheels. There was far too much to take in given an hour let alone a few moments, but little to be gained by hesitating. If I could get the machine to make some sort of demonstration, it would surely provoke the Navy out of their enforced passivity.

I pressed the top button under the legend, and the button immediately lit up: Manual Override, it flashed obediently, and directly below a screen glowed, frizzled and then settled down to an extensive array of digital read-outs. Heading 065, Speed 00, Depth S-10, INS Co-ordinates, Hydroplane angles 00, Reactors 1, 2, 3, Standby. Faults: Radionics, Sonics, Proximity Sensors, DME. Systems negative: AD, SD.

In some confusion, I looked down at the rest of the panel, found a knob saying Ahead and Astern and moved it gingerly to Ahead, Min., and, as I did so, lights flashed and beepers beeped by each of the controls marked as faulty on the screen. I switched them all off and the noise continued, but on the screen they had now joined the Systems negative. In their place there flashed on the screen, Reactor Override, Error. I searched the panel for a clue, found none and started to hunt among the other panels. Then I got anxious again and clambered back up the ladder for a look at the weather, in case it had cleared. It hadn't, it was worse and the wind was clearly audible before I reached the top. Heavy rain still fell, and the wind was lashing it about. I could only see just beyond the submerged end of the hull, where water still heaved in oily response to the slight movements of the ship.

Quickly I scurried back down again, sliding the last few feet. After continuing my search, I found control panels for each of the three reactors, each panel showing three controls separate from the remainder, at the top, marked Centre Control, Manual Override (Centre Monitor) and Manual Override (Operator Monitor). On the assumption that the computer would take care of whatever happens in a reactor, I pressed in each case Manual Override (Centre Monitor) and returned to the first panel. The Error light had stopped flashing, but up on the screen instead it said: Reactors 1, 2, 3, Standby, followed by 04,42, which I assumed was minutes and seconds since the right-hand digits steadily reduced at the familiar rate. I suppose it was ridiculous, but I fumed and ranted at the fact that a machine like this took five whole minutes to get steam up. I simmered down after a bit, still fretting at the delay, but using the time to examine as much of the panel as I could.

I assumed that Depth, S-10, meant that the ship was ten feet below her fully surfaced level and that if she started moving, the nose might have a down tendency, because of its apparent shape from outside. Just to be sure, I turned the forward hydroplane control to +5 degrees, but the screen beeped at me again saying Error. I took another walk and eventually found Hydroplanes, and on that panel lighted buttons showed Folded, for both fore and aft planes. I pressed the one next to it, for the forward planes, marked Extended, and returned to the Manual Centre. The screen read Hydroplanes, Fwd, +5, Aft 00. Satisfactory so far, in different circumstances I could have played with it all day, but in the acute anxiety and exhaustion there was no pleasure.

I found a heading control and turned it to 060, and the screen promptly lit up the rudder angle, which increased slowly up to thirty-five degrees port until I returned it to 065. There was no point in it bursting a gut trying to turn when we had no forward movement. In fact, I was surprised it hadn't shouted Error at me, and reasoned that it wouldn't be programmed to expect me to be so stupid.

The countdown for the Reactors passed the two-minute mark, and I thought of going up again for another look, but I knew it was a waste of time. I walked through to the base of the sail and from there I could hear the wind and rain outside. I went back in and the beeping noise was going again. I ran over to the screen and under Reactor Standby and the time, now 00.55, there flashed on and off insistently: Operator, punch Ready, S. by punch Turbine Run. I recalled those from my search along the panel, though it took some twenty seconds to find them again. I obeyed the first instruction and the beep and flash stopped. After that I stayed glued to the countdown, waiting for the moment to obey the second.

How time hangs in such moments. I would have sworn the digit counter had slowed down, it positively crawled its way to zero. When at last it did, I was instantly beeped at again, and pressed Turbine Run.

For a long moment, nothing happened, but slowly I became aware of a very muffled building up of sound from somewhere back aft and sensed movement in my feet.

The screen showed Speed: 0·2, then 0·3, increasing very slowly, so impatiently I turned the Ahead knob to Max. Centre said No to that, beeping in reproof and stating Insufficient Power. I wound the knob back until it was satisfied, between Min and One-Third, then I dialled in 060 on the heading, which was roughly the downwind direction previously given by Mother. Then I found another little wheel bearing the legend, Pre-set Speed Override, and put it to six knots. I looked at the screen for disapproval, and got none, in fact next to the speed read-out of 1·6 knots it actually stated six knots pre-set, so I left it at that and went up top again.

The scene was much the same, very poor visibility and driving rain, but the wind had not increased any further. Movement through the water was still slow but quite apparent, water sliding aft off the submerged bows instead of the thick, limpid movement of before.

Checking my watch, I saw that I had been on board for thirty-eight minutes, or at least since I had had my last sight of the Teal. With the increased wind, Cleodie would not have been able to keep tacking for too long, and her drift could well be up to three knots, which would put her a mile and a half to two miles downwind. Because the ship's speed was increasing steadily, I would not know how far it had travelled without a constant, so I went back down to see if the machine could tell me. I recalled a button marked INS (Inertial Navigation System) Link read-out, found it quickly and pressed it. The screen promptly showed distance travelled in last twenty-four hours, 6·3 miles. Not much use, as that showed yesterday's and last night's drift. I pressed it again and got the read-out for the last twelve hours, and finally,

182

after another press, last 01 hours, 0·3 miles. I gazed at it in relief and it slipped to 0·4. The speed showed 3·2, heading 060. Satisfied, I returned to the sail-top and to peering anxiously through the murk. Also to a creeping multi-horned dilemma, whose facts and questions piled up on me suddenly in far less time than it takes to tell:

a) The longer the Teal was exposed to this worsening weather, the less chance of survival. b) I might not find her, in which case it was time wasted. c) Mother was holding station, that is steaming constantly in a given area and might not notice for a while the small directly downwind movement of UNS 1 on her screens. d) If I found her in a water-logged condition the battery would be underwater and therefore the radio U/S. e) If I found her either water-logged or buoyant I would not be able to effect a rescue myself anyway, since there was no question of getting her into the submarine in the prevailing conditions of weather and her own injuries. f) Therefore, the only way Cleodie could be rescued was by helicopter. g) A helicopter with search equipment would find her straight away, provided she was still with the aircraft. UNS 1 was not equipped with radar, being strictly an underwater vessel.

She would have understood why I had to be logical about it and not passionate, also that I settled for a small but possibly fatal compromise; to continue downwind for a good two miles, turn to port for half a mile in case the wind backing had added extra northing to her drift, then, if unsuccessful, to double back towards the carrier at best possible speed until someone decided it must be safe to come and talk to me. I haven't checked over it, but it could be that the time required to develop full power from the reactors made the result just about the same anyway.

On a reasonable estimate that the ship was now up to five knots, I stayed on the sail for a further twelve minutes, saw a dozen imaginary Teals but no real ones, then I gave it a further five before dashing down and switching the heading to 330, or ninety degrees to port. The rudder must have been very deep or some other system involved, because the ship banked sharply to port like an aircraft and wasted no time or space in the turn at all. The INS link had shown just over two miles at the point of turn, which was the maximum I felt she could have drifted in the time. I gave it five minutes, or half a mile on the northerly leg, straining my eyes both upwind and down, then slid back to the control-room, turned the heading through 180 degrees and clambered immediately back up again. I drew a blank on both legs, after which point the decision had to be made. I held the third leg for six minutes to allow for the turn and for perhaps too much northing on the first, downwind, leg, then snaked back down again, set the heading at 240, the reciprocal of the first leg, took out the Pre-set Override and turned the Ahead Control to Max. This time there was no protest from the machine and the effect was quite dramatic.

By the time I got back up on the sail, spray was flying aft in great crashing gouts, the hydroplanes were trying to ride the wave-crests and the nose was canted out of the water like some enormous, starving leviathan going for the Big Kill. For the first minute I kept a careful lookout all round, but still the small, grey circle of ocean stayed pathetically empty.

Back down below again, it became almost impossible to keep my feet, but I was very careful, knowing that disaster was certain if anything should happen to me and I couldn't stop her. To my knowledge, the only remaining object between me and the North American continent was the pride of the British Navy. Clinging to the alloy tubing by the main console, I saw a reset button next to the INS link, so I pressed it and got an immediate time check followed by distance travelled, 00. It changed at once to 0·01 then 0·02, which puzzled me until I looked at the speed read-out: thirty-eight knots! The motion was absolutely horrifying and I thought she might break up. For the ship itself, I can't say I cared that much, but there seemed little point in breaking her back. She should only be pushed at those kind of speeds down in the unruffled depths. Forward in the next compartment, the loose wreckage was crashing about, so I changed the forward hydro-plane setting to +1, and the motion eased off immediately.

When I got my eyes back to the screen, the speed read-out showed forty-six knots, distance travelled from reset 3·6 miles. I went back up to have a look, the wind howling savagely inside the sail.

The wafer-thin steel tower was cutting through the water like a well-honed machete, but the forward part of the hull was entirely underwater, and, except for occasional glimpses where it passed a deep trough, invisible. But when I looked to each side, I could see that it was supporting or displacing a huge mound of grey-black sea along its whole length. Behind was the scene of a maelstrom, an evil place like the meeting of storms and malignant currents, a whitened, boiling turmoil of terrible power, which continued to heave and seethe and throw up unexpected spouts long after we had passed. The equipment down below was measuring speed through the water, but up there on the sail, the relative wind-speed must have been well over seventy knots and still increasing, tearing at my hair and clothing and making ghastly shrieking noises as it swirled round the openings. The extraordinary thing was that there was no machinery noise or vibration, no other sound but the wind and water, no slighter movement than the momentous heaves from the ship's heavily stabilised motion.

I went back down below once more, into comparative quiet, and checked the data on the screen. Heading 240, Speed, stupefyingly, fifty-five knots! Distance from reset, 9·6 miles. They must be on their way soon, I thought, and wondered how to stop her when the time came. It looked simple enough, for underneath the Ahead/Astern control was a button marked Stop, in white like the others. Next to it was a red button, imprinted Crash Stop, and I was wondering about that when the beeper came on again. Stabiliser Lag, Surface Overspeed, flashed the screen, and above it the speed read-out showed fifty-eight knots. I turned the Ahead knob down to about three-quarters, the speed began to drop instantly and the beeper subsided. Distance from reset, 11·2 miles, which gave us about ten or eleven miles to the carrier. They must have seen it now on their screens, and I could imagine the pandemonium it would be causing on their bridge. The radar would reflect only the sail and it would show as a very small echo because of its slim section, but it was approaching at the speed of a torpedo. I hoped it was causing the right kind of stir and that they were launching everything that could be made to fly. I hastened up the ladder once again, and just as I reached the top, a Vixen flashed overhead very low, and disappeared astern. Spray was whipping up occasionally from where water boiled up around the leading edge of the sail, but the rain had stopped and I could see quite a bit further. I looked round to see if the Vixen was coming back, but it didn't appear again, and peering forward I could see the reason why. Two helicopters came into view, a Whirlwind and a Sea-King. I fancied that the Vixen had been sent on a possible Kamikaze mission to see if his presence made the sub blow up, and once established as safe, it was clear for the choppers to come in.

In my mind every second counted heavily and with mounting desperation, I slid back down again, ran to the Manual Console, turned the Ahead knob to zero and pressed Crash Stop. It's the kind of action you expect to result in thundering noises and alarm bells, but down there it was quite silent and nothing happened for about five seconds. Then I was suddenly and viciously plucked clean off my feet; the nose must have dipped because I didn't touch the deck at all before coming to rest with a clangorous impact against the forward bulkhead. Fortunately I had curled into a ball as soon as I became airborne and my feet and backside struck the bulkhead together, missing both the open hatch and its curved locking levers by about eighteen inches. There was a second jarring thump as I hit the deck a moment afterwards, and I heard the rushing of water as I tried to struggle upright. I was still pressed hard against the bulkhead as I looked and saw water flooding in through the after hatchway – which meant the top of the sail had to be underwater, unless the whole thing had been torn off.

The press of deceleration kept me immobile for about five seconds longer, staring in horror at the huge amount of water being forced down the hatchway. She must have nose-dived, and I would never be able to climb the ladder against the force of the flooding. Oh, Moses, what action then? No chance of shutting the hatch. Remember those wartime submarine stories, Blow all main Ballast! No, there was a quicker way than that, especially with all the power at hand. I got away from the bulkhead and limped uphill towards the console, wondering how to negate the Crash Stop. Its red light was still showing, so I pressed it again and it went out. Water was swirling around my legs as I switched the forward hydroplanes to +20 and the Ahead knob to Max. Gripping the bars, I searched the screen for information, and there it was: Depth S-85, then I noticed movement and it went *down* to 90, 95, 100. The roaring of water was deafening now, but I could feel the ship start to come level. The depth went down to 125, stayed there for a few moments and then quickly began to diminish as the up-angle increased alarmingly. Imagining she might be going for the loop, I turned the hydroplane angle quickly back to zero, the tilt stayed where it was, and the depth reading reduced at great speed. At forty feet I switched the speed to Min, since the log was already showing sixteen knots, and the inrush of water had fallen right off. I didn't want her to leap out of the water and go down in two halves, so before the depth recorder reached zero I turned back the Ahead control and pressed Stop, the ordinary one this time, as the ship came horizontal with a vast shuddering heave. I checked the Distance from Re-set at 13·2 miles, and then left it to its many devices.

Utterly weary, I waded over to the hatch, noticing that most of the water had drained away downwards, and made my way up the long, narrow, hateful ladder for the last time. I emerged to find the Whirlwind hovering directly overhead. Within thirty seconds I was in the harness and being winched aboard, where I had to shout down the crew's delighted exclamations and descriptions of the dramatic dive and re-surface, not to mention my own appearance.

In spite of my pleading, they said they had their instructions to put me on board the carrier at once, but at least the Sea-King was detailed to go and search the whole area surrounding my only point of reference, thirteen plus miles, north-east, 060. With my fervent wishes, it banked sharply away and disappeared downwind.

Fourteen

As we touched down on the carrier's flight deck, the pilot turned to me and said, "They want you up in Flyco straight away. The Brass is here."

I jumped quickly out of the open hatchway, not waiting for a ladder, and ran across to the tower, up several flights of stairs and through the already open door marked Flying Control. They must have heard me coming and were lined up in almost ordered, dour ranks.

I burst out at once. "Can I report later, please, I want to go out there and look for her?"

"Sit down," thundered a commanding voice. "The boys know their job, and you wouldn't be able to do any better."

"Look, I've got to –"

"NO! They'll find it if it's still there," added the voice, from behind the others. They made a space for him to come through, another admiral, a towering bull of a man who eclipsed Feather completely.

Someone slid a chair up to me, then thoughtfully covered it with a newspaper. I was dripping on the floor and reeling, and the man held my arms and guided me into the chair. Only then did I become fully conscious of biting pain in my left arm, from where I'd fallen in the darkened radio-room, and it made me jump as he gripped it.

They grilled me between them, the Admiral and a couple of boffins in civvies, for what seemed like eternity, and when I'd finished describing the condition of the ship when I found it, they couldn't seem to agree that it made sense. I was frantic to get out of there.

The first boffin, a thin twittery man with a long narrow nose, tried to explain to the Admiral that the degree of impairment to the communications-room should have caused the ship to self-destruct. The second one, heavy and ill-dressed with bulging pockets and a battered pipe, tried to explain to the Admiral that there was nothing in the Com. Centre that could cause an explosion of that extent.

"Suppose," said the Admiral, "the air-conditioning had packed up in there, could there have been a build-up of explosive gases?"

The boffins shook their heads and turned to me again. I was only half listening to them because I was anxiously waiting for news over the radio. I'd already heard SK 258 report square search completed, and the controller had told him to repeat and extend the pattern.

They both started to speak at once, but I held my hand up.

"It must have been sabotage. A gas explosion wouldn't have hurled all the port side equipment across the floor. Besides, one of the SD switches was off."

"OFF? That's impossible . . . all right, which one?"

"RadCom, I think it said."

"A-ha," said the thin boffin, while the big one puffed his pipe and they looked at each other. The Admiral looked at both of them, then turned to me again.

"We have to thank you, you did very well, very well indeed."

"How many men did you lose trying to get aboard?"

He looked uncomfortable and said, "Why do you ask?"

"Well, one of them nearly made it. He was stuck on the ladder, drowned."

"Can you describe him? I don't imagine he's still there."

"No, but he was washed away before I started her up. He was face down and wearing a black wetsuit."

A captain stepped forward in response to the unspoken enquiry. "No, sir, certainly not one of ours. The parachute idea was definitely abandoned."

There was silence for a moment, then I strained to catch a voice on the loudspeaker, but it was the Vixen coming back in.

Rather off-handedly, I remarked, "It's a good thing I'm not a

189

Russian, I'd be well on my way to Murmansk by now. You really should rig up an ignition key for that thing."

"Enough of that," commanded the Admiral. "There's a team of engineers and naval architects that I've kept away from you, they want to nail your hide to the crosstrees, they're on the sub now." He grunted and went on, "Do you realise you travelled thirteen nautical miles in just over nineteen minutes? They were up here screaming at me, and I had to throw them out. What happened at the end, by the way? You disappeared for a minute, two minutes."

"I did a crash-stop and she dived a bit."

"Well, for heaven's sake, don't tell them."

"I'm afraid they'll find out, the hatch was wide open and she went down to a hundred and twenty-five feet."

They all stared at me in horror, and pipe-boffin said slowly, "Salt water and electronics don't get on."

There were nods of agreement and plenty of heavy frowning.

I said, "If you send me a bill, I'll put in for salvage. Can we send out another chopper on that search, please, and let me go with it?"

"We'll send another, but you'll go to the MO and get yourself patched up. Really, you wouldn't be any use. See sense, man."

"Did you keep the aircraft on radar?"

"Well, we did for a while, but we lost it shortly after you started moving. The two echoes sort of merged, and we didn't pick it up again."

I knew what he was thinking immediately, that I had run down the Teal whilst I had been below getting the submarine started. My head reeled with a terrible nausea, the thought too unbearable to entertain. With dreadful effort, I gripped the arms of the chair and tried to get control of myself, but it took some while. I looked up into their concerned and embarrassed faces, shaking my head.

"No, I could *not* have run it down. The speed was minimal, and I went straight up on the sail after she got started. I'm quite certain of this. Are you sure the blips didn't separate again?"

The controller answered, "No, they didn't, but they were both very tiny, and became difficult to spot once the weather worsened. The screen was a bit snowy. As you know, we couldn't overfly to keep track with an aircraft. We even missed the initial movement of the sail."

"Everyone tried damned hard," the Admiral finished lamely.

I got up and turned to go. The Lieutenant who had brought the chair said he would take me to the sick-bay, and the controller promised to send word the moment they had anything. I nodded my thanks and asked him if he'd arranged the call to Mrs McNeil.

He smiled and said, "It's arranged, but it's not 8.30 yet."

"Well, you'd better cancel it until we hear something."

The thought persisted that I might have run her down, but I could hardly bear to consider it. I'd been on the sail the whole time, except for the three course-changes ... I pleaded silently that I'd only been below for thirty seconds on each one, and at less than six knots, I couldn't have, surely, surely ...

I went out feeling numb and barely living, in the hardening knowledge that we were not going to hear anything. The Teal could not have stayed buoyant that long, I was certain, and even if in her injured state Cleodie had managed to get out, her survival time in the water would be half an hour at the outside.

On the way to the ship's hospital, one of Feather's staff accompanied us and asked for a brief run-down on the events of the night. When I'd finished I asked him to call the bridge again but there was still no news of Cleodie.

Defeated, I let the doctor give me some aspirin, but it must have been horse sedative and I didn't come round for fifteen hours. Then, horrified, I got out of the bunk and reeled around shouting, and a moment later someone came in with a tray of food. I made him put it down and call the Flyco, and, after a while, the doctor came in shaking his head. He told me that the search with two helicopters had continued for over seven hours and covered many square miles. He said they'd been very thorough, they'd even found a small black cushion and were sending it down to me.

I waited until it was brought and in my recognition of it as coming from the Teal lay my final acceptance. Feeling infinitely sad, I asked to be taken ashore, and the messenger went out saying he would pass on the request. In the doorway, he looked back and said quietly, "They also found a body, a frogman. He'd been dead for some time."

I pushed the food away and stared blankly at the ceiling until there was a commotion outside, hushed talking and then a familiar voice.

"*Cer*tainly. Shan't be long."

Jack Plumley appeared in the doorway, fingers to his lips and

191

a bottle of Scotch in the other hand. At the sight of me, he turned his mouth down and ogled. I hadn't troubled to look at myself, but I could feel thick bandages on my head and arm and multiple small dressings on my face and hands. Then he brightened and said, "Could have been worse!"

I didn't answer him. My thoughts were miles away.

"I *thought* it was you. We got a bleat from Lossie about someone buggering about the Hebrides in the middle of the night, so they sent me over to have a look. I had you on radar and watched you go down next to that little island, then buzzed over you."

I didn't answer, finding his bonhomie rather shocking, though it didn't seem to matter. He rattled on unaware.

"Did you hear me, then? You couldn't have done unless – you didn't by any chance have your engine switched off?"

I nodded and he puffed out his cheeks in disbelief, shaking his head like a scandalised confessor. "It's a bit like jumping into a tiger-trap and hoping to fall between two spikes, or were you still plastered, whaw?"

I shook my head and was about to say something when he went on.

"What did the boys in the chopper say to you when they came over?"

"Nothing. They got chewed up."

"Golly. Well, then, I came back here but I was still the standby and they sent me up again when you were reported heading this way. When you neared the twenty-mile limit, I was told to shoot you down."

"What? Why didn't you?"

"Fire control malfunction!" he grinned cryptically. "Actually I did think it was a pretty unsporting way of taking out a rival suitor. Was anyone with you, by the way?"

"Yes, *she* was."

"Cleodie? Good God, where is she, I must go and see her?"

"Haven't you heard?" I said to him aghast.

"I've been in the sack since the early hours. What is it, what's happened?"

"She's gone. She was in the Teal when the wind came. They've spent half the day looking for her, but they only found that cushion. It's from the Teal. They also found a dead frogman."

He was silent for a very long time, then he got two glasses from the shelf, filled them and passed one to me. We sipped in silence for a while, then he asked me to tell him the whole story.

I gave him a flat, detached outline, but I wasn't really thinking about it. Something was nagging at me, a feeling that the Teal could not have sunk so quickly, and yet the facts were irrefutable. There had come a point when it was no longer visible on the radar screens and I didn't have any doubt whatsoever that, if it had been afloat, they would have found it during the search.

But it still didn't make sense. They'd found a frogman and even a tiny black cushion, but Cleodie had been wearing an orange lifejacket and should have been spotted even if dead from hypothermia.

Unless the Teal had gone down very quickly and she'd been unable to get out because of her injuries. Then why the cushion? She might have got the window half-open and then got stuck. I baulked once again at the thought, something inside me nearly bursting.

Jack interrupted me, saying my answers weren't making sense. I hadn't really been aware of him asking me questions. I asked him to get me a pen and paper, and shortly there was an argument outside the door. Eventually he was allowed in again and I resented the invalid treatment. I didn't want to be dry and warm and bandaged, I wanted to put things right and it was too late. I felt frantically close to the edge of hysteria but after a while I fought it down. I expect the whisky on top of the sedative probably helped. As a partial distraction I worked with the pen and paper, muttering to Jack about the figures. I suppose it was futile but I had to do it.

"The fuel tanks were empty," I said, "and the caps are sealed. The breathers are led down nearly to the water-line so they couldn't have filled with water. So even if the hull was waterlogged, that's sixty-five gallons of sealed buoyancy space. Water weighs ten pounds a gallon so the tanks alone could have supported six hundred and fifty pounds displacement."

"I dare say, but the aircraft weighs much more than that, surely?"

"Yes, about fourteen hundred pounds, so there's no equation there, but recalling how much space the tanks take up in the wings, there'd be room at least for another three in each wing, a total of a hundred and twenty gallons. I know the wings aren't sealed but they've only got tiny holes at the trailing edge for pressure equalisation apart from the cable holes at the wing-roots, and they're about half-way up. So let's halve it, that gives us another six hundred pounds buoyancy. That's twelve hundred and fifty. Still not enough – but then what about the semi-sealed compartments in the back of the fuselage?"

Jack stopped me with a hand on my shoulder. "This is rather pointless, you know."

"Yes." We lapsed into silence again.

"Are the tip-floats sealed?" he asked unexpectedly.

I nodded and stared at him, baffled, "I reckon they'd hold about fifteen gallons each – that's another three hundred pounds! It's well over. This is crazy."

"Well, in that case the storm must have broken it up."

"No, not in the time. I know it was blowing half a gale later but the sea hadn't got up enough. The only way I can figure it is if the cockpit filled suddenly and the buoyancy in the tail made her tip until the engine was over the centre of gravity. With the tail in the air, the rear compartments could fill via the control cables and the wings empty through the breathers. But it would still take time . . . " I trailed off hopelessly.

It would only have been a matter of minutes before the wings lost enough buoyancy to overcome the equilibrium. And after this, the judgement. Trapped inside, she'd have been in sight of the surface all the time she was drowning; the final bewilderment, only one arm, the hatch stuck, Seamus, please help me, Seamus, where are you . . .

But it wasn't the right picture. With the precious courage of her youthful zest, she would more likely have been yelling at the elements or cursing me good-humouredly for my tardiness. She would not have been bleating, I was sure, and I think it was then, with that thought, that I felt the lowest point of life. Something seemed to snap, the optimistic connection, whatever it was that could link me to a purpose or a meaning. In trying to stay alive, I had been wasting time and effort. They were compulsive thoughts, mean and selfish, and now there was her mother, to whose distress mine should be hardly comparable. There was one last thing for me to do, to see her and tell her how Cleodie had been just before she died and throughout the ordeal. Pride might give her a vestige of comfort. I hauled myself away from the other dead-end thoughts, since there would be time enough for them later.

"What are you doing?" asked Jack, as I started pulling my clothes on.

"Carruthers. I'll have to go and tell her. How do I get off this hulk?"

"Crikey, I don't know. It's ten o'clock at night and we're steaming north. Depends how much pull you've got."

"Well, don't drink any more. I'll get on the blower and perhaps we can check out. Have they mended your machine?"

"How do you mean?"

"That malfunction you had, with the Fire Control."

He gave me a conspiratorial wink and shook his head. I stared at him in disbelief, he'd taken a terrible chance. As it happened, UNS 1 did not blow, but only because of the sabotage, and he wasn't to know that. I felt it would have been a merciful and quick relief if he'd obeyed his orders, though no better for Carruthers.

Admiral Feather listened sympathetically to my request, then held up a flaccid hand.

"We had no reply from Mrs McNeil; we asked the police to go round there. She'd left a note for her daughter, slightly acid about being out all night and saying that she'd gone down to Glasgow to see a specialist. From there we traced her to the Southern General Hospital about to have an emergency operation for an abdominal tumour. That'll be this evening sometime. No, wait, don't interrupt. It's a touch-and-go situation, I gather, and she won't be allowed visitors for at least forty-eight hours."

He paused to let me digest this and then changed the subject. "As for Breac, the Marines went in to clean up and they were a bit thorough, I'm afraid. Most of McHarg's lot were killed, one badly wounded, and he was apparently made willing to identify the others. Two of them were Russians and they were all part of an infiltration network set up specifically to penetrate the UNS1 project. He also named a couple of deep-cover operators in Glasgow."

"What about McHarg?"

"He wasn't there and we think he got away across the sandspit. I'm sure the pick-up would have been aborted – anyway there were no submarine approaches to the island. Naturally, we have an all-points-alert for McHarg and we know he didn't take the Uist ferry because it wasn't running."

"Check the movements of the HALOS helicopters from Aberdeen."

"Thank you."

"What happens if you find him?" I asked, feeling true and bitter hatred for the first time in my life. "Will he stand trial?"

"Unlikely," he answered in a matter-of-fact tone. "Look, I'm sorry you didn't get our co-operation earlier, it would have saved a lot of mess."

"Mess," I repeated dully. I wanted to smash his face in, but it was pointless venom.

"Where do you want to go now?" he asked, but I just shrugged hopelessly and went out. I found myself by an open rail, watching the dusk-grey seas sliding past the hull about eighty feet below. The ship seemed to have such a sense of purpose that I wanted to step off and not be part of her. I was actually considering it when the thought struck me that Cleodie would resent and scorn such a craven act, and I gained something from the thought – perhaps a pride that her life had touched mine and conferred on it a greater value.

There was a hand on my arm and Plumley led me away in silence up to the briefing. He handed me a set of flying kit, which I was helped to put on, then he led me up to the flight deck, to the cockpit of 002.

Strings were pulled and the puppets danced, and fate looked on unheeding. Within minutes, the most powerful taxi in the Western World gathered with me its awesome fury, hunched and quivering, then slammed off the catapult and went howling through the night sky at twice the speed of a scream. For a short while I was pure animal, hunted, cornered and certain of dying.

On our left, the Aurora Borealis twinkled its romantic mirage with a lustre that had no meaning for me except as a mockery of caring in the face of elemental unconcern.

Beneath us lay the great, black graveyard, the rolling soulless sea, the spirit of unrelenting callousness, too disembodied for anyone's hatred and serenely impervious to vengeance.

Above us, an infinity so unthinkable that it seemed impossible for our futile microcosm to be detected, let alone be the subject of benign patronage, a knowing of each mortal's waking and sleeping, thoughts and motives and weaknesses. How could it hear? How could it possibly care? So how could we?

196

In pure self-defence, I switched off all my reflective processes and became one with the Phantom, an unthinking, hawk-eyed predatory machine which man had perfected simply for acts of destruction. My mind went as cold as the computer's abstract calculating, but it was not transcendence, it was more a seeping, abject slide into sub-humanity. It isn't true that when you reach bottom, the only way is up. You can stay there and decompose.

It was an effort not to think of Briggs as a messenger of death. He actually looked as though he had lost more weight, his eyes impenetrable in their deep sockets. He met us at Lossiemouth on the tarmac, which gleamed black under the soft rain; then he led me into a stark, bright office while Jack went off to find a bed. He started to show concern for my apparent injuries, but in fact I wasn't any more interested than he was and we quickly dropped the subject.

"Right then," he said. "There's been a further development because, as soon as we lifted the two Reds from Glasgow, Moscow came up with a deal. We lost a network over there just recently and they want to do a trade, three of ours for two of theirs. Want a job?"

"Not particularly."

"Thing is, we've picked up McHarg, outside Aberdeen. We're holding him at Wick with the other two."

The thought of that man boiled the murderous hatred in me once more. Briggs picked it up immediately.

"Small clean-up job you could help me with. The arrangements are for shortly after dawn, we have to dump our two on a currently deserted exploration rig in the Beryl field, and they'll be picked up from there by a Russian trawler. Our chaps are in Berlin now and will be put through Charlie at the same time, exactly. We have agreed not to interrogate."

"And McHarg?"

"Yes. It seems they don't particularly feel that he would enhance their society, but for HMG he's a big embarrassment, because that's not his real name. He changed it several years ago after a manslaughter charge, you may recall it if I tell you that his brother is a Cabinet Minister. I'd like you to come with us to the rig, to see that all goes smoothly."

I looked carefully at him. There was quite a lot unspoken, but no mockery in his face.

197

"Was this Poofy's idea?" I asked.

"In a sense, yes. He perhaps feels he owes you something."

"Elevation to Refuse Disposal Officer," I said drily.

"In a way. At least you'll be sure that it's all nicely tied up."

"OK," I said dully, to hide my savage feelings. "When do we go?"

"Get a couple of hours' sleep. You'll be called."

The Sikorsky's rotors were already turning when I climbed in. As soon as I had the door shut, we lifted off and thrashed away northwards across the Moray Firth, just visible in the pre-dawn. It looked as cold and dreary as slate. Briggs was up in the cockpit with the pilot, but I hadn't acknowledged his gesture when I stepped aboard. Getting up after two hours' sleep can feel like crawling out of your grave.

Twenty minutes later we set down at Wick, high up on the north-east coast. Two men stepped aboard, silent but unfettered, followed by a handcuffed and dishevelled McHarg. There was still a spring in his movements and arrogance in his face, but he was very startled to see me. Briggs had come aft and taken another pair of handcuffs from the Naval guard with which he fixed McHarg to an eyebolt on the fuselage. While he was doing this, the guard handed a package through the open door, grunting slightly. I took it from him, underestimating the weight. I guessed it was lead, about thirty pounds of it, and there was no question about its purpose. McHarg hadn't noticed and was trying to be spry with Briggs, who ignored him and went forward, stooping his long, thin frame.

As we lifted off for the final leg, I sat down opposite McHarg. We were all silent, the Russians stiffly upright on the bench looking malevolent, and I became very aware of the atmosphere.

Eventually, McHarg spoke. He was grimy, stained and bruised, especially under the chin, and he didn't meet my eyes.

"What now, do you know?" he asked, speaking very quietly.

"I don't know."

"Can I do a deal?" came the urgent whisper. "I know a lot of names."

"You can try, I suppose. Do they speak English?"

He nodded so I signalled to the two men to move away to the rear of the machine, then I glanced forward. Briggs was peering round at us but speaking on the radio. I went up forward and stood next to him.

"Hold One," he said into the microphone, lifted off the headphones, then said to me, "everything all right?"

"Yes. McHarg wants to do a deal. Can you come back?"

"Thought he might. Can't you handle it?"

"I don't know what to ask him."

"Well, I can't leave the set. Just get names – and bring them to me so I can have them checked."

"What does he get in exchange?"

"Anything you like. Say a trip abroad and don't come back."

"Got a gun?"

"What for?"

"The others might try to stop him."

He nodded and handed me his Navy Colt. I suppose in his job he had to be a ruthless cynic; he turned back to the radio and dismissed me with an apologetic hand. I took pen and paper and went back to my seat.

"If they see me talking to you, they'll hunt me down wherever I go," said McHarg, indicating the Russians.

"I expect they will anyway. As far as they're concerned, you're an expensive write-off. Why didn't they want you back if you know so much?"

"They don't know that I know."

"We'll see. OK, shoot."

He gave a resigned shrug after I told him the terms and then began to speak while I scribbled furiously. One of the Russians stood up and came over to me.

"There is to be no interrogation," he said in perfect English.

"This man is not part of the deal. Sit down or I'll blow your knee off."

He stood there defiantly until I put the muzzle of the Colt against his knee-cap and looked him in the eyes. He could tell I meant it, and after a moment he backed away and sat down. He spoke to his compatriot but we couldn't hear over the engine noise, so McHarg began again. He spoke steadily for three or four minutes and also explained how one of the seamen had placed the charge in UNS1 right at the end of sea-trials, in his capacity as Master-at-Arms ensuring that no one was left on board. They'd had access to the shore computer and communications centre, but instead of first steaming north as originally intended, UNS1 had

had a last-minute programme change for security reasons and the charge had gone off in the wrong place. The Royal Navy had thus been able to reach her first and set up the cordon. The top-secret power station at Dounreay, where amongst other things the nuclear fuel was processed, had also been infiltrated.

When he'd finished, I had some two dozen names and asked, "What was their hold on you, just money?"

He nodded. "I hope that's enough – it's all I can remember but it should be very useful."

I was still no less hostile to him and said, "Enough? It could never be enough, not for me." I stood up to go forward.

"What's your beef?" he asked in a querulous voice. "You've won out, cracked it all wide open and got your girl back as well, very dramatic. And a very pretty piece, I wouldn't have minded . . . "

With my fingers round his windpipe, he had to stop speaking. I was absolutely on fire with rage, and hissed at him furiously.

"She was badly injured by your people, then wounded by machine-gun fire, and finally drowned because she couldn't get out of the aircraft."

His face went ashen, then he spluttered as I released my grip. After a moment, he met my eyes levelly.

"That's my pay-off, isn't it?"

"Yes."

"Do I go in the drink?"

I didn't answer but went forward and handed Briggs the list. He took it with a sly smile, nodded once in approval and turned back to the radio once more. The pilot turned round and signalled to us, then pointed out through the screen. Distantly, we could see a spidery-looking rig and a big trawler holding station about a mile and a half from it, and as we drew closer we could see a smaller boat close by the base of the structure.

Once overhead, Briggs said to him, "Put down and we'll offload. Then we have to wait for another signal. Something's happening simultaneously." Then to me, "I'll have to stay here. Will you show them out?"

The landing platform was raised and cantilevered out over the side of the rig. Down on the main deck, two figures waited in yellow oil-skins, while a third was at the rail winding vigorously on a hand-crank.

I opened the door and beckoned the two Russians out and they stepped down in silence. I stood and watched them go down the steel ladder. I glanced at McHarg, but he was slumped in his seat gazing at the floor.

When the three reached the deck, one of the men in oil-skins beckoned to me. I hesitated a moment, then went down the ladder, with difficulty because there was no pull in my left arm.

On the main deck, they were talking in a group, then the one who had beckoned spoke to me in Russian.

"We have a delivery for you to make. Wait please."

He went over to the rail to help the man who had been cranking, and in a moment they came across carrying a light structure of alloy tubing with a heavily wrapped parcel on it, tightly roped and zipped. There was a pronounced lump in the middle of it. I glanced at the spokesman suspiciously, but with a motion of his hand he invited me to inspect. Hardly visible at the nearest end of it was a very small slit. I looked at the man again but he was quite impassive. I heard Briggs shout down from the helipad, asking what was going on, but I ignored him.

I peered cautiously into the slit and a single eye looked back at me unblinking.

"Well, who is it?" I asked him impatiently.

"Ask", he said. "We do not know. Our orders were to deliver."

I looked into the slit again, baffled, then I said, in English, "Who are you?" and a small, muffled voice answered, "Don't you recognise me, my darling? You ought to come in here, it's lovely and warm."

I had already started to reel back as she spoke, the improbability of her survival and my deep conviction of her loss wrestling inside my head with what I had heard, the unmistakable voice and the typical words themselves. I must have reached the last stages of pessimism and despair because my first thought was of a sadistic joke. Then the whole world turned upside down like a toppled gyroscope.

For a long moment, I just looked down into the tiny aperture, but I cannot describe my feelings. I couldn't even say anything, but just mouthed her name silently. Eventually I looked up at the spokesman and croaked, "Thank you. Will you help me up with her, please?"

Anxiously I followed the two of them up the awkward ladder, but they were seamen and handled the stretcher with ease. They placed it in the helicopter and, with a short bow, turned away. Briggs was watching with a scowling expression.

"What's going on? There was no other arrangement." He strode over and tried to stop me as I was widening the aperture to see her face.

Squatting, I turned my body to come between us so that he couldn't interfere.

"Look, I have to know."

"It's Cleodie," I beamed up at him.

"McNeil? Oh, good, very good, delighted." Without glancing at McHarg he added, "Those names all exist. Well done."

He strode quickly back to the cockpit and his radio. I had a sudden thought and glanced out of the doorway. The last Russian sailor was about to descend the ladder. I gave a short whistle.

"Zhdeetye pozhalsta," I called, "wait, please," then I went forward to the cockpit. Briggs was bent over the radio set, listening intently.

"Give me the keys to the handcuffs, will you? I want to move him so she can lie down properly."

Without looking up, he pulled them out of his pocket and handed them to me.

McHarg was still sitting slumped and defeated. He looked wildly about when I unhooked him, urged him upright and pushed him out through the door, his hands still fastened behind his back. The other sailor had joined the one waiting outside.

"A delivery for you to make. Here are the keys. Watch out for him." Cleodie was still wrapped up and she and McHarg didn't see each other.

"He's not so pretty," said one of the men, giving a short bark which I took to be a laugh.

McHarg asked in a shaky voice what was going on.

"I've got the girl back. You're going with them."

"But they're . . . they're Reds!"

"Yes. Aren't you?"

He shook his head numbly and stammered about deals and clemency, and how they would probably put him away. I badly wanted him to be gone.

"Briggs wanted me to dump you out there. Tied and weighted. You've got your clemency, it's all I can give you. Go quickly, before he stops me."

He began to struggle against the two trawlermen, who were

202

clearly puzzled what to do. I reached into the helicopter and took out the packet of weights, split it and dropped the halves into his jacket pockets. He tried to strain away but they held him firmly.

I nodded to one of them and said, "Walk him near the edge and he won't give you any trouble."

One of them made that curious bark again, then they turned away and helped him down the ladder to the drilling deck.

I closed the door and looked towards the cockpit. Briggs was still sitting with narrowed eyes, presumably waiting for the all-clear. I didn't want any changes so I went forward.

"All OK," I said, and slipped a hand into his side pocket as if returning the keys. He nodded without looking up.

Through the screen, I saw the trawlermen start to lower McHarg on the hand-crank, but suddenly it ran away with them, the handle spinning furiously. Weighted as he was, he stayed a long time underwater until they stopped laughing and wound him out again for the waiting launch.

I hurried back to Cleodie, hearing Briggs call out, "Let's go," as I did so, and shortly afterwards we lifted off and whickered away to the south.

I swear there was Handel in my head, the piece we had both wanted to play again on that first evening together. As I unwrapped her, I was dying to ask her to explain the miracle, but I was having difficulty in speaking, just gazing at her foolishly as I got the covering away from her head. She grinned and spoke first.

"That's better. How will I ever forget your look of horror when you first heard me, or was it my wicked suggestion in front of all those foreigners? And you look like a battle-hero."

"What's this big lump in your stomach?"

"Not what you think, it's your anorak. I insisted on saving it, it looks like an old favourite."

"Please tell me what happened to you. Are your injuries all right?"

"Oh yes. I was given a truth drug, it was ghastly, like being drunk, only worse."

"But where, how? Please tell me how this is possible."

"In the submarine. Don't you know anything about what's happened to me?" I shook my head, still completely mystified.

"Well, marriage and babies is going to be terribly boring after all this. I've been beaten up, broken and dislocated, shot to bits, flown around in the dark half the night, drowned, ogled through a periscope, spent three days in a submarine with over a hundred sweaty, silent men, been injected, inspected and detected, then transferred to a ship reeking of fish, then to a small boat, then hauled up on a crane, then the man I thought quite liked me gives me a look as though I was a dead squid being hauled out of the sea, and now I think I'm in a helicopter! But I was warm and well-fed, courteously treated once they'd discovered I wasn't a spy, and the surgeon set my arm and shoulder and sewed up my tummy. Now I'm ready for anything."

She stopped then and tried to sit up, but I hadn't got all the straps off.

"What about Carruthers? Does she think I'm – ?"

"No, she doesn't know anything, just that you were out all night, probably on the tiles. I'll explain later."

She smiled wickedly but I steered her away.

"Did the Teal sink?"

"No, at least not at first. The rain came and I lost sight of you. I had to let her go head to wind because she wouldn't tack any more – if you can call it that. The leeward wing was half in the water at one stage. She seemed to drift very quickly and all of a sudden I was scared rigid. It got rougher too, with the water slopping under the screen, though I tried to stop it with the anorak. It was up over the floorboards and then a wave pushed the whole screen in. That's how I got out. I've still got your funny little gun. Boris roared with laughter at it, especially when I told him it didn't mean you weren't a VERY dangerous fellow." Her eyes twinkled at me.

"Who's Boris?"

"The captain. Isn't it too perfect?"

"What happened then?"

"I was in the water, unbelievably cold, I don't know how you managed that swim. The Teal was full up but still floating with the wings just sitting on the water. I managed to climb up and sit on top. I was feeling a bit depressed by then. I sat there for twenty minutes, half an hour."

"How long had you drifted before that?"

"About the same, at a guess, perhaps longer. Well, anyway, about a hundred yards off, this little thin stick comes out of the water and turns its beady eye on me. It's amazing how long it took me to realise it was a submarine, and of course I was ecstatic and waved like crazy. Then it disappeared, though I carried on waving at nothing, but I had to stop because of my stomach, you know, where the –"

"Yes, I know."

"Um. Well, the next thing is a big black fin comes up, much nearer, then a man climbs out and jumps in the water and swims towards me. I'd already inflated the life-jacket, so I got off the wing when he came and he gave me a tow back. Other people helped me up, but the first man swam to the Teal. I saw him take the caps off the fuel tanks and then he drove a big spike into the wings. He kept doing it. I tried to tell him to stop it, but they took me down this great long black hole. That really hurt, but they couldn't see I was crying because I was so wet anyway.

"They patched me up and then started with the questions. I gave them a lot of silly answers which they didn't like, and then they gave me a needle which *I* didn't like. The captain spoke good English and told me it was a Russian submarine, but that was after they'd drugged me and found out I didn't know anything. Don't stop doing that, I like it."

I carried on stroking her forehead. "A truth drug? What did you tell them?"

"The truth, of course. They showed me a transcript of what I'd said, but couldn't understand why I laughed at the answers. I said, I love Seamus, about six times, so there's the truth . . . and I said, he'll come and get you and then you'll be sorry, 'cos he was very fond of that aeroplane and me as well, I hope. Later on, I asked him why he'd done it, to the plane I mean, and he said they'd come into the area silently, just using momentum to get as near as possible, and they'd been waiting three days with everything shut down, unable to use anything but the periscope – and they'd lost a frogman trying to get your submarine; anyway, he said that the Teal had been close enough to look like the same radar-blip as his conning-tower when he surfaced, and his idea was to replace the Teal on everybody's radar screens."

"They let me think that I'd run you down and that's why the blip disappeared."

"Oh, poor you. I can just see it." She smiled gently, then went on. "When the man came back from sinking it, there was a big alarm and the sonar men started shouting, men came tumbling down the hatch and we dived at once. He said there was another submarine bearing down on us."

"That was me. I was looking for you."

"Ah, thank you. You'd have found me too, presumably. It's a good thing I didn't know, I might have run amuck with a can-opener. Boris told me that it had carried out a brief search – hey, why brief, anyway? I was very upset about that."

"Well, even if I'd found you I wouldn't have been able to pick you up. I went off to get help."

"Yes, he did say then that you went off and they tried to follow, submerged of course, but then he couldn't catch you. He kept shaking his head when he told me, said he couldn't believe his instruments, that no displacement craft could move that fast. I didn't know you could drive one of those things."

"Neither did I. The computer does most of it."

"Was it very fast?"

"Unbelievable. About seventy mph, and it would be faster underwater. I was just going flat out trying to attract some attention."

I told her the rest of it, including the crash-stop and the seven-hour search. We both did our best to be lighthearted about my believing her lost, but she couldn't hide the emotion in her eyes. Meanwhile, I unstrapped the parcel and got her into a seat, the pilot looking back with great interest because she was laughing at herself dressed in a seaman's jersey and trousers, cut off at the bottoms and tied round her bandaged waist with coarse string. She asked about my injuries and I reassured her.

"But you do look silly grinning at me like that, with your hair sticking out through the top of your bandage. Have you looked at yourself?" I shook my head and she asked, "Did you really miss me?"

I could only acknowledge dumbly. I had never been so pleased about anything in my whole life, at the same time terrified at the thought of ever losing her again.

"It's like Jonah and the whale, isn't it?" She smiled for a moment and then went all stern and schoolmarmish. "Now, are you going to give up all this nonsense and settle down? Your children won't think much of you if you're always disappearing and then coming home cut to ribbons – they'll think you're a loser and they'll get all insecure and fractious."

I folded her to me, my face muscles aching with grinning, and she spent the rest of the flight making detailed plans and asked me if Jack would be best man. As long as he has nothing to do with

206

giving out the drinks, I thought. I told her what he had done for us, and we decided to buy him a new car with the numberplate FCM for Fire Control Malfunction.

There was a lengthy pause while she looked at me, quizzical but smiling.

"Well?" she asked.

"Yes, thanks."

"I meant, are you going to settle down?"

"Yes, of course. What do you take me for?"

"For good," she sighed contentedly.